RAVE REVIEWS FOR GARY A. BRAUNBECK!

"Braunbeck is, quite simply, one of the best storytellers working in this genre—or any other."
—Briane Keene, Bram Stoker Award–winning
Author of *Urban Gothic*

"Braunbeck's fiction is absolutely essential reading for anyone who values dark literature."
—*Cemetery Dance*

"Braunbeck is much more than a superbly skilled storyteller. Popular fiction doesn't get any better than this."
—William F. Nolan, Author of *Nightworlds*

"Braunbeck is one of the brightest talents working in the field."
—Thomas Monteleone, Author of
The Blood of the Lamb

"A phenomenally talented writer who never seems to make a misstep."
—Shocklines

"Gary A. Braunbeck is simply one of the finest writers to come along in years."
—Ray Garton, Author of *Ravenous*

"Braunbeck's power is that he can see our fear and our pain, and he can bring it to life in a way that can be both terrible and beautiful at the same time. But he can also see light in the darkness, and his stories and novels, no matter how bleak they may become, also contain a kernel of hope, of humanity."
—Horror World

"Gary A. Braunbeck is one
writers, writing dark noir th
the lights on and jumping o

D0377595

THE REAL STORY

Death-Metal spoke up again: "So are you gonna tell us, or what?"

Sure, I thought. *And maybe we'll even speak of other ghosts and buried things and a lost circus and a great, grotesque, horribly magnificent honest-to-God monster that still walks the woods at night.*

"The offer to write anyone a pass for Study Hall still stands if you find you can't . . . well, listen anymore. With that said . . .

"If a happy ending depends on where you choose to stop the story," I said, "it matters just as much where you decide to start it. This one starts with ghosts.

"Don't say I didn't warn you. . . ."

FAR DARK FIELDS

GARY A. BRAUNBECK

LEISURE BOOKS   NEW YORK CITY

A LEISURE BOOK®

August 2009

Published by

Dorchester Publishing Co., Inc.
200 Madison Avenue
New York, NY 10016

ISBN 10: 0-8439-6190-2
ISBN 13: 978-0-8439-6190-4

The name "Leisure Books" and the stylized "L" with design are trademarks of Dorchester Publishing Co., Inc.

Printed in the United States of America.

10 9 8 7 6 5 4 3 2 1

Visit us online at www.dorchesterpub.com.

DEDICATION

To all the readers who have followed the Cedar Hill Cycle over the years; I thank you from the bottom of my heart. We're not quite out of the woods just yet, so stay tuned. . . .

I would like to thank Don D'Auria for his continued faith in this odd little town I've created; Vince Singleton for being my most Constant Reader; Sara Larson, for being the first to read this and offer words of support; Michael Kelly, for giving some excellent suggestions and much-needed input early on; and, of course, my wife, Lucy Snyder, for . . . well, *everything*.

FAR DARK
FIELDS

"If I could break away to some long-gone year I'd try it;
Find a quiet town where you'd know no fear inside it . . ."
—John Nitzinger, "One Foot in History"

"In the dark night we call to one another for help across
far dark fields, while the ghost of Death stands in our
midst stretching his black wings over us and, with his
iron hands, pushes our souls into the abyss."
—Kahlil Gibran

"The wonder is not that there is so much darkness; the
wonder is that there is any light at all."
—Graffiti on a wall in Coffin County

Recapitulation

Hoopsticks

"It is strange that the Mind will forget so much, and yet hold a picture of flowers that have been dead thirty years and more."
—Richard Llewellyn, *How Green Was My Valley*

"If we lived long enough to see the result of our actions it may be that those who call themselves good would be sickened with a dull remorse, and those whom the world calls evil stirred by a noble joy."
—Oscar Wilde, *The Critic as Artist*

Here is a story; if you listen carefully, at the end, you'll be someone else.

Cedar Hill Division of Police
Division of Evidence
Inter-Office Memo re: Exhibit D
Case #HPS713-60
Attn: Det. William Emerson

Attached are photocopies of the articles found on the suspect at the time of his apprehension. As per your request, they are in the same order here as when found in his pocket.

From the *Cedar Hill Ally*, December 25, 1988:

BURIED CARNIVAL WAGONS POSE LOCAL PUZZLE
ROAD CREWS UNEARTH RUSTED VEHICLES, AS WELL

By KEN WILLIS
Ally **Feature Reporter**

A curious footnote in the history of local road construction is buried not far from the site of the Old County Home.

Road crews reinforcing the embankment along Route 37 have uncovered a row of rusted carnival wagons, as well as vehicles used to transport them.

Cedar Hill resident Cletus Walters, a foreman on the road crew, was the first to see the odd buried treasures. Walters said a row of nine vehicles—five cars and four wagons—is visible, their left sides and one-quarter of the rear exposed. "You can even read some of the writing on the side of one of the wagons," he said. "It says something about a 'Two-headed' something 'wonder.' My guess is that was a sideshow attraction."

He theorized they might have been placed there to help stop erosion. "It looks almost as if they stopped there for traffic at the tracks," he said, alluding to the nearby railroad tracks.

"One sure looks like an old Model-T truck," he added.

In the floods this past July, Raccoon Creek overflowed, washing out a half-mile section of Route 37, which passes through the area. Ohio Road and Bridge has been hired as subcontractor to drive pylons into the embankment to build a steel wall to protect against erosion, according to Licking County road superintendent Bryce Fortney.

The wagons and vehicles became exposed as the mud was washed away, Fortney said, adding that he was surprised to find that the half-buried junk he saw there was actually a line of circus vehicles.

The sides of the wagons and the chassis of the cars could at first barely be made out because the color of the mud and the rust were so similar.

According to Licking County engineers' records, that area of Route 37 was built in 1935, then widened and repaired in 1970. Licking County commissioners' records confirmed this.

"Since there's been no work done there since

1970," said Fortney, "then it stands to reason that the vehicles were utilized at that time, though there's no record of it."

A historian with the Circus World Museum in Baraboo, Wisconsin, has been contacted in an effort to discover with which carnival the wagons might have traveled.

From the *Columbus Dispatch*, July 13, 1992:

MYSTERIOUS HIDDEN "CHAMBER" BAFFLES EXPERTS

CEDAR HILL (AP) — A mysterious underground discovery is so fresh it hasn't yet been named. Archaeologists are calling it simply "the chamber."

What little that is known is this: it's completely underground, circular, some 180 feet across, and is surrounded by a series of now mostly collapsed tunnels.

Using powerful sensors and scientific instruments that capture geophysical energy, government archaeologists made the discovery this summer in the heart of Licking County in central Ohio.

National Park Services officials recently confirmed the find and stated they plan to formally announce the discovery at a scientific convention this September.

Plans on how exactly to excavate "the chamber" are still under discussion.

Researchers stated that the underground chamber is in a region of Ohio that has long been combed for ancient artifacts. The locale in Cedar Hill under which "the chamber" was discovered is called Moundbuilder's Park, and is dotted with Indian mounds, all of which are aboveground and shown on maps. The land was recently added to the Hopewell National Culture Historical Park Registry, created by Congress in 1992. The area is known for artifacts of the Hopewell (named after the farmer on whose land their remains were first found), a lost civilization that built hundreds of mysterious objects across Ohio before vanishing about 1,500 years ago.

All summer, National Park Service archaeologists have been using the technology to explore the various Indian mounds and earthworks in this region of the state, looking for small artifacts like arrowheads, pottery, fire pits, and wooden posts. When a circle popped up June 29 on computer screens analyzing the data, researchers were stunned.

"We don't know the age of it," said one park service researcher. "We're uncertain of the overall composition. We don't know the depth. We don't where the tunnels lead or even if they were dug out from inside the chamber or vice versa. We don't even know what it might have been used for. At this point, there's no end to the questions."

From the *Cleveland Plain Dealer*, October 2005:

PREHISTORIC GRAVES YIELD MYSTERY MORTUARY PRACTICES FOUND NEVER BEFORE SEEN IN OHIO

LICKING COUNTY (AP) — Archaeologists are still trying to figure out what they found more than a year ago when they unearthed prehistoric graves at the site of a five-acre plat near Dawe's Arboretum.

"It's just amazing," Randall Pape, an Ohio Historical Society field archaeologist in charge of the dig, told the *Cedar Hill Ally* for an article Sunday. "We're seeing here some mortuary practices never before seen in Ohio."

The dig uncovered the remains of adults and children that had been carefully dismembered and distributed across twelve burial pits. The sex of the individuals has not yet been established.

"From what we've seen so far, it was a place of interment for around thirty to thirty-two individuals in a fairly small area," said Amy Winters, the society's project chief for the site. "There's lots of weird stuff like two people in one grave pit with no heads. There's also the skeleton of a child placed on a set of adult arms which seem to be cradling it, but the rest of the adult is not there. Nobody's seen this kind of thing before."

Some skeletons have no skulls, some skulls have no bodies, and many body parts don't seem to match up. Buried with the bones were about fifty artifacts including a trophy ax, beads, antler-bone points, shells, grinding tools, and bear and rodent teeth used for ornamentation.

The most unusual burial has arms from two bodies arranged on each side of what appears to be an ax, as if caught by death in the act of exchanging a baton. Pape said, "It reminded me of those jugglers you see in circuses who throw flaming torches back and forth at each other. We were just astounded when we uncovered these particular burials with these arm features."

Winters is doing doctoral work at Ohio State University focusing on how prehistoric people reflected their cultures in their mortuary practices.

She presented her preliminary findings on the site last April at the Society for American Archaeology meeting in New Orleans.

When asked if this was a Hopewell ritual, Winters replied that grave sites for the Hopewell—a historic people who occupied Ohio about 1,500 years ago—have contained only trophy skulls that might have been souvenirs of war or ancestral worship. The skulls or bones of ancestors might have been kept as family heirlooms and buried later with their descendants, she added.

"I don't think it represents that they were being grotesque or brutal to their people. I think this was more a respectful way to be left for the afterlife."

Professor Tracy Castle, curator of archaeology at the historical society and former site chief for the disastrous "chamber" dig of 1995, said the artifacts found at the site strongly indicate the graves date to an era before the Hopewell existed.

The trophy ax, made of soft limestone with a flattened blade, is an extremely rare relic used for ceremony rather than work or fighting. This may be the first ax of its kind found in Ohio, Castle said.

Adding to the allure of this recent discovery is the local legend of the area itself, known as either "The Nest" or "Audubon's Graveyard." Since the spring of 1957, those five acres of county-owned land have been the sporadic focus of several official investigations conducted by the Ohio State Department of Health as well as federal hazmat teams. Twice every year, during spring and winter, for a period lasting about three weeks, every bird that flies over that area drops from the sky, dead. Records show the soil has annually been tested for contaminants, as has the air, the small creek that runs parallel, and even the wild-life inhabiting the woods surrounding the plat. Nothing else has ever been found to have been infected, and only birds die during this time.

In every case, the birds' hearts have exploded. No cause for this phenomenon has ever been determined.

Archaeologists were called to the site when a local man hired to clear away the bodies of the birds discovered loose bones along the creek's embankment.

Castle has spent the last year preparing and cataloging the materials. A survey of the area is now being conducted using a ground-penetrating scanner, but Castle doesn't know whether or not there will be further excavations.

"If it were up to me, I'd leave it for people two hundred years from now who'd have better instruments," he said. "It's that important of a site."

From the *Cedar Hill Ally*, June 23, 197—

ADOPTION PICNIC SET FOR SEPT. 16

Licking County Children's Services will sponsor its annual Adoption Picnic on Sept. 16 from 2 to 6 P.M. at Moundbuilder's Park. The free, public event includes entertainment, games, nearby rides, prizes, face painting, music, and a free picnic for children. The event is a chance for interested couples to meet the eighty children awaiting adoption. For more information, please call the offices of Judge Arthur Buchanan at the Cedar Hill Courthouse between 9 A.M. and noon.

"There's been a shooting here. . . ."

CHAPTER ONE

Violence never really ends, no more than a symphony ceases to exist once the orchestra has stopped playing; bloodstains and bullet holes, fragments of shattered glass, knife wounds that never heal properly, nightmarish memories that thrash the heart, countless other weapons of diminishment . . . all fasten themselves like a leech to a person's core and suck their spirit bit by agonized bit until there's nothing left but a shell that looks like it once might have been a human being.

My God, what do you suppose happened to that person?

I heard it was something awful. I guess they never got over it—hell, you can just look at them and know that.

Drop a pebble in a pool of water and the vibrations ripple outward in concentric circles. Some physicists claim that the ripples continue even after they can no longer be seen.

Ripples continue.

A symphony does not cease.

And violence never really ends.

It took over half my life to learn that.

Don't misunderstand; I haven't spent the entirety of my years in single-minded pursuit of this knowledge—I don't have it in me to be that monomaniacal—but it, I now suspect, probably spent just as long, if not longer, in pursuit of me. If teaching high-school English for the past twelve years has shown me nothing else, it has affirmed that a lesson can be learned even when the student isn't aware that it's being conducted, individual stubbornness be damned.

I was such a student where this newly acquired knowledge was concerned (to bring this embarrassingly self-conscious metaphor to its anemic conclusion); for me, acts of grotesque violence—a mother drowning her small children, school shootings in Colorado, a man torturing his entire family to death—were something on the periphery of life, headlines on page one, single-column articles buried in the middle of the "National" section, or stories on the eleven o'clock news read by well-coiffed, somber-faced anchors with their heads tilted just so in order to convey the proper balance of sympathy and professionally detached outrage. Like many, I encountered such stories, *tsk*'d or gasped appropriately, then moved quickly on to news about a train wreck in Iran or a flood in Brazil or food riots in India or the NASDAQ figures for the week, all the while so very *aware* that there was no proper way to express grief or sympathy, that unless you were from the place where this violence occurred, or in some way knew one of the victims or the person or persons who killed them, it was impossible to truly understand how someone, a *normal enough* someone, a someone like you and me, could do such a horrible thing. It's easier by far to understand the complicated financial maneuvers of Wall Street kingpins than an isolated burst of homicidal rage in a small Midwestern city . . . which is where much of this story begins and ends and—if there exists that place where mysteries, symphonies, and ripples go—continues in its own way.

My name is Geoff Conover and I live in a suburb of

Dayton, Ohio, where I am employed at the local high school. I am married to a wonderful woman named Yvonne who is six and a half years my junior and is the news director at the local television station. She is about to give birth to our first child, a boy. Yvonne has a six-year-old girl from her previous marriage; her name is Patricia and I love her very much and she loves me and we both love her mother and are looking forward to having a brand-new addition to our family.

I am an unremarkable man who, until two years or ten days ago (maybe even three decades, depending on where this story really starts), led a solid, stable, unremarkable life. I am not a leader of men, nor am I a visionary, a poet, an artist, composer, or great philosopher: I am simply a high-school English teacher whose unremarkable life is now something I struggle on a daily—sometimes hourly—basis to protect and maintain. There is nothing so slender or delicate as the imaginary veil that separates us from genuine chaos. Look up information on fractal patterns in an encyclopedia and you might have some idea what I mean.

CHAPTER TWO

It happened like this:

Last Friday night, a student from my high school named Bruce Dyson—seventeen, member of the drama club, a commentator at his church, not particularly popular but far from an outsider—walked into a local restaurant/ice-cream parlor shortly after our football team won its fifth straight game of the season. The atmosphere was festive not only because of the win, but also because it was snowing and the Christmas/New Year's break was only six days away. Bruce brushed the snow from his hair, waved at some friends he recognized, smiled at the hostess, then pulled a semiautomatic rifle from underneath his coat and opened fire, killing nine people (two of them small children) and wounding seven others. He then got back into his car, drove to the I-70 on-ramp, and headed toward Columbus. It would be another thirty-eight minutes before police had enough information from survivors and confused witnesses to piece together most of his license plate number, another five to confirm that it belonged to a car registered to Dyson's parents (both of whom he had killed before going to the ice-cream parlor), and—because of decreased visibility due to the snow and wind—nearly half an hour more before his car was spotted by the highway patrol.

It took three cruisers twelve minutes to run him off the road. Before officers could get to him, Dyson took a Smith & Wesson Ladysmith .38 Special from either his coat pocket or the car's glove compartment (officers on the scene weren't able to tell for certain), shoved the business end into his mouth, and blew out the back of his skull along with a good portion of his brain tissue.

But he didn't die.

He was still breathing when EMTs arrived on the scene, so he was taken by Life Flight helicopter to the nearest hospital, Cedar Hill Memorial. (It was later established that Cedar Hill was definitely his destination: he'd stopped for gas at a mom-and-pop station and checked for directions; the attendant—one of those sad, lonely sorts whose only company at night is a police scanner that is never turned off—heard the APB just as Dyson was pulling out, got the license number, and called the authorities.) Dyson was still registering EEG activity even though nearly a third of his brain was gone. He was moved to ICU and placed on life support where he lingered for thirty-six hours before finally dying, but not before delivering one last dose of damage.

That he shot himself in the head wasn't made public until a few months after his death; what few specifics were released presented the facts in a piecemeal manner, deliberately out of sequence and so easily misinterpreted; the official story remains that Dyson was wounded during a police pursuit and died at the hospital a day and a half later: the madman is dead, justice has been dealt, let us sigh in relief, sad story over.

Except, of course, for the violence, which never really ends.

I did not know Bruce Dyson, except for having seen him in the halls, as well as the drama club's fall production of *Spoon River Anthology*, and as Howie Newsome, the milkman in *Our Town*, the previous school year. He was never in any of my classes, and I honestly don't think we ever so much as said hello to one another.

Three hours after the killings I was called, along with all other teachers, to an emergency meeting at the high school where a team of psychologists explained to us how and why we had to resume something akin to normalcy as soon as possible. When classes began on Monday grief counselors would be available to students and faculty both. As teachers we were being urged to get the students talking about what happened; if traditional classroom activities needed to be suspended, that was fine. We spent several hours mapping out the "healing plan," as the psychologists called it.

By the time I got back home, Bruce Dyson was under armed guard in the ICU at Cedar Hill Memorial Hospital.

"How are *you*?" was the first thing Yvonne asked me as I came through the door. Her tone said all her words did not: *I know so many people are dead, and I know there are a lot of soul-sick, grieving families out there tonight, but I'm not married to any of them, I'm married to* you, *and later my heart will crack for them, but right now I'm going to be selfish because you're the one who's looking hobbled so it's you I'm crying for and you I'll care for.*

I looked at her and could only shrug. "I just . . . I still can't fathom it, y'know?"

She pulled me to her as if she had no plans of ever letting go. "I keep thinking about the families and friends of all the victims, what they must be going through. God, Geoff, there's this sudden, horrible, empty *space* in their lives that will always be with them. 'He used to sit there,' or 'That was her favorite spot for reading' or

'That's where he took his first steps.' Empty spaces that are going to be so *loud* with the absence of the person who used to fill them. It's so damned *sad*."

I placed my hand on the back of her head. Her cheek against my chest felt like a heart suddenly beating again after the paddles were applied. I couldn't think of anything to say to make it seem all right, because it never would be; better, yes, eventually, a little, perhaps, but never all right.

She fixed me a cup of hot chocolate (melting the chocolate before adding the milk, none of that instant crap for my wife) then sat silently holding my hand while I drank it. When I took a shower a few minutes later she put down the toilet lid and sat there, just so I'd know she was nearby if I needed a hug. When we climbed into bed she snuggled close but took care not to hold on too tightly, as if she knew there was something in me that might break in half if even the slightest pressure were imposed. Not once during all of this did she press me for details of the meeting or demand that I "share" my feelings with her *this instant*; not once did she look at me and say, "This *has* to be bringing up all the Cedar Hill stuff again, why not admit it?" (She would have been right to assume that.) Yvonne knew me well enough to sense that there are times when tender silence is the only salve that works. Somewhere around 2:00 A.M. consciousness and I parted on friendly terms.

Odds are you've seen the movie *Searching For Survivors*, considering that it grossed something along the lines of two hundred million dollars at the box office, was nominated for nine Academy Awards, and walked off with five of them (Cinematography, Music, Adapted Screenplay, Supporting Actor, Director). I didn't read the book when it came out twenty-odd years ago (I still haven't) and didn't want to see the film when it played in theaters, but Yvonne insisted that it might be "therapeutic" for me to see others' vision of the tragedy. I reminded her that there had been a howlingly awful made-for-television movie about it back in the '70s that I had seen but barely remembered, but that wasn't much of an argument against seeing the new film, so one night in early September of last year, after the initial crowds began tapering off, my wife and I went to our local multiplex, bought our tickets, popcorn, and sodas, then settled into our seats.

Somewhere in the middle of the "No Talking During the Movie, Please" animation that followed the previews I began to sweat. Not *perspire*, mind you—sweat. By the time the opening credits began, I was drenched.

"Is it one of your headaches?" Yvonne whispered. I suffer from severe cluster headaches that my doctor treats as outright migraines. These attacks are always prefaced by two things: the sweats and the shakes. Always. This was the first time I'd ever broken into the sweats without benefit of their cohort.

"I don't think so," I said, and was *Shh*'d by someone sitting one row behind us. Just to be safe, I reached into my pocket and removed the small emergency bottle of meds I make it a rule to carry at all times; in it I keep one Zoloft (for anxiety and depression, 200 mg), one Naproxen (for tendinitis, 375 mg), and one Percocet (for pain, 650 mg). I took the Percocet, wiped my face down with my handkerchief, gobbled a couple handfuls of popcorn, and finished in time to see the rest of the credits.

The first half hour of the film is glorious. Most of the exteriors were filmed on location in Cedar Hill and the filmmakers display a real affection and fascination with everyday life in a small Midwestern city. There's none of the idealized, sweetness-and-light small-town America that Frank Capra invented (this said as an avid Capra fan, just so you know), nor does it flirt with the nauseating, obsidian, look-at-the-moral-and-spiritual-corruption-under-the-surface tone of something like *Blue Velvet* (said as a hit-and-miss admirer of David Lynch); no, *Searching For Survivors* presents an honest and nonjudgmental portrait of this place and its people. Though the entire movie has a deliberate documentary-like feel to it, nowhere is it more effective than this first half hour.

I talk about those first thirty minutes because they are all I remember of the film. As soon as the actor portraying the murderer makes his first appearance (the scene with the little boy who's lost his toy gun), I . . . faded. That's the only word for it. My body was there, I continued sipping my soda and eating my popcorn and holding my wife's hand after I finished snacking, but it was autopilot time. I was *aware* of the movie, of its music and dialogue and images, but each element was completely disconnected in my mind; it was like trying to discern a newspaper photo solely on the basis of the individual dots that compose it: holistically, the film did not exist for me.

I know what you're thinking—it must have been the Percocet. Sorry. I won't lie to you—I get a mild buzz from the pills whenever I take them (which isn't that often), but I have never just stoned-out on them. Never.

When I told my doctor about it a few days later, she said: "First of all, you missed a damn good movie, it should've won Best Picture, you ask me. Secondly, you blacked out."

"But I remember *being there*. I remember the sounds and—"

"—and the popcorn and the soda and all the rest of it, yes. But too many people associate the term 'blackout' with alcoholics or people with brain tumors. You're not a drunk and you don't have a brain tumor, but you blacked out nonetheless."

I stared at her for a moment, and then said: "You *know* you can't leave it at that."

She rubbed her eyes, chewed her lower lip for a moment, then exhaled. "Bear in mind I'm a GP, not a psychologist—I say that to cover my butt because my horrifyingly expensive malpractice insurance requires me to, *capiche*? All righty, then. My guess is you blacked out because you saw something in that first half hour that triggered every defense mechanism you've got. I won't even try to take a stab at what—you'd be surprised at how insignificant some triggers appear on the surface—but whatever it was, it brought everything back and you couldn't deal with it at that moment, so your perception became fragmented. That's why you can quote lines from the middle of the movie and yet have no idea how they fit into the overall narrative. Same thing with the music, individual images, all of it. Perceptual fragmentation is as much a form of blackout as an alcohol-induced fugue state. The difference is you were *aware* of it as it was happening. And, no, it has nothing to do with the headaches. This was a PTSD episode."

I groaned and shook my head. We'd had this discussion too many times for my liking. "I'm not suffering from post-traumatic stress disorder."

"Says you. I'm the one with medical degrees covering up the holes in the plaster. You're sure nothing else happened?"

"I'm sure."

"You've been sleeping all right?"

"Yes."

"And you're *certain* that—?"

"*Nothing*, I'm telling you!"

She smiled again, albeit cautiously. "Says you. By the way, in the movie, were you—?"

"—yes," I said, rubbing my eyes. "That was supposed to be me."

For a moment she stared at me with an odd kind of quiet awe. "Wow."

"That's what everyone says when they find out."

As Yvonne and I left the movie theater that night, she squeezed my hand and said, "I have to tell you, Geoff, that was a *lot* better than I was expecting it to be. They didn't go nearly as far with the violence as I was afraid they would. And it sure didn't seem like it was two hours and forty-five minutes long. "

I nodded. It sure *didn't* seem that long.

"Are you okay?"

"I am resplendent in my normalcy."

"So that's a 'yes'? I really need to know, Geoff. I know you didn't feel like seeing this and that I kind of bullied you into it, so if it's, y'know, brought up anything, I want you to tell—"

"I'm okay, honey. Really."

"Did you like it at all?"

"I'm not sure," I said. "But that first half hour was great."

"*Wasn't* it? Oh, Geoff, I never imagined that Cedar Hill was so *pretty* in places. Those sculptures around the courthouse lawn . . ." And that was all that was ever said between us about the movie. At least until the damn thing was released on DVD ten days ago and a student by the name of Bruce Dyson was among the first to buy a copy. *That* little tidbit of information didn't surface until the first series of funerals was under way. By then— thanks to several students and a couple of loudmouthed faculty members desperate to see their names in print— our local newspaper knew my connection to the events portrayed in the movie and took great care in the article to mention me by name five times, Yvonne three times, and Patricia once. Not once did the paper contact me for any comments, or to ask permission to use the names of my family members.

Yvonne and I have since had to change our phone number because of the threatening late-night calls— most of which were of the "You were there for both of them so you *have* to be at least somehow partly respon- sible" variety. ("They're desperate for a scapegoat, for someone *living*, to blame," Yvonne said. "By the way, I canceled our newspaper subscription.") We double-check before going out of the house in the morning to make sure no one has engaged in a little "harmless" vandalism while we were asleep; toilet paper and dog shit seem to be the weapons of choice for the most part. We no lon- ger open the curtains at night. When I take Patricia to preschool I walk her all the way into the classroom, and Yvonne picks her up right outside the same door. Patricia carries an emergency pager attached to her Scooby-Doo fanny pack; she knows how to use it and, more impor- tantly, *when*. Some of the threats have been directed at her, and her teacher keeps an extra-careful eye focused for any problems. Some of my students drive by every night to make sure no one is lurking about outside the house. I wish I could say that all of these precautions make us feel safe.

Safe.

That word seems as foreign to me now as a quantum equation. The last time I felt I understood its meaning, I had just fallen asleep on the evening of the Dyson massacre.

CHAPTER THREE

Yvonne heard the knocking before I did; I was aware only that the night had begun to strobe. I opened my eyes and saw the pirouetting patterns of visibar lights brushing against our window from outside.

"Geoff," whispered Yvonne, shaking me fully awake. "*Geoff!* The police are here."

Downstairs, the knocking on the door became louder, more insistent.

Patricia wandered into our room, rumpled and sleepy-eyed, rubbing at her face and asking what was wrong.

I climbed out of bed and threw on my bathrobe while at the same time turning on the bedside light, losing my balance only once and amazed I managed even *that* much grace for having been awake less than a minute. The officer or officers at the door evidently realized that someone was up because the knocking immediately stopped.

Yvonne looked at the clock: 3:41 A.M. "What could they want at this hour?"

I tried to smile at her and failed. "Somehow, I don't think the hour is the central issue."

"I'm scared, Geoff, don't be a wise-ass."

Patricia giggled. "You said *ass.*"

"Yes, I did, honey, and I'm sorry."

"'S'okay."

This time my smile made it all the way to the surface. I quickly fixed my bed-head hair as best I could and went down to answer the door.

Front porch lights were on at several of our neighbors' homes and I could see their faces looking out from behind curtains; a few of the braver souls even stepped out on their front porches for a better view despite the cold and snow. I didn't blame them; I might have done the same thing if the object of curiosity weren't myself—but it was, and I felt suddenly exposed, vulnerable, embarrassed . . . and maybe even a little guilty; after all, the police don't pull up in front of your house at close to four in the morning with lights blazing to congratulate you for not being a litterbug.

Two cars were parked directly in front of our house; a police cruiser and an unmarked car with an inactive cherry dome attached to the roof on the passenger side.

A well-dressed man who appeared to be my age (but looking slightly more frayed around the edges) tried to smile as I opened the door; his smile, like mine, failed.

"Geoffrey Conover?"

"Yes?"

He looked past me to where Yvonne and Patricia were paused halfway down the stairs. "I can't apologize enough for our less-than-covert entrance here, but I need—oh, sorry, forgot something." He produced his shield and ID. "I'm Detective Phil Varrasso, state police." He offered his ID and shield for closer inspection; since I have no idea what these are supposed to look like, I made a small show of examining them as if I'd be able to spot phonies from a mile away. He was considerate enough to join in my little skit and act as if he believed I knew what I was doing. I nodded and handed them back to him.

"Mr. Conover, I need you to get dressed and come with me."

The alarm on my face must have been visible from space, because he immediately looked over his shoulder at the growing number of spectators, then signaled the police cruiser to kill the visibar lights. "You're not in any trouble, sir, I'm not here to arrest you or anything like that, but—look, can I come inside?"

"Please." I closed the door behind him. He smiled at Yvonne and Patricia.

"You a p'liceman?" asked my daughter.

"I sure am. I'm here because I need your daddy's help with something."

Patricia's eyes and mouth opened wide at hearing that: a *policeman*? Here in the middle of the night because he needed her daddy's *help*? Wow—you must be *really* special, Daddy. Are you some kind of secret agent or superhero? Is being my daddy your *secret identity*?

How much more wondrous the world would be if we could see ourselves the way our children do when we surprise or impress them.

"Why?" I asked Varrasso. "What's going on?"

"I don't know all the specifics—things still haven't settled down—but I need you to come with me right away."

Yvonne chimed right in: "Where are you taking him?"

"The airport. There's a helicopter fueled and waiting to"— he turned back to me—"fly you to Cedar Hill. The authorities there need you as soon as humanly possible. I really can't emphasize this enough."

Yvonne and I looked at one another the moment he said *Cedar Hill*. Her eyes flashed an anxious *God, you just got over the* last *time*. I had yet to tell her about everything that happened two years ago—most of it, yes, but not quite all; even now, I was still processing much of it myself.

"I'd really appreciate it if you'd agree to come with me, Mr. Conover," said Varrasso. "They handed me a court order before I got in the car and I'd actually feel kind of lousy if I had to serve it to you."

"You won't have to. Of course I'll come with you."

Yvonne took Patricia's hand and started back upstairs. "I'll get some clothes for you. How long do you think he'll be gone, Detective? Do I need to pack an overnight bag?" She was already out of sight by the time she asked this second question.

Varrasso, not the least bit self-conscious, leaned forward and called up: "Three or four hours, probably. Maybe a little longer if the weather doesn't let up."

"Why now?" I asked. "It's close enough to four in the morning to call it."

He looked up the stairs again to assure himself we had a few moments to ourselves, then said in a half whisper, "Bruce Dyson regained consciousness about fifteen minutes ago. The doctors don't know how long it's going to last. He's in pretty bad shape. He's refusing to answer any questions until he speaks to you."

"*Me*? I hardly know the kid—scratch that, I don't know him *at all*, I've just seen him around school and—"

"All I can tell you is that Dyson's condition is critical enough that he isn't expected to last very long—from what I hear he should've been dead hours ago—so if we're going to get any answers we need to get them *now*, while he's still conscious and lucid. He won't talk to us, but he says he'll talk to you. My job is to help get you to Cedar Hill Memorial before he loses consciousness again or dies."

Yvonne called down that my clothes were ready. I excused myself and went to dress. I was starting to put on my shirt when Patricia tugged on my pant leg.

"You comin' back?"

"You bet."

"Promise?" There was a note of genuine fear in her voice.

I brushed some hair from her face and kissed her forehead. "I promise. Why wouldn't I?"

"Just to be a pain."

I laughed. *Just to be a pain* was Yvonne's and my catchall response to any question we were mentally ill-equipped to answer at the time. Patricia must have heard us throw it at one another a hundred times, but this was her first test drive with it. I pulled her close for a hug and quick dose of the noogies.

Patricia held on to me a moment longer and whispered, low enough for me but not Yvonne to hear: "The Graveyard People are coming back, Daddy. To keep you safe."

I leaned closer and looked into her eyes. "Are you sure?"

She nodded her head, so serious and brave.

"How do you know this, hon?"

"Your snowflake is all pink."

My "snowflake," as Patricia and Yvonne both call it, is a patch of scar tissue on my left side, between my chest and hip. It's more oval than round, and is roughly the size of my hand. It sometimes swells up in hot weather, and it looks like an old burn mark—albeit a serious burn.

"Did it do that last time? I don't remember."

Patricia nodded again, her eyes unblinking. "I thought it was going to turn into a big old pink grapefruit." Then she giggled.

I was glad one of us was keeping our nerve.

Back downstairs, Varrasso was already waiting on the front porch. I grabbed my coat from the hall tree, blew Yvonne a kiss, and closed the door, taking an extra second to make sure it had locked behind me.

Walking toward the car, I saw how dense the crowd was becoming; even though my neighbors remained on their porches or behind their windows, there was still an impressive crowd lining the walk and milling by the curb. I recognized most of them from two years before, but between some there were now gaps in which the churning snow was giving form to the new arrivals, to those who'd joined their ranks only this evening. I didn't have to look to know Varrasso couldn't see them, nor could any of the neighbors. When I got back I'd have to ask Patricia how she'd known the "Graveyard People" (a phrase she'd made up on her own) would be waiting outside to grant me safe passage. When they'd first shown up two years ago, she hadn't been afraid for even a second; she was in truth really tickled by them: it's not every kid who gets to see an honest-to-goodness gathering of ghosts.

Varrasso climbed into the front passenger seat of the unmarked vehicle and gestured for me to take a seat in the back; he then nodded at the driver—who didn't say a word the entire drive—and activated the portable cherry dome. The police cruiser hit its visibar lights (but not the siren), pulling out at least twenty miles per hour with Varrasso's car right on its tail. In less than a minute we pulled onto the highway, the siren was activated, speed was picked up, and we headed toward the airport going close to seventy. I hoped both cars had damned good snow tires.

Varrasso put on a small communications headset and radioed that I was in transit and could be expected in three to five minutes.

One of the great charms about this area, regardless of where in the city you live, is that once you hit the highway you're close to everything, and even if you get lost within the city, the road signs will eventually take you back to where you started. Yvonne and I didn't live all that far from Dayton International Airport in the first place, but from the way both cars were burning rubber you would have thought we needed to cover a quarter of the state in that time instead of half a dozen miles.

After he finished speaking with whomever had organized things at the airport, he was transferred to someone else. "Yeah?" He leaned forward, placed his fingers against the earpiece, and said, "Could you repeat that?" Then: "You're sure that's what he—yes, of course." He signed off and looked back at me. "I cannot believe that you're not wearing your seat belt."

"It's jammed."

"Yeah, shit—sorry," he replied. "Been meaning to get that fixed."

It was at that moment the driver followed the cruiser into a semisharp turn that flung me across the length of the backseat and plastered me against the door.

"Seat belt on *that* side works fine," said Varrasso. I quickly pulled it down and across, locking it solidly into place.

The snow and wind and darkness outside merged to cast a spectral fairy-tale glow over the world, making it a blurred thing of wistfulness and dream, not something I was a part of or would ever be.

Varrasso said: "Are you okay?"

"Yeah . . . yeah," I said, rubbing my cheek and realizing I needed a shave. The shape of my face felt alien, a mask, a surgical mishap, John Randolph waking up to find he'd metamorphosed into Rock Hudson in John Frankenheimer's *Seconds*, my favorite film.

"You sure?"

I nodded.

Varrasso pointed toward something in the distance. "You can see the lights of the control tower. Kind of pretty, I think."

The recurrent blinking of those two beams against the spiraling snow was oddly compelling, even hypnotic, and for a moment I imagined their rhythm was accompanied by one of those mellifluous, too-well-modulated voices you find reading books on tape, but this voice spoke only two words: *Going back . . . going back . . . going back . . .*

I closed my eyes and stretched my neck muscles. I heard things cracking beneath the skin, felt tissue twisting itself out of and then back into position. Christ, I hadn't realized I was this tense.

The cars made another turn—this one much less jarring—as we passed through a set of open security gates; I caught passing glimpses of figures in bulky coats and heavy woolen caps waving us on with burning flares in their gloved hands, and then I saw with a start that we were on the runway and driving straight toward a 747. The police cruiser killed its lights and siren and moved over so that we could pass, which we did, making a sharp left directly underneath the tail of the plane and heading toward an area about a hundred feet away where a series of ignited flares had been arranged in a large circle. Their flames snapped and spit against the cold and snow, being pressed against the ground by the force of the wind beating down from the rotating blades of the bubble-fronted helicopter that sat in the center.

Varrasso looked back at me with an anxious half grin. "Your limo awaits."

"I've never been in one of those things."

"They scare the hell out of me—don't get me wrong, Brian there's the department's best pilot, but I like for there to be more between me and a thousand-foot drop than an inch and a quarter of Plexiglas."

"I can't tell you how reassuring that is."

He looked at his watch. "A minute ahead of schedule." The car made one last turn and came to a smooth, assured stop with my door facing toward the helicopter. Varrasso released his seat belt and turned fully around, offering me his hand over the seat. "On behalf of the Ohio State Police I'd like to thank you for your cooperation, Mr. Conover. Remember to keep your head down while you're both approaching and exiting the helicopter. There'll be a car waiting here to take you home when you get back."

I released my own seat belt, leaned forward, and shook his hand. "Would you think less of me if I said I was so scared that"—I shook my head and shrugged—"that I'm just scared, that's all."

"I find that's usually enough," he replied, squeezing my hand a little tighter before letting go. "If it's any help, just remember that there are people out there tonight in your community who're in a lot of misery because they've lost a loved one, and they need *some* kind of answer, some reason why this happened. It won't bring back the dead, and it sure as hell won't blunt the immediate pain, but maybe it'll help give them enough resolve to get through the worst of the next few days. When someone dies as horribly as those people did, the survivors want to know why. They'll never *understand* the reasons, but at least they'll have them. You're going to find out for them, hopefully. Think about that as you're lifting off and maybe it'll make takeoff easier."

I almost laughed. He'd thought I was talking about being scared of flying in the helicopter.

I opened the door and was starting to climb out when Varrasso gently gripped my forearm. "Listen, I have to tell you something. A minute or two ago Dyson asked when you were coming. He knows you're en route. He said to give you a message."

I blinked against the freezing wind. *"And . . . ?"*

"'Hoopsticks.'"

Talk about triggers. Nothing fragmented, but suddenly the cold outside was nothing compared to the center of my chest. "Are you . . . are you *certain* that's what he said?"

"Two officers and a nurse heard him clear as a bell. 'Hoopsticks.' Do anything for you?"

I nodded. "You have no idea."

A beat, then Varrasso said: "You're not going to tell me, are you?"

"I've never even told my wife the whole story." Time was not my friend here; I should have already been strapped into the helicopter and flying the friendless skies but I knew he and I weren't quite finished yet.

He did not blink when he said: "It must've been something pretty terrible."

"How could you know?"

"Your face. There's a famous photo of a French guy who's crying as the Nazis march into Paris—you know the one I mean? Black-and-white. The camera's almost flat against the guy's nose. Looks like he's watching dogs chew a baby to death. I used to wonder what his face looked like the second *before* he broke down. I don't have to wonder anymore. I just have to say 'Hoopsticks' and look at you. *That's* why I'm sure it was something terrible."

I looked directly into his eyes. For some reason I couldn't begin to fathom, I knew at that moment I would have trusted Varrasso with my life. "I'll tell you. When I get back. I think I need to tell someone, finally."

"I'll pick you up myself, then."

"I look forward to it."

"Me, too. Sincerely."

And with that I climbed out, closed the door, bent over, and ran toward the helicopter. The pilot reached across and opened the door, helped me to both climb in and secure the heavy safety belt, then instructed me on how to put on and operate the communications headpiece.

"We're cleared to go. All set then, Mr. Conover?"

"As much as I can be, I guess."

"This is your first time in one of these, right?"

"Yes."

"You're going to experience a really hard lurch in your stomach when we lift off, might even feel like you're going to upchuck. It's a typical reaction and nothing to worry about, I guarantee."

"Got it."

We lifted off, my stomach lurched, and for a moment I thought I was going to upchuck, but it had little to do with there only being an inch and a quarter of Plexiglas between me and one mother of a swan dive; what made me feel like I was about to vomit up everything I'd eaten since the age of five was the word Dyson had spoken and the hypnotic blinking of the control tower lights accompanied by some voice whispering: *Going back . . . going back . . . going back . . .*

CHAPTER FOUR

It had probably always been there, but it wasn't until the autumn of 1924 that the people of Cedar Hill began to call him or it "Hoopsticks." Said to roam the streets of West Cedar Hill, he was the nightmare dread of every child, an umbrella repairman whose deformed twin brother, Gash, grew out of his back. The two of them wore a quiver slung over their shoulder, and that quiver was said to be filled with the severed spinal cords of unruly youngsters.

I'd heard the legend, as well as countless (and sometimes absurd) variations on it throughout my childhood and adolescence. Anyone who'd lived in or near Cedar Hill since the late 1800s had encountered some form of the legend; a few even took the time to write it down for posterity—after all, what better way to scare your children into behaving themselves than to threaten them with a visit from Hoopsticks if they didn't do as they were told?

I'd always thought it was just a local (albeit intensely centralized) myth that was given life after something terrible or tragic took place before the existence of the Internet or television or radio—or even printed newspapers, for that matter. (According to documents I came across at the local historical society, there was indeed a grisly mass murder during the early days of Cedar Hill's settlement, and the profoundly superstitious settlers—as profoundly superstitious settlers are wont to do—invented a "curse" to serve as an explanation for something that *had* no explanation; otherwise, the mass murder itself would have to be accepted at face value; it would have meant they suffered the wrath of God . . . but surely they had done nothing to deserve it. Amazing how effectively a well-placed parable can replace the burden of a conscience.)

A surprising amount has been written about good old Hoopsticks over the last two centuries, some of it fascinating, some of it sickening, some of it outright silly, all of it to be taken with a grain of salt and a "nice little story" grin. Because such things can't actually exist. You're an adult, you know the difference between myth and everyday truth; you can tell where to draw the line between the factual and fanciful; and you *damn well* understand that there is a proper time and appropriate place for the telling of tall tales. In short: you know a whimsical bit of deceit when you encounter it.

Hoopsticks = horseshit.

That assumption = wrong. So very wrong.

As the helicopter banked farther up into the night and began leveling out, I pressed my fists against my knees and tried to slow my breathing to a normal pace.

Only six people knew the truth about Hoopsticks; I was one of them; the other four, I knew, would never talk about it outside of their tight little group, and the sixth was dead.

None of the others had known Dyson; even if via some Möbius-strip hiccup in space-time any of them had somehow known him, *that name* was something they would never have spoken aloud; not to Dyson or anyone who *wasn't there* . . . not after what happened during the last and dreadful twenty-four hours I'd spent in Cedar Hill two years ago.

(The Graveyard People are coming back, Daddy. . . .)

So how the hell had Bruce Dyson known the name of one of the few things in this world that truly frightened me?

I'd find out soon enough. I'd talk to him, and I'd ask him why he did what he did, and I would listen carefully to what he said, but he was going to tell me where he'd heard *that goddamn name* and—

—and we need to leave me up there for a while, flying through the night winter sky toward my return visit to Cedar Hill, my balls in my throat and an inch and a half of Plexiglas separating me from the mother of all swan dives; we need to leave me like this because I left part of myself up there, though I didn't know it at the time; we need to jump ahead a little before going back even further; only in this way can we safely return to this moment and know that *here* is where we were meant to be, from the beginning. So wave good-bye for now; I'll just wait here.

There are more things you should know, not the least of which is the *other* possible beginning to this story— and that only occurred to me the following Monday morning, after I'd listened to the message Dyson had kept himself alive long enough to deliver to me. That's when the Graveyard People returned once again to my classroom.

PART ONE

GRAVEYARD PEOPLE

"Sometime then there will be every kind of a history of every one who ever can or is or was or will be living. Sometime then there will be a history of every one from their beginning to their ending. Sometime then there will be a history of all of them, of every kind of them, of every one, of every bit of living they ever have in them, of them when there is never more than a beginning to them, of every kind of them, of every one when there is very little beginning and then there is an ending, there will then sometime be a history of every one there will be a history of everything that ever was or is or will be them, of everything that was or is or will be all of any one or all of all of them . . ."
—Gertrude Stein, *The Making of Americans*, page 308

"These be
Three silent things:
The falling snow . . . the hour
Before dawn . . . the mouth of one
Just dead."
—Adelaide Crapsey, *Cinquain: Triad*

CHAPTER ONE

Weekend newscasts about the Dayton killings were quick to mention Cedar Hill, of course, and to draw tenuous parallels between what took place there and what happened here—after all, central Ohio has only known two simultaneous mass murders (the FBI's official term for describing these types of killings) in the last thirty-five years, so why shouldn't have newscasts revisited the first one? When one of my students asked me if I was "around" for the Cedar Hill murders I laughed—not raucously, mind you, but enough to solicit some worried glances.

"Yes," I said. "I was around. Please excuse . . . excuse my laugh, I know it has to seem thoughtless and in bad taste . . . it's just that no one has ever asked me that before.

"Do any of you want to discuss what happened Friday night?"

Listen to their silence after I asked this. Individual class periods had been abandoned for this Monday, so each teacher would spend the entire day with only the students in their homeroom. If any of them asked to see a grief counselor, they were to be sent at once. The point was to try and get everyone to talk about their anger, their grief, their confusion. If this silence was any indication of what the rest of the day was going to be like, I was dead in the water with iron boots and an anchor around my neck.

"Look, I don't want to make anyone feel uncomfortable, but odds are someone in this room knew at least one of the shooting victims. Believe me when I tell you—because I know from experience—you don't want to keep this to yourself. It's important to talk about what you're thinking and feeling."

Nothing—a nervous shrug, perhaps, a lot of downcast stares, even a quiet tear from someone in the last row of desks, but no one spoke.

I rubbed the side of my neck and looked toward the back wall where the ghosts of the Cedar Hill dead were assembling once again.

Go on, they whispered. *Remember us to them. It's the only way.*

"No one's going to laugh at or judge you. Twelve people are dead and some of them were your friends. You have to feel *something*."

Still nothing.

"Come on, folks, this isn't a pop quiz. There's no wrong answer." I realized I was coming dangerously close to doing the one thing we'd been warned not to do—forcing them to talk. I had to be careful.

A girl in one of the middle rows slowly raised her hand. "Could you . . . could you maybe tell us about Cedar Hill? How did you deal with it?"

I smiled my thanks to her, as did the ghosts. "I still *am* dealing with it. I went back there a couple of years ago, in fact, to find some of the survivors and talk with them. I needed to put certain things to rest and—wait a second."

As they had outside my home forty-eight hours ago, the ghosts of the newly dead locals—except for Bruce

Dyson—joined those from Cedar Hill. All of them smiled at each other like old friends.

I wished I could have known them.

Tell them everything.

Go on.

I nodded my head to the ghosts and then said to the class: "Okay, I thought this might happen, so . . . I had a meeting with the principal and superintendent before classes began this morning, and I told them that if my talking to you about Cedar Hill would get you to open up about what happened Friday night, then I'd tell you— and I wouldn't whitewash anything. They gave me permission. You need to know that some of this gets a little . . . actually, it gets *really* ugly in places and might upset you, and I'm sorry about that. If at any time any of you feel like you can't listen anymore, just let me know and I'll write a pass for you to go to study hall.

"So let's make the deal official. Since we're going to be stuck with each other for the entire day, I'll tell you about Cedar Hill only if you agree to at least *try* to talk about what happened Friday night. I promise I won't force the issue again, just think about it, okay? Maybe getting things out in the open will make it easier to live with. How's that sound?"

Another student raised her hand and asked, "Why do you suppose somebody'd do something like that?"

Tell them, demanded the ghosts.

"I went back to Cedar Hill in hopes of answering some questions about the night of the killings. I talked to witnesses and survivors over the telephone, at their jobs, in their houses, over lunches, and in nursing homes. I dug through dusty files buried in moldy boxes in the basements of various historical society offices. There were decades-old police reports to be found, then sorted through and deciphered. I tracked down over two hundred hours' worth of videotape, and then subjected my family to the foul moods that resulted from my watching those tapes. Dozens of old transcribed statements had to be located and copied, and a couple of times I had to bribe a certain seedy individual—who I'm guessing has had only a passing acquaintance with soap during his life—into leaving me alone for a couple of hours with several boxes of old and not particularly well-preserved evidence. There were graves I had to visit, names I needed to learn, individual histories lost among bureaucratic paper trails that I had to assemble, only to find they yielded nothing of use—and I'd be lying through my teeth if I said that I didn't feel more than a little guilty in deciding that so-and-so's life didn't merit so much as a footnote.

"These weren't the only ways I managed to piece everything together, so you'll excuse me if I skip over several of the more banal events of the visit and offer up what you might call the 'Good Parts' version."

That got a couple of soft laughs from around the room.

I do not purport to have sorted everything out as a result of my research. In some instances the gaps between facts were a little *too* wide and I had to fill them with conjectures and suppositions that, to the best of my knowledge and abilities, provided a *rightness* to the story that the facts did not. Yvonne says that I did it in an effort to forgive myself for having survived. She may be right. No one asked me to do it; nonetheless, certain ghosts demanded it of me—and I say this as a man who, before, never thought of himself as being particularly superstitious.

That morning, when my students asked to hear the tale, I hoped that its telling would in some way release us all from the shame and anger and guilt that threatened to forever diminish us—and "diminish" was the right word; if I had any doubts about that, I had only to remember my conversation with Bruce Dyson less than fifty hours before.

"Here is a story; if you listen carefully, at the end, you'll be someone else," I whispered to myself, and then cleared my throat, smiled at the ghosts in the back of the room, and said, "In order for you to understand . . ."

Chapter Two

... what took place in Cedar Hill, you must first understand the place itself, for it shares some measure of responsibility.

If it is possible to characterize this place by melting down all of its inhabitants and pouring them into a mold so as to produce one definitive citizen, then you will see a person who is, more likely than not, a laborer who never made it past the eleventh grade but who has managed through hard work and good solid horse sense to build the foundation of a decent middle-class existence; who works to keep a roof over his family's head and sets aside a little extra money each month to fix up the house, maybe repair that old back-door screen or add a workroom; who has one or two children who aren't exactly gifted but do well enough in school that their parents don't go to bed at night worrying that they've sired morons.

Perhaps this person drinks a few beers on the weekend—not as much as some of their rowdier friends but enough to be social. They've got their eye on some property out past the county line. They hope to buy a new color television set. They usually go to church on Sundays, not because they want to but because, well, you never know, do you?

This is the person you would be facing.

This is the person who would smile at you, shake your hand, and behave in a neighborly fashion.

But never ask them about anything that lies beyond the next paycheck. Take care not to discuss anything more than work or favorite television shows or an article from this morning's paper. Complain about the cost of living, yes; inquire about their family, by all means; ask if they've got time to grab a quick sandwich, sure; but never delve too far beneath the surface, for if you do the smile will fade, that handshake will loosen, and their friendliness will become tinged with caution.

Because this is a person who feels inadequate and does not want you to know it, who for a good long while now has suspected that his life will never be anything more than mediocre. He feels alone, abandoned, insufficient, foolish, and inept, and the only thing that keeps him going sometimes is a thought that makes him both smile and cringe: that maybe one of *his* children will decide for themselves, Hey, Dad's life isn't so bad, this burg isn't such a hole in the ground so, yeah, maybe I'll just stick around here and see what I can make of things.

And what if they do? How long until they start to walk with a workman's stoop, until they're buying beer by the case and watching their skin turn into one big nicotine stain? How long until they start using the same excuses he's used on himself to justify a mediocre life?

Bills, you know. Not as young as I used to be. Too damn tired all the time. Work'll by God take it out of you.

Ah, well . . . at least there's that property out past the county line for him to keep his eye on, and there's still that new color television set he might just up and buy. . . .

This is the person who would look back at you, whose expression would betray that they'd gotten a little lost in their own thoughts for a second there.

It happens sometimes.

So they'll blink, apologize for taking up so much of your time, wish you a good day, and head on home because the family will be waiting for supper. It was nice talking to you.

Meet Cedar Hill, Ohio.

Let us imagine that it is evening here, a little after 10 P.M. on the seventh of July, and that a pair of vivid headlight beams have just drilled into the darkness on Merchant Street. Seen from behind the safety of living room windows, the magnesium-bright strands make one silent, metronomelike sweep, then coalesce into a single lucent beacon that pulls at the vehicle trailing behind.

Imagine that although the houses along Merchant are dark, no one inside them is asleep.

The van, its off-white finish long faded to a dingy gray, glides toward its destination. It passes under the diffuse glowing cone from the sole streetlight, and the words DAVIES' JANITORIAL SERVICE painted on its side can be easily read.

The gleam from the dashboard's gauges reveals the driver to be a tense, sinewy man whose age appears to fall somewhere between a raggedy-ass forty-five and a gee-you-don't-look-it sixty. In his deeply lined face is both resignation and dread.

He was running late, and he was not alone.

A phantom, head half bowed and tilted slightly to the side, its face obscured by alternating knife-slashes of light and shadow, sat on the passenger side. Three other phantoms rode in the back, none of whom could summon enough nerve to look beyond the night at the end of their nose.

The van came to a stop, the lights were extinguished,

the engine grumbled and complained, and with the click of a turned key Merchant Street was again swallowed by the baleful graveyard silence that had recently taken up residence there.

The driver reached down next to his seat and grabbed a large flashlight. He turned and looked at the phantoms, who saw his eyes and understood the wordless command.

The driver climbed out as the phantoms threw open the rear double doors and began unloading the items needed for this job.

Merchant Street began to flicker as neighbors turned on their lights and lifted small corners of their curtains to peek at what was going on, even though no one really wanted to look at the Leonard house, much less live on the same street.

The driver of the van walked up onto the front porch of the Leonard house. His name was Jackson Davies and he owned the small janitorial company that had been hired to scour away the aftermath of four nights earlier when this more-or-less peaceful industrial community of 42,000 had been dragged kicking, screaming, and (most of all) bleeding into the national spotlight.

Davies turned on his flashlight, gliding its beam over the shards of broken glass that littered the front porch. As the shards caught the beam, each glared at him defiantly: *Come on, tough guy, big macho Vietnam vet with your bucket and Windex, let's see you take us on.*

He shifted his position, moving the beam to his right where it landed squarely on the bay window—which, like all the first-floor windows of the Leonard house, was covered by a large sheet of particleboard crisscrossed by two strips of yellow tape. A long, ugly stain covered most of the outside sill, dribbling over the edge in a few places

and down onto the porch in thin, jagged streaks. Tipping
the beam, Davies followed the streaks to another stain,
darker than the mess on the sill and wider by a good 50
percent. Just outside of this stain was a series of receding
smears that stretched across the length of the porch and
disappeared in front of the railing next to the glider.

Footprints.

Davies shook his head in disgust. Someone had tried
to pry loose the board and get inside the house. Judging
by the prints, they'd left in one hell of a hurry, running
across the porch and vaulting the rail—scared away, no
doubt, by neighbors or a passing police cruiser. Probably
a reporter from one of those goddamn tabloids, eager to
score a hefty bonus by snapping a few graphic photos of
the Infamous Scene.

Davies swallowed once, loud and hard, then swung
the light over to the front door. Spiderwebbing the frame
from every conceivable angle were more strips of yellow
tape emblazoned with large, bold black letters: **KEEP
OUT BY ORDER OF THE CEDAR HILL PO-
LICE DEPARTMENT**. An intimidating, hand-size
padlock held the door securely closed.

As he looked at the padlock, a snippet of a Rilke poem
flashed through his mind: *Who dies now anywhere in the
world, without cause dies in the world, looks at me*—

—and Jackson Davies, dropout English Lit. major, recent ex-husband, former Vietnam veteran, packer of
body bags into the cargo holds of planes at Tan Son
Nhut, one-time cleaner-upper of the massacre at My Lai
4, hamlet of Son My, Quang Ngai Province (after Lt.
William Calley, Jr. and company finished their legendary testosterone tantrum), a man who thought there was
no physical remnant of violent death he didn't have the

stomach to handle—this same Jackson Davies heard himself muttering, "Goddamn, god*damn*, *goddamn*," and felt a lump dislodge from his gut and bounce up into his throat and was damned if he knew why, but suddenly the thought of going into the Leonard house scared the living shit out of him.

Unseen by Davies, the ghosts of Irv and Miriam Leonard sat on the glider a few yards away from him. Irv had his arm around his wife and was good-naturedly scolding her for slipping that bit of poetry into Davies's head.

—I can't help it, Miriam said. And even if I could, I wouldn't. Jackson read that poem when he was in Vietnam. It was in a little paperback collection his wife gave to him. He lost that book somewhere over there, you know. He's been trying to remember that poem all these years. Besides, he's lonely for his wife and maybe that poem'll make it seem like part of her's still with him.

—Could've just gone to a library, said Irv.

—He did but he couldn't remember Rilke's name.

—Think he'll remember it now?

—I sure do hope so. Look at him, will you? Poor guy, he's so lonely, God love 'im.

—Seems nervous, don't he?

—Wouldn't you be? asked Miriam.

—That was really nice of you, hon, giving that poem back to him. You always was one for taking care of your friends.

—Charmer.

—What can I say? Seems my disposition's improved something considerable since I died.

—Oh, now, don't go bringing that up. There's not much we can do about it now.

—How come that doesn't make me feel any better?

—Maybe this'll do the trick: *Who laughs now anywhere in the night, without cause laughs in the night, laughs at me,* said Miriam.

—Don't tell me, tell the sensitive poetry soldier over there.

—I just did. I think. I know that *someone* picked it up.

They watched Davies for a few more seconds; he rubbed his face, lit a cigarette, leaned against the porch railing, and looked out into the street.

—It's not right, said Irv to his wife. What happened to us, it just wasn't fair.

—Nothing is, dear. But we're through with all of that, remember?

—If you say so.

—Worrier.

—Yeah, but at least I'm a charming worrier.

—Shhh. Did you hear that?

—Hear what?

—The children are playing in the backyard. Let's go watch.

A moment later, the wind came up and the glider swung back, then forward, once and once only, with a thin-edged screech.

Startled by the sound, Jackson Davies dropped his cigarette and decided, screw this, he was going to go wait down by the van.

He turned to leave the porch and ran smack into a phantom. Davies recoiled slightly. The phantom stepped from the scar of shadow and into the flashlight's beam and became Pete Cooper, one of Davies's crew managers.

Davies, through clenched teeth, said, "It's not a real good idea to sneak up on me like that. I have a tendency to hurt people when that happens."

"Shakin' in my shoes," said Cooper. "You gettin' the jungle jitters again? Smell that napalm in the air?"

"Yeah, right. Whacked-out 'Nam vet doing the flash-back boogie, that's me. Was there a reason you came up here or did you just miss my splendid company?"

"I just . . ." Cooper looked over at the van. "Why'd you bring the Brennert kid along?"

"Because he said yes."

"C'mon, fer chrissakes! He was *here*, you know? When it happened?"

Davies sighed and dug a fresh smoke from his shirt pocket. "First of all, he wasn't here when it happened, he was here *before* it happened. Second, of my forty-eight loyal employees, not counting you, only three said they were willing to come out here tonight, and Russell was one of them. Do you find any of this confusing so far? I could start again and talk slower."

"What're you gonna do if he gets in there and sees . . . well . . . *everything* and freezes up or freaks or some-thing?"

"I talked to him about that already. He says he won't lose it and I believe him. Besides, the plant's going to be laying his dad off in a couple of weeks and his family could use the money."

"Back up," said Cooper. "You're telling me that you couldn't find anyone else who wanted to make three hundred bucks for a couple of hours' work?"

"Not for this house, I couldn't."

"Yeah, well, Brennert's *your* problem, okay? I'll keep the other guys in line, but he's all yours."

"Fine. Anything else? The suspense is doing wonders for my colon."

"Just that this seems like an odd hour to be starting."

Davies made a quick, sweeping gesture with his arm that drew Cooper's attention back to the street. "Look around us, Pete. Tell me what you don't see."

"I'm too tired for your goddamn riddles."

"You never were any fun. What you don't see are any *reporters* or any trace of their nauseating three-ring circus that blew into this miserable burg a few nights back. The county is paying us, and the county decided that our chances of being accosted by reporters would be practically nil if we came out late in the evening. So here we are, and I'm no happier about it than you are. Despite what people say, I do have a life. Admittedly, it isn't much of one since my wife decided that we get along better living in separate states, but it's a life, nonetheless. I just thank God she left me the cats and the Mitch Miller sing-along records or I'd be a sorry specimen right about now. To top it all off, I seem to have developed a retroactive case of the willies, which is why I'm prattling on like this. Please tell me to be quiet."

"But it's so entertaining."

"Of course. Wouldn't be a traffic accident without innocent bystanders."

They watched as a police cruiser pulled up behind the van.

"Ah," said Davies. "That would be the keys to the kingdom of the dead."

"You plan to keep up the joking?"

Davies's face turned into a slab of granite and his voice dropped to a deadly whisper. "You bet your ass I do, Pete. And I'm going to keep on making jokes until we're finished with this job and loading things up to go home. The sicker and more tasteless I can make them, the better. Don't worry if I make jokes. Worry if I stop."

They went to meet the police officers, unaware that as

they came down from the porch and started across the lawn they walked right through the ghost of Andy Leonard, who stood looking at the house where he'd spent his entire, sad, brief, and ultimately tragic life.

CHAPTER THREE

On July fourth of that year Irv Leonard and his wife were hosting a family reunion at their home at 182 Merchant Street. All fifteen members of their immediate family were present and several neighbors stopped by, at the Leonards' invitation, to visit, watch some football, enjoy a hearty lunch from the ample buffet Miriam had been preparing since early in the week, and see Irv's newly acquired pearl-handled antique Colt Army .45 revolvers.

Irv, a retired steelworker and lifelong gun enthusiast, had been collecting firearms since his early twenties and was purported to have one of the five most valuable collections in the state.

Neighbors later remarked that the atmosphere in the house was as pleasant as you could hope for, though a few did notice that Andy—the youngest of the four Leonard children and the only one still living at home—seemed a bit "distracted."

Around 8:45 that evening Russell Brennert, a friend of Andy's from Cedar Hill High School, came by after getting off work from his part-time job. Witnesses described Andy as being "abrupt" with Russell, as if he didn't want him to be there. Some speculated that the two might have had an argument recently that Andy was still sore about. In any case, Andy excused himself and went up-stairs to "check on something."

Russell started to leave but Miriam insisted he fix himself a sandwich first. A few minutes later, Andy—apparently no longer upset—reappeared and asked if Russell would mind driving Mary Alice Hubert, Miriam's mother and Andy's grandmother, back to her house. The seventy-three-year-old Mrs. Hubert, a widow of ten years, was still recovering from a mild heart attack in December and had forgotten to bring her medication. The seventeen-year-old Brennert offered to take Mary Alice's house key and drive over by himself for the medicine, but Andy insisted Mrs. Hubert go along.

"I thought it seemed kind of odd," said Bill Gardner, a neighbor who was present at the time, "Andy being so bound and determined to get the two of them out of there before the fireworks started. Poor Miriam didn't know what to make of it all. I mean, I was on my way out and didn't think it was any of my business, but you'd think *somebody* would've said . . . I don't know . . . said something about it. Andy started getting outright rude. If he'd been my kid I'd've snatched him bald-headed, act-ing that way. And after his mom'd gone to all that fuss to make everything so nice."

Mrs. Hubert prevented things from getting out of hand by saying it would be best if she went with Russell; after all, she was an "old broad," set in her ways, and ev-erything in an old broad's house had to be *just so* . . . besides, there were so many medicine containers in her cabinet Russell might just "bust his brain right open" trying to figure out which was the right one.

As the two were on their way out, Andy stopped them at the door to give Mrs. Hubert a hug.

According to her, Andy seemed ". . . really sorry about something. He's a strong boy, an athlete, and I don't care what anyone says, he should've got that scholarship. Okay, maybe he wasn't as bright as some kids, but he was a fine athlete and them college people should've let that count for something. It was terrible, listening to him talk about how he was maybe gonna have to go to work at the factory to earn his college money . . . everybody knows where that leads. I'm sorry, I got off the track, didn't I? You asked about him hugging me when we left that night . . . well, he was always real careful when he hugged me never to squeeze too hard—these old bones can't take it—but when he hugged me then I thought he was going to break my ribs. I just figured it was on account he felt bad about the argument. I didn't mean to create such a bother, I thought I had the medicine with me, but I . . . well, I forget things sometimes.

"He kissed me on the cheek and said 'Bye, Grandma. I love you.' It wasn't so much the words, he always said that same thing to me every time I left . . . it was the way he said them. I remember thinking he was going to cry, that's how those words sounded, so I said, 'Don't worry about it. Your mom knows you didn't mean to be so surly.' I told him that when I got back we'd watch the rest of the fireworks and then make some popcorn and maybe see a movie on the TV. He used to like doing that with me when he was littler.

"He smiled and touched my cheek with two of his fingers—he'd never done that before—and he looked at Russ like maybe he wanted to give him a hug, too, but boys that age don't hug each other, they think it makes them look like queers or something, but I could see it in Andy's eyes that he *wanted* to hug Russ.

"Then he said the strangest thing. He looked at Russ

and kind of . . . *slapped* the side of Russ's shoulder—friendly, you know, like men'll do with each other when they feel too silly to hug? Anyway, he, uh, did that shoulder thing, then looked at Russ and said, 'His quiver is empty, and that will not do.' I figured it was a line from some movie they'd seen together. They love their movies, those two, always quoting lines to each other like some kind of secret code—like in *Citizen Kane* with 'Rosebud.' That kind of thing.

"It wasn't until we were almost to my house that Russ asked me if I knew what the heck Andy meant when he said that.

"I knew right then that something was awful wrong. Oh Lord, when I think of it now . . . the . . . the *pain* a soul would have to be in to do something . . . like that. . . ."

Russell Brennert and Mary Alice Hubert left the Leonard house at 9:05 P.M. As soon as he saw Brennert's car turn the corner at the end of the street, Andy immediately went back upstairs and did not come down until the locally sponsored Kiwanis Club fireworks display began at 9:15.

Several factors contributed to the neighbors' initial failure to react to what happened. Firstly, there was the thunderous noise of the fireworks themselves. Since White's Field, the site of the fireworks display, was less than half a mile away, the resounding boom of the cannons was, as one person described, ". . . damn near loud enough to rupture your eardrums. Some folks was even stuffing cotton into their ears."

Secondly, music from a pair of concert hall speakers that Bill Gardner had set up in his front yard compounded the glass-rattling noise and vibrations of the cannons. "Every Fourth of July," said Gardner, "WLCB (a local low-wattage FM radio station) plays music to go along with the fireworks. You know, 'America the Beautiful,' 'Stars and Stripes Forever,' stuff like that, and every year I tune 'em in and set my speakers out and let fly. Folks on this street want me to do it, they all like it. How the fuck was I supposed to know Andy was gonna flip out?"

Third and lastly, there were innumerable firecrackers being set off by neighborhood children. This not only added to the general racket but also accounted for the neighbors ignoring certain visual clues once Andy moved outside. "You have to understand," said one detective, "that everywhere around these people, up and down the street, kids were setting off all different kinds of things: firecrackers, sparklers, bottle rockets, M-80s, for God's sake! Is it any wonder it took them so long to tell the difference between the burst of a firecracker and the muzzle flash from a gun?

"Andy Leonard had to've been planning this for a long time. He knew there'd be noise and explosions and lights and a hundred other things to distract everyone from what he was doing."

At exactly 9:15 P.M. Andy Leonard walked calmly downstairs carrying three semiautomatic pistols stuffed into his belt—a Walther P38 9mm Parabellum, a Mauser Luger 7.65mm, and a Coonan .357 Magnum—and was carrying a Heckler & Koch HK53 5.56mm assault rifle that he laid across the top of the dining room table. He had taken the weapons from his father's massive oak gun cabinet upstairs after forcing open one of its doors with a crowbar.

Of the thirteen other family members present at that time, five—including Irv Leonard, sixty-two, and his oldest son, Chet, twenty-five—were outside watching the fireworks. Andy's two older sisters—Jessica, twenty-nine, and Elizabeth, thirty-four (both of whose husbands

were also outside)—were in the kitchen hurriedly help-
ing their mother put away the buffet leftovers so they
could join the men on the front lawn.

Jessica's three children—Randy, age seven; Theresa,
four; and Joseph, nine months—were in the living room.
Randy and his sister were just finishing changing their
baby brother's diaper and were in a hurry to get out and
see the fireworks, so they paid no attention to their uncle. They were strapping Joseph into his safety seat. The
infant thought they were playing with him and giggled
a lot.

Elizabeth's two children—Ian, twelve, and Lori,
nine—were thought to be already outside but were upstairs in the makeshift game room—which contained,
among other items, a pool table, a large color television,
and a massive component stereo system.

By the time Andy walked downstairs at 9:15, Ian and
Lori were already dead, their skulls crushed by repeated
blows with, first, a gun butt, then a pool cue, and, at the
last, with billiard balls that were crammed into their
mouths after their jaws were wrenched loose.

Laying the HK53 across on top of the dinner table,
Andy walked into the kitchen, raised the .357, and shot
his sister Jessica through the back of the head. She was
standing with her back to him, in the process of putting
some food into the refrigerator. The shot blew out most
of her brain and sheared away half of her face. When she
dropped she pulled two refrigerator shelves and their
contents down with her.

Andy then shot Elizabeth—once in the stomach, once
in the center of her chest—then turned the gun on his
mother, shooting at point-blank range through her right
eye.

After that things happened very quickly. Andy left the

kitchen and collided with his niece, who was running toward the front door. He caught her by the hair and swung her face-first into a thirty-inch-high cast-iron statue that sat against a wall in the foyer. The statue was a detailed reproduction of the famous photograph of the American flag being raised on Mount Suribachi at Iwo Jima.

Theresa slammed against it with such force that her nose shattered, sending bone fragments shooting backward down her throat. Still gripping her long strawberry blonde hair in his fist, Andy lifted her off her feet and impaled her by the throat on the tip of the flagstaff. The blood patterns on the wall behind the statue indicated an erratic arterial spray, leading the on-scene medical examiner to speculate she must have struggled to get free at some point; this, along with the increase in serotonin and free histamine levels in the wound, indicated Theresa had lived for at least three minutes after being impaled.

Seven-year-old Randy saw his uncle impale Theresa on the statue, then—grabbing the carrying handle of Joseph's safety seat—picked up his infant brother and ran toward the kitchen. Andy shot him in the back of his right leg. Randy went down, losing his grip on Joseph's safety seat, which skittered across the blood-sopped tile floor and came to a stop inches from Jessica's body. Little Joseph, wide-awake, frightened, and helpless in the seat, began to cry.

Randy tried to stand but his leg was useless, so he began moving toward Joseph by kicking out with his left leg and using his elbows and hands to pull himself forward.

Nine feet away, Andy stood at the kitchen entrance watching his nephew's valiant attempt to save the baby.

Then he shot Randy between the shoulders.

And the kid kept moving.

As Andy took aim to fire again, the front door swung

open and Keith Shannon, Elizabeth's husband, stuck his head in and shouted for everyone to hurry up and come on.

Shannon saw Theresa's body dangling from the statue and screamed over his shoulder at the other men out on the lawn, then rushed inside, calling out the names of his wife and children.

He never stopped to see if Theresa was still alive.

Andy stormed across the kitchen and through the second, smaller archway that led into the rooms on the front left side of the house. As a result of taking this shortcut he beat Shannon to the living room by a few seconds, enabling him to take his brother-in-law by surprise. Andy emptied the rest of the Magnum's rounds into Shannon's head and chest. One shot went wild and shattered the large front bay window.

Andy tossed the Magnum aside and pulled both the Mauser and Walther from his belt, holding one pistol in each hand. He bolted from the living room, through the dining room, and rounded the corner into the foyer just as Irv hit the top step of the porch.

Andy kicked open the front door and for the next fifteen seconds, while the sky ignited and some country singer wailed how God should bless this country he loved, God bless the USA, the front porch of the Leonard house became a shooting gallery as each of the four remaining adult males—at least two of whom were drunk—came up onto the porch one by one and were summarily executed.

Andy fired both pistols simultaneously, killing his father, his uncle Martin, his older brother Chet, and Tom Hamilton, Jessica's husband.

A neighbor across the street, Bess Paynter, saw Irv's pulped body wallop backward onto the lawn and yelled for her husband, Francis. Francis took one look out the window and said, "Someone's gone crazy." Bess was already calling the police.

Andy went back into the house and grabbed the rifle from the dining room table, then headed for the kitchen where Randy, still alive, was attempting to drag Joseph through the back door. When he heard his uncle come into the kitchen, Randy reached out and grabbed a carving knife from the scattered contents of the cutlery drawer that Miriam had wrenched loose when she fell, then threw himself over his infant brother.

"That was one goddamn brave kid," an investigator said later. "Here he was, in the middle of all these bodies, he had two bullets in him so we know he was in a lot of pain, and the only thing that mattered to him was protecting his baby brother. An amazing kid. His folks would've been proud. Hell, it makes me proud. If there's one bright spot in all this shit, it's in knowing that that kid loved his brother enough to . . . well . . . ah, hell, I can't talk about it anymore."

For some reason Andy did not shoot his nephew a third time. He came across the kitchen floor and raised the butt of the rifle to bludgeon Randy's skull, and that's when Randy, in his last moments, pushed himself forward and jammed the knife deep into his uncle's calf. Then he died.

Andy dropped to the floor, screaming through clenched teeth, and pulled the knife from his leg. He grabbed his nephew's lifeless body and heaved it over onto its back, then beat its face in with his fists. After that, he loaded fresh clips into the pistols, grabbed Joseph, and stumbled out the back door to the garage and drove away in Irv's brand-new pickup.

At 9:21 P.M. the night-duty dispatcher at the Cedar Hill Police Department received Bess Paynter's call. As was SOP, the dispatcher, while believing Bess had heard gunfire, asked if she was certain that someone had been shot. This dispatcher later defended their actions by saying, ". . . every year we get yahoos all over this city who decide that the Kiwanis's fireworks display is the perfect time to go out in their backyard and fire their guns into the air—well, the Fourth and New Year's Eve, we get a lot of that. We had all our units out that night, just like every holiday, and there were drunks to deal with, bar fights, illegal fireworks being set off—M-80s and such, traffic accidents . . . holidays tend to be a bit of mess for us around here. Seems that's when everybody and their brother decides to act like a royal horse's ass.

"The point is, if we get a report of alleged gunfire during the fireworks, we're required to ask the caller if anyone has been hurt. If not, then we get to it as soon as we can. It may take a while, but we'll get there. If we had to send a cruiser to check out every report of gunfire that comes in during the fireworks on the Fourth of July, we'd never get anything else done. I didn't do anything wrong. It's not my fault."

It took Bess Paynter and her husband the better part of three minutes to convince the dispatcher that someone had gone crazy over at the Leonard house and shot everyone. The dispatcher agreed to send a cruiser to check it out.

Francis, red-faced with fury at this point, screamed at the dispatcher that they'd better make it fast because he was grabbing his hunting rifle and going over there himself, goddammit.

And he did just that.

The first cruiser was dispatched at 9:24 P.M.

At 9:27 a call came in from the Leonard house; by noon the next day, that phone call would be heard by most of the nation, courtesy of all three networks, as well as newscasts from hundreds of local stations across the country:

"This is Francis Paynter. My wife and I called you a couple of minutes ago. I'm standing in the . . . the kitchen of the Leonard house . . . that's 182 Merchant Street . . . and I've got somebody's brains stuck to the bottom of my shoe.

"There's been a shooting here. A little girl's body is impaled on a statue in the hallway and there's blood all over the walls and the floors and I can't tell where one person's body ends and the next one begins because everybody's dead. I can still smell the gunpowder and smoke.

"Is that good enough for you to do something? C-c-could you maybe please if it's not too much trouble send someone out here NOW? It might be a good idea, because the crazy BASTARD WHO DID THIS ISN'T HERE—and I think he might've took a baby with him."

By 9:30 P.M. Merchant Street was clogged with police cruisers.

By then Andy Leonard was halfway to Moundbuilder's Park, where the Second Presbyterian Church was sponsoring parish family night. Over one hundred people had been gathered at the park since five in the afternoon, picnicking, tossing Frisbees, playing checkers or flying kites. A little before nine, the president of the parish council had arrived with a truckload of folding chairs that were set up in a clearing at the south end of the park.

By the time Francis Paynter made his famous phone call, 107 parish members were seated in twelve neat little rows watching the fireworks display.

Between leaving his Merchant Street house and arriving at Moundbuilder's Park, Andy Leonard shot and killed six more people as he drove past them. Two were in a car, the other four had been sitting out on their lawns watching the fireworks. In every case, Andy simply kept one hand on the steering wheel while shooting with the other through an open window. One witness along the route said they thought they heard him shouting about quivering or something being empty.

At 9:40 P.M., just as the fireworks kicked into high gear for the grand finale, Andy drove his father's pickup truck at eighty miles per hour through the wooden gate at the northeast side of the park, barreled across the picnic grounds, over the grassy mound that marked the south border, and went straight down into the middle of the spectators.

Three people were killed and eight others injured as the truck plowed into the back row of chairs. Andy threw open the door and leapt from the truck and opened fire with the HK53. The parishioners scrambled in panic, many of them falling over chairs. Of the dead and wounded at the park, none was able to get farther than ten yards away before being shot.

Andy stopped only long enough to yank the pistols from the truck. The first barrage with the rifle was to disable; the second, with the pistols, was to finish off anyone who might still be alive.

At 9:45 P.M. Andy Leonard crawled up onto the roof of his father's pickup truck and watched the grand finale of the fireworks display. The truck's radio was tuned in to WLCB. The bombastic finish of the *1812 Overture* erupted along with the fiery colors in the dark heaven above.

The music and the fireworks ended.

Whirling visibar lights could be seen approaching the park. The howl of sirens hung in the air like a protracted musical chord.

Andy Leonard shoved the barrel of the rifle in his mouth and blew most of his head off. His nearly decapitated body fell backward on the roof, then slid slowly down the hood of the truck, smearing a long trail of gore down the center of the windshield.

Twenty minutes later, just as Russell Brennert and Mary Alice Hubert turned onto Merchant Street to find it blocked by police cars and ambulances, one of the officers on the scene at Moundbuilder's Park heard what he thought was the sound of a baby crying. Moments later, he discovered Joseph Hamilton, still alive and still in his safety seat, on the passenger-side floor of the pickup. The infant was clutching a bottle of formula that had been taken from his mother's baby bag.

CHAPTER FOUR

I stopped at this point and took a deep breath, surprised to find that my hands were shaking. I looked to the ghosts and they whispered *Courage*.

I swallowed once, nodded my head, then said to my students: "I suspect a lot of you probably already know from the news and the movie, but I'm just going to say it outright so there's no confusion on the point: that baby—Joseph Hamilton—was me.

"I have no idea why Andy didn't kill me. I was taken from the hospital and then placed in the care of Cedar Hill Children's Services." I opened my briefcase and removed a file filled with photocopies of old newspaper articles and began passing them around the room; I had brought several pieces of my research along that morning in case I'd need them to prompt discussion among my students. "The details of how I came to be adopted by the Conovers are written about in these articles. Suffice to say that I was arguably the most famous baby in the country for the next week or so."

One student held up a copy of an article and said, "It says here that the Conovers took you back to Cedar Hill six months after the killings. Says you were treated like a celebrity."

I looked at the photo accompanying the article and shook my head. "I wasn't even a year and a half old. I have no memory of that at all. At home, in a box I keep in my filing cabinet, are hundreds of cards I received from people all over the country, not just those who lived in Cedar Hill at that time. Most of the Cedar Hill people are either dead or have moved away now, and when I went back there two years ago I could only find a handful of them.

"It's odd to think that, somewhere out there, there are dozens, maybe even hundreds, of people who prayed for me when I was a baby, people I never knew and never will know. For a while I was at the center of their thoughts. I like to believe these people still think of me from time to time. I like to believe it's those thoughts and prayers that keep me safe from harm.

"But as I said, this story isn't about me. Maybe it never was. Some mysteries interwoven with one's heritage have to be confronted even if there's no possible chance of finding an answer. Since I'm not arrogant enough to say, 'Listen: I know everything now,' I don't have much choice but to offer this as something of a folktale, because that's what it's always been to me. Thinking of it in those terms helps me to live with it. I suspect it'll be this way until I die. If there's any Great Truth to be found, I'm not the one to tell you what it might be. From the moment that nameless police officer found a squalling baby on the floor of a murderer's truck I ceased to be a part of the story. But it's never stopped being a part of me."

Details were too sketchy for the eleven o'clock news to offer anything concrete about the massacre, but by the time the local network affiliates broadcast their news-at-sunrise programs, the tally was in.

Counting himself, Andy Leonard had murdered thirty-two people and wounded thirty-six others, making his spree the largest single mass shooting to date in the U.S. (Some argued that since the shootings took place in two different locations they should be treated as two separate incidents, while others insisted that since Andy had continuously fired his weapons up until the moment of his death, including the trail of shootings between his house and the park, it was all one single incident. What could not be argued was the body count, which made the rest of it more than a bit superfluous.)

Those victims were what the specter of my uncle was thinking about as Jackson Davies and Pete Cooper walked through him.

Andy's ghost hung its head and sighed, then took one half step to the right and vanished back into the ages where it would relive its murderous rampage in perpetuity, always coming back to the moment it stood outside the house and watched as two men passed through it on their way toward a police officer.

Russell Brennert looked at the two other janitors who'd come along tonight and knew without asking that neither one of them wanted him to be here. Of course not; *he* had known the crazy fucker, *he* had been Andy Leonard's best friend, *his* presence made it all just a bit more real than they wanted it to be. Did they think that some part of what had driven Andy to kill all of those people had rubbed off on him, as well?

He finished unloading the last of the wheeled buckets, then filled each one with towels, scrub sponges, one-quart bottles of industrial cleaner concentrate, wax remover, finish-stripping liquid, a pair of yellow rubber gloves, fiberglass face masks to protect against chemical fumes, a roll of paper towels, a spray bottle of Windex, an extra mop head and, of course, a mop. There were five buckets in all, so this took a few minutes—during which neither of his coworkers offered to help, for which Russell was grateful; at least he wouldn't have to stand here and try to make conversation with . . . with . . .

Christ, he couldn't even remember their names. Not that it was any big deal, mind you. He'd seen these guys around school often enough but never in any kind of a social situation. They passed in the halls during class change, stood in line in the cafeteria; Russell had homeroom with one of them—

—hell with it, he thought. Call them Mutt and Jeff and leave it at that. Odds were they wanted even less to do with him than he did with them.

He checked (for the third or fourth time) to make sure each plastic barrel had plenty of extra trash bags. Then Mutt came over and, fighting the smirk trying to sneak onto his face, asked, "Hey, Brennert—that's your name, right?"

"Yeah."

"We were just wonderin' if, well . . . if it's true, y'know?"

"If *what's* true?"

Mutt gave a quick look to Jeff, who turned away and oh-so-subtly covered his mouth with his hand.

Russell dug his fingernails into his palms to keep from getting angry; these guys were going to pull something, or say something, he just knew it.

Mutt sniffed dryly as he turned back to Russell. He'd given up trying to fight back the smirk on his face.

Russell bit his lower lip. *Stay cool, you can do it, you need the money.*

"We'd just been wonderin'," said Mutt, "if it's true that you and Leonard used to . . . go to the movies together."

Jeff snorted a laugh and tried to cover it up by coughing.

Russell held his breath. "Sometimes, yeah."

"Just the two of you or you guys ever take dates?"

You're doing fine, just fine, he's a mutant, just keep that in mind.

"Sometimes it was just him and me. Sometimes he'd bring Barb along."

"Yeah, yeah . . ." Mutt leaned in, lowering his voice to a mock-conspiratorial whisper. "The thing is, we heard that the two of you went to the drive-in together a couple of days before he shot everybody."

Fine and dandy, yessir. "That's right. Barb was going to come along but she had to babysit her sister at the last minute."

Mutt chewed on his lower lip to bite back a giggle. Russell caught a peripheral glimpse of Davies and Cooper heading back up to the porch with one of the cops.

"How come you and your buddy went to the drive-in all by yourselves?"

Russell blinked, then swallowed. Once. Very hard. "We wanted to see the movie." *Jesus, Jackson, get down here, will you?*

Russell didn't hear all of the next question because the pulsing of his blood sounded like a jackhammer in his ears.

". . . thigh?"

Russell blinked, exhaled, and dug his nails in a little deeper. "I'm sorry, could you run that by me again?"

"I said, last week after gym when we was all in the showers I noticed you had a sucker-bite on your thigh."

"Birthmark."

"You sure about that? Seemed to me it looked like a big ol' hickey."

"Stare at my thighs a lot, do you?"

Mutt's face went blank. Jeff jumped to his feet and snarled, "Hey, watch it, motherfucker."

"Watch what?" snapped Russell. "Why don't you feebs just leave me alone? I've got better things to do than be grilled by a couple of redneck homophobes."

"Ha! Homo, huh?" said Mutt. "I always figured the two of you musta been butt-buddies."

"Fag-bags," said Jeff; then the two flaming wits high-fived one another.

Russell suddenly realized that one of his hands had reached over and gripped a mop handle. *Don't do it, Russ, don't you dare, they're not worth it.* "Think whatever you want. I don't care." He turned away from them in time to see a bright blue van pull up behind the police cruiser. A small satellite dish squatted like a gargoyle on top of the van and Russell could see through the windshield that Ms. Tanya Claymore, Channel 9's red-hot newsbabe, was inside.

"Oh shit," he whispered.

One of the reasons he'd agreed to help out tonight— the money aside—was so he wouldn't have to stay at home and hear the phone ring every ten minutes and answer it to find some reporter on the other end asking for Mr. Russell Brennert oh this is him I'm Whatsis-name from the In-Your-Face Channel, central Ohio's News Authority and I wanted to ask you yadda-yadda a few questions about Andy oogity-boogity Leonard, cha-cha-cha.

It had been like that for the last three days. He'd hoped

that coming out here tonight would give him a reprieve from everyone's constant questions but it seemed—

—put the ego in park, Russ. Yeah, maybe they called the house and Mom or Dad told them you'd be out here, but it's just possible they came out in hopes of getting inside the house for a few minutes' worth of video for tomorrow's news.

He thought about it another moment and decided that his second notion was the right one. The police hadn't let any reporters see the inside of the house and had even posted guards to make sure no one tried to sneak in. News vans had police scanners, didn't they? Tanya Claymore and her crew had probably heard the cops in the cruiser radio that they were going over to let the janitors into the house.

"Hey, ass-bandit!"

Russell looked down at his hand on the mop handle and smiled, but there was not one ounce of humor in it.

Mutt smacked the back of his shoulder much harder than was needed just to get his attention. "Hey, yo! Brennert, I'm talking to you."

"Please leave me alone. Please?"

All along the murky-death membrane that was Merchant Street porch lights snapped on and ghostly forms shuffled out in bathrobes and housecoats, some with curlers in their hair or shoddy slippers on their feet.

Mutt and Jeff both laughed, but not too loudly.

"What's it like to corn-hole a psycho, huh?"

"I—" Russell swallowed the rest of the sentence and started toward the house, but Mutt grabbed his arm, wrenching him backward and spinning him around.

One of the tattered specters grabbed her husband's arm and pointed from their porch to the three young men by the van: did it look like there was some trouble?

The ghosts of Irv and Miriam Leonard, accompanied by their grandchildren Ian, Theresa, and Lori, stood off to the side of the house and watched as well. Irv shook his head in disgust and Miriam wiped at her eyes.

—Just breaks your heart, doesn't it? she whispered to her husband. The way they're treating him. And he's such a nice, respectful boy.

—I always thought a lot of him, replied Irv. Shit, if I had actual hands I could use, I'd go down there and wring those other two boys' necks.

On the porch of the Leonard house, an impatient Jackson Davies waited while the officer ripped down the yellow tape and inserted the key into the lock.

"Jackson?" said Pete Cooper.

"What?"

Cooper cleared his throat and lowered his voice. "Do you remember what you said about no reporters being around?"

"Yeah, so wha—" Then he saw the Channel 9 News van. "Ah, fuck me with a fiddlestick. They plant a homing device on that poor kid or something?" He watched Tanya Claymore slide open the side door and lower one of her too-perfect legs toward the ground like some Hollywood starlet exiting a limo at a movie premiere.

"Dammit, I *told* you bringing Brennert along would be a mistake."

"Thank you, Mr. Hindsight. Let *me* worry about it?"

Cooper gestured toward the news van and said, "Aren't you gonna do something?"

"I don't know if I can." Davies directed this remark to the police officer unlocking the door. The officer looked over his shoulder and shrugged, then said, "If she interferes with your crew performing the job you pay them for, you've got every right to tell her to go away."

"Just make sure you get her phone number first," said Cooper.

Davies turned his back to them and stared at Tanya Claymore. If she even so much as *looked* at Russell, he'd drop on her like a curse from heaven.

Down by the trash barrels and buckets, Mutt was standing less than an inch from Russell's face. "All right, asshole-licker, let's get to it. People're sayin' that you maybe knew what Andy was gonna do and didn't say anything."

"I didn't," whispered Russell, more to himself than anyone. "I didn't know."

Some part of him realized that Tanya's cameraman had turned on his light and was taping them, but he was backed too far into a corner to care right now.

"Yeah," said Mutt contemptuously. "I'll just bet you didn't."

"I *didn't* know, all right? He never said . . . never said a thing to me."

"According to the news, he was in an awful hurry to get you out before he went ape-shit."

For a moment Russell found himself back in the car with Mary Alice, turning the corner and being almost blinded by visibar lights; then that cop came over and pounded on the window and said, "This area's restricted for the moment, kid, so you're gonna have to—" and Mary Alice shouted, "Is that the Leonard house? Did something happen to my family?" and then the cop shone his flashlight in and asked, "You a relative, ma'am?" and Mary Alice was already in tears and Russell felt something boiling up from his stomach because he saw one of the bodies being covered by a sheet and then Mary Alice screamed and fell against him and a sick cloud of pain descended on their skulls—

"I had no idea, okay?" The words fell to the ground in a heap. Russell thought he could almost see them groan before the darkness put them out of their misery. "Do I have to keep on saying that or should I just write it in Braille and shove it up your—"

"—you knew, you *had* to know!" The mean-spirited mockery of earlier was gone from Mutt's voice, replaced by anger with some genuine hurt wrapped around it. "He was your best friend!"

You need the money, Russell.

"Two of 'em was always together," said Jeff, just loud enough for the microphone to get every word. "Everybody figured that Brennert here was queer and in love with Andy."

Three hundred dollars, Russell. Grocery money for a month, if you use sale coupons. Mom and Dad will appreciate it.

It seemed that both of his hands were gripping the mop handle, and somehow that mop was no longer in the bucket.

He heard a chirpy voice go into its popular singsong mode: "This is Tanya Claymore. I'm standing outside the house of Irving and Miriam Leonard at 182 Merchant Street where—"

"You wanna do something about it?" said Mutt, pushing Russell's shoulder. "Think you're man enough to mess with me?"

Russell was vaguely aware of Davies coming down from the porch and shouting something at the news crew; he was only dimly aware of the second police officer climbing from the cruiser and making a beeline to Ms. Newsbabe; and he was only abstractedly aware of Mutt saying, "How come you came along to help with the cleanup tonight? Idea of seeing all that blood and brains get you hard, does it? You a sick fuck just like Andy?"; but the one thing of which he was fully, almost gleefully aware, was that the mop had become a javelin in his hands and he was going to go for the gold and hurl the thing right into Mutt's great big ugly target of a mouth—

—*Three hundred dollars should just about cover the emergency room bill*—

—then a hand clamped down so hard on Mutt's shoulder Russell thought he heard bones crack.

Jackson Davies's smiling face swooped in and hovered between them. "If you're finished with this nerve-tingling display of machismo, we have a house to clean, remember?" Still clutching Mutt's shoulder in a Vulcan death grip, Davies hauled the boy around and pushed him toward one of the barrels.

"Hey, we were just—"

"I know what you were *just*, thank you very much. I'd appreciate it"—he gestured toward Jeff—"if you and Swamp Thing here would get off your asses and start carrying supplies inside." Russell reached for a couple of buckets but Davies stopped him. "You stay with me." Mutt and Jeff stood staring as Ms. Newsbabe came jiggling up to Russell in all of her journalistic glory.

Davies glowered at the two boys and said, "Yes, her bazooba-wobblies are very big and no, you can't touch them. Now get moving before I become unpleasant."

They became a blur of legs and mop buckets. Russell said, "Mr. Davies, I'm sorry but—"

"Hold that thought."

Tanya and her cameraman were almost on top of them; a microphone came toward their faces like a projectile.

"Russell?" said Tanya. "Russell, hi. I'm Tanya Claymore and—"

"A friend of mine once got in the way of a claymore," said Davies. "Made his sphincter switch places with his eardrums. I was scraping his spleen off my face for a week. Please don't bother any member of my crew, Ms. Claymore."

The reporter's startling green eyes widened. She made a small, quick gesture with her free hand, and her cameraman swung around to get Davies into the frame.

"We'd like to talk to *both* of you, Mr. Davies—"

"Go. A. Way." Davies looked at Russell and the two of them grabbed the remaining buckets and barrels and started toward the house.

Tanya Claymore sneered at Davies's back, then turned around and waved to the driver of the news van. He looked over and she mimed talking into a telephone receiver. The driver nodded his head and grabbed the microphone from the radio unit inside. Tanya gave her microphone to the cameraman and took off after Davies.

"Mr. Davies, please, could you—dammit, I'm in heels! Would you *wait* a second?"

"Oh yeah, she wants me," whispered Davies to Russell. "We've got this whole Tracy-Hepburn thing going already, can you feel it?" Despite everything, Russell gave a little smile. He liked Jackson Davies a lot and was glad this man was his boss.

Tanya stumbled up the incline of the lawn and held out one of her hands for Davies to take hold of and help her.

"Are those fingernails real or press-ons?" asked Davies, not making a move.

Russell put down his supplies and gave her the help she needed. As soon as she reached level ground she offered a sincere smile and squeezed his hand in thanks.

Davies said, "What's it going to take to make you leave us alone?"

Her eyes hardened but the smile remained. "All I want is to talk to the both of you about what you're going to do."

"It's a little obvious, isn't it?"

"Central Ohio would like to know."

"Oh," said Davies. "I see. You're in constant touch with central Ohio, are you? Champion of the common folk in your fake nails and designer dress and tinted contacts?"

"Does all of that just come to you or do you write it down ahead of time and memorize it?"

"You're not being very nice."

"Neither are you. And they're not contacts."

They both fell silent and stood glaring at one another.

Finally, Davies sighed and said, "Could we at least move our stuff inside and get started first? I could come out in a half hour and talk to you then."

"What about Russell?"

Russell half raised his hand. "*Russell* is right here. Please don't talk about me in third person."

"Sorry," said Tanya with a grin. "You haven't talked to *any* reporters, Russell. I don't know if you remember, but you've hung up on me twice."

"I know. I was gonna send you a card to apologize. We always watch you at my house. My mom thinks you look like a nice girl and my dad's always had a thing for redheads."

Tanya leaned a little closer to him and said, "What about you? Why do you like watching me?"

Russell was glad that it was so dark out because he could feel himself blushing. "I, uh . . . I—look, Ms.

Claymore, I don't know what I could say to you about what happened that you don't already know."

The radio in the police cruiser squawked loudly and the officer down by the vans leaned through the window to answer the call.

"All right," said Tanya, looking from Davies to Russell, then back to Davies again. "I won't bullshit you guys. The news director would really, really prefer that I come back tonight with some tape either of Russell or the inside of the house, preferably both. I almost had to beg him to let me do this. Don't take this the wrong way—especially you, Russell—but I'm sick to death of being a puff-piece talking head. Don't ever repeat that to anyone. If—"

"Oh, allow me," said Davies. "If you don't come back tonight with a really boffo piece so everyone will be calling you 'Scoop' Claymore tomorrow, you'll be stuck reading teleprompters and covering new mall openings for the rest of your career, right?"

Tanya said nothing.

Russell looked over at his boss. "Uh, look, Mr. Davies, if this is gonna be a problem I can—"

"She's lying, Russ—or at the very least rearranging the facts to form a more convenient truth. Her news director is all hot to trot for some shots of the inside of the house and he'll do anything for the exclusive pictures, won't he? Up to and including having his most popular female anchor lay a sob story on us that sounds like it came out of some overbaked 1940s melodrama. Nice try, though. Goddammit—it wouldn't surprise me if you and your crew were the ones who tried to break in."

Tanya started. "What? Someone tried to break into the house?"

"Wrong reading, sister. Don't call us, we'll call you."

The hardness in Tanya's eyes now bled down into the rest of her face. "Fine, Mr. Davies. Have it your way."

The officer in the cruiser walked up to his partner on the porch and the two of them whispered for a moment, then came down toward Davies and Tanya.

"Mr. Davies," said the officer who'd unlocked the door, "we just received orders that Ms. Claymore and her cameraman are to be allowed to photograph the inside of the house."

Behind her back, Tanya gave a thumbs-up to the driver of the news van.

"What'd you do," asked Davies, "have your boss call in a few favors or did you just promise to fuck the chief of police?"

"Watch it, Mr. Davies," said one of the officers. The offense and warning in his voice was quite clear. "Ms. Claymore can photograph only the foyer and one other room. You'll all go in at the same time. I am to personally escort Ms. Claymore and her cameraman into, through, and out of the house. She can only be inside for fifteen minutes, no more." He turned toward Tanya. "I'm sorry, Ms. Claymore, those're our orders. If you're inside any longer than that, we're to consider it to be trespassing and are to act accordingly."

"Well," she said, straightening her jacket and brushing a thick strand of hair from her eye, "it's nice to see that the First Amendment's alive and well and being slowly choked to death in Cedar Hill."

"You should attend one of our cross burnings sometime," said Davies.

"You're a jerk."

"How would you know? You never come to any of the meetings."

"That's enough, boys and girls," said Officer Lock & Key. "Could we move this along, please?"

"One thing," said Tanya. "Would it be all right if we got some shots of the outside of the house first?"

"You'd better make it fast," said Davies. "I feel a record-breaking cleaning streak coming on."

"Or I could get them later."

Davies stood in place for a moment, and then took a deep breath and said: "Ms. Claymore, I sincerely apologize for that last remark. It was cruel and disrespectful and you didn't deserve it. It's not your fault you were elected to be another pain in my ass tonight. We're all a bit . . . edgy about what has to be done."

Tanya stared at Davies for a moment as if trying to decide whether or not he was being truthful. "Are you setting me up with this?"

Davies grinned, embarrassed. "No, I'm not—but it sure would be a *good* setup if that were the case, huh?" He took a step closer and offered his hand. "I don't know that I've *ever* said anything that foul and vicious to a woman before, and I'm really ashamed. Please accept my apology?"

Tanya looked at his hand, then into his eyes. "Apology accepted." She shook his hand.

Russell walked away from the group and began setting his supplies on the porch. The front door was open and the overhead light in the foyer was turned on. He caught sight of a giant red-black spider clinging to the right-side wall and turned quickly away, pressing one of his hands against his stomach.

Mutt and Jeff laughed at him as they walked into the house. Pete Cooper shook his head and dismissed Russell with a wave of his hand. The ghosts of the Leonard family surrounded Russell on the porch, Irv placing a reassuring hand on the boy's shoulder while Miriam stroked his hair and the children looked on in silence. Tanya Claymore's cameraman caught Russell's expression on tape. It wasn't until Jackson Davies came up and took hold of his arm that Russell snapped out of his fugue and, without saying a word, got to the job.

And all along Merchant Street, shadowy forms in their housecoats and slippers watched from the safety of front porches.

CHAPTER FIVE

Even more famous than Francis Paynter's phone call is Tanya Claymore's videotape of that night. It ran four and a half minutes and was the featured story on Channel 9's six o'clock news broadcast the following evening. Viewer response was so overwhelming that the tape was broadcast again at seven and eleven P.M., then at six A.M. and noon the next day, then again, reedited to two minutes, forty-five seconds, at seven and eleven P.M. The story won Tanya a local Emmy Award and caught the attention of a network executive who flew her to Los Angeles later that month for an audition. She was offered a network job and accepted it.

She credited all of her success to the "Cleanup" tape.

It is an extraordinary piece of work, one that was painstakingly recreated in part (or so I'm told) in *Searching For Survivors*, but that day I showed my students the real thing. I doubt any of them had seen it before, only the truncated movie version. I eventually received an official reprimand from the school board—several of the students had nightmares about it, compounding those about the Dyson killings—but I thought they needed to see and hear other people, strangers, express what they themselves were feeling.

The ghosts wanted to see it again, as well.

As did I—and why not? In a way it is not so much about the aftermath of a tragedy as it is a chronicle of my birth, a point of reference on the map of my life: *This is where I came in*.

The tape opens with a shot of the Leonard house, bathed in shadow. Dim figures can be seen moving around its front porch. Sounds of footsteps. A muffled voice. A door being opened. A light coming on. Then another. And another.

Silhouettes appear in an upstairs window. Unmoving.

The camera pulls back slightly. Seen from the street the lights from the house form a pattern of sorts as they slip out from the cracks in the particleboard over the downstairs windows.

It takes a moment, but suddenly the house looks like it's smiling. And it is not a pleasant smile.

All of this takes perhaps five seconds. Then Tanya Claymore's voice chimes softly in as she introduces herself and says, "I'm standing outside the house of Irving and Miriam Leonard at 182 Merchant Street where, as you know, four nights ago their son Andy began a rampage that would leave over thirty people dead and over thirty more wounded."

At that very moment, someone inside the house kicks against the sheet of particleboard over the front bay window and wrenches it loose while a figure on the porch uses the claw end of a hammer to pull it free. The board comes away and a massive beam of light explodes outward, momentarily filling the screen.

The camera smoothly shifts its angle to deflect the light. As it does so, Tanya Claymore resolves into focus like a ghost on the right side of the screen. Whether it was purposefully done this way or not, the effect is an eerie one.

She says, "Just a few moments ago, accompanied by two members of the Cedar Hill Police Department, a team of janitors entered the Leonard house to begin what will most certainly be one of the grimmest and most painful cleanups in recent memory."

She begins walking up toward the front porch and the camera follows her. "Experts tell us that violence never really ends, no more than a symphony ceases to exist once the orchestra has stopped playing."

As she gets closer to the front door the camera moves left while she moves to the right and says, "And like the musical resonances that linger in the mind after a symphony, the ugliness of violence remains."

By now she has stepped out of camera range and the dark, massive bloodstain on the foyer wall can be clearly seen.

At the opposite end of the foyer, a mop head drenched in foamy soap suds can be seen slapping against the floor.

It makes a wet, sickening sound. The camera slowly zooms in on the mop and focuses on the blood that is mixed in with the suds.

The picture cuts to a well-framed shot of Tanya's head and shoulders. It's clear she's in a different room but which room it might be is hard to tell. When she speaks her voice sounds slightly hollow and her words echo.

"This is the only time that a news camera will be allowed to photograph the interior of the Leonard house. You're about to see the kitchen where Miriam Leonard and her two daughters, Jessica Hamilton and Elizabeth Shannon, spent the last few seconds of their lives, and where seven-year-old Randy Hamilton, with two bullets in his small body, fought to save the life of his infant brother, Joseph.

"The janitors have not been in here yet, so you will be seeing the kitchen just as it was when investigators finished with it."

For a moment it looks as if she might say something else; then she lowers her gaze and steps to the left as the camera moves slightly to the right and the kitchen is revealed.

The sight is numbing.

The kitchen is a slaughterhouse. The contrast between the blood and the off-white walls lunges out at the viewer like a snarling beast escaping from its cage.

The camera pans down to the floor and follows a single splash pattern that quickly grows denser and wider. Smeary heel- and footprints can be seen. The camera moves upward: part of a handprint in the center of a lower counter door. The camera moves farther up: the mark of four bloody fingers on the edge of the sink. The camera moves over the top of the sink in a smooth, sweeping motion and stares at a thick, crusty black whirlpool twisting down into the garbage disposal drain.

The camera suddenly jerks up and whips around, blurring everything for a moment, a dizzying effect, then comes to an abrupt halt. Tanya is standing in the doorway of the kitchen with her right arm thrust forward. In her hand is a plastic pistol.

"This is a rough approximation of the last thing Elizabeth Shannon saw before her youngest brother shot her to death."

She remains still for a moment. The viewer cannot help but put themselves in Elizabeth's place.

Tanya slowly lowers the pistol and says, "The question for which there seems to be no answer is, naturally, 'Why did he do it?'

"We put that question to several of the Leonards' neighbors this evening. Here's what some of them had to say about seventeen-year-old Andy, a young man who now holds the hideous distinction of having murdered more people in a single sweep than any killer in this nation's history."

Jump-cut to a quick, complicated series of shots:

Shot #1: An overweight man with obviously dyed hair saying, "I hear they found a tumor in his brain."

Insert shot: Merchant Street as it looked right after the shootings, clogged with police cruisers and ambulances and barricades to keep the ever-growing crowd back.

Shot #2: A middle-aged woman with curlers in her hair: "I'll bet you anything it was his father's fault, him bein' a gun lover and all. I heard he beat on Andy a lot."

Insert shot: Lights from a visibar rhythmically moving over a sheet-covered body on the front lawn.

Shot #3: An elderly gentleman in a worn and faded smoking jacket: "I read there were all these filthy porno magazines and videotapes stashed under his mattress, movies of women having relations with animals and pictures of babies in these leather sex getups . . ."

Insert shot: Two emergency medical technicians carrying a small black body bag down the front porch steps.

Shot #4: A thirtyish woman in an aerobic body leotard: "I felt that he was always a little *too* nice, you know? He never got . . . angry about anything."

Insert shot: A black-and-white photograph of Andy taken from a high school yearbook. He's smiling and his hair is neatly combed. He's wearing a tie. The voice of the woman in Shot #4 can still be heard over this photo, saying, "He was always so calm. He never laughed much, but there was this . . . *smile* on his face all the time. . . ."

Shot #5: A little girl of six, most of her hidden behind a parent's leg: ". . . I heard the house was haunted and that ghosts told him to do it. . . ."

Insert shot: A recent color photograph of Andy and Russell Brennert at a Halloween party, both of them in costume; Russell is Frankenstein's monster, and Andy, his face painted to resemble a smiling skeleton, wears the black hooded cloak of the Grim Reaper. He's holding a plastic scythe whose tip is resting on top of Russell's head. The camera moves in on Russell's face until it fills the screen, then abruptly CUTS TO:

A shot of Russell in the foyer of the Leonard house. He's on his knees in front of the massive bloodstain on the wall. He's wearing rubber gloves and is pulling a large sponge from a bucket of soapy water. A caption at the bottom of the screen reads: RUSSELL BRENNERT, FRIEND OF THE LEONARD FAMILY.

He squeezes the excess water from the sponge and lifts it toward the stain, then freezes just before the sponge touches the wall.

He is trembling but trying very hard not to.

Tanya's shadow can be seen in the lower right-hand corner of the frame. She asks, "How do you feel right now?"

Russell doesn't answer her, only continues to stare at the stain.

Tanya says, "Russell?"

He blinks, shudders slightly, then turns his head and says, "Wh—what? I'm sorry."

"What were you thinking just then?"

He stares in her direction, then gives a quick glance to the camera. "Does he have to point that thing at me like that?"

"You have to talk to a reporter eventually. You might as well do it now."

He bites his lower lip for a second, then exhales and looks back at the stain.

"What're you thinking about, Russell?"

"I remember when Jessie first brought Theresa home from the hospital. Everyone came over here to see the new baby. Oh, you should've seen Andy's face."

Brennert's voice begins to quaver. The camera slowly moves in closer to his face. He is oblivious to it.

"He was so . . . *proud* of her. You'd have thought she was *his* daughter."

He reaches out with the hand not holding the sponge and presses it against the stain. "She was so tiny. But she couldn't stop giggling. I remember that she grabbed one of my fingers and started . . . chewing on it, you know, like babies will do? Andy and I looked at each other and smiled and yelled, 'Uncle Attack!' and he s-started . . . he started kissing her chubby little face and I bent down and put my mouth against her tummy and started blowing real hard, you know, making belly farts, and it tickled her so much because she started giggling and laughing and squealing and farting and k-kicking her legs . . ."

The cords in his neck are straining. Tears well in his eyes and he grits his teeth in an effort to hold them back.

"The rest of the family was enjoying the hell out of it and Theresa kept squealing . . . that delicate little-baby laugh. Jesus Christ . . . he *loved* her. Her loved her *so much* and I thought she was the most precious thing . . . she always called me 'UncleRuss'—like it was all one word."

The tears are streaming down his cheeks now but he doesn't seem aware of it.

"I held her against my chest. I helped give her baths in the sink. I changed her diapers—and I was a helluva lot better at it than Andy ever was . . . and now I gotta . . . I gotta scrub this off the wall."

He pulls back his hand, then touches the stain with only his index finger, tracing indiscernible patterns in the dried blood.

"This was her. This is all that's . . . that's left of the little girl she was, the baby she was . . . the woman she might have grown up to be. He loved her." His voice cracks and he begins sobbing. "He loved all of them. And he never said anything to me. Not a *thing*! I didn't know, I swear to *Christ* I didn't know, I didn't know! This was her. I—oh *Goddammit*!"

He drops down onto his ass and folds his arms across his knees and lowers his head and weeps.

A few moments later Jackson Davies comes in and sees him and kneels down and takes Russell in his arms and rocks gently back and forth, whispering, "It's all right now, it's okay, it's over, you're safe, Russ, you hear me? Safe. Just . . . give it to me, kid . . . you're safe . . . that's it . . . shhh, there, that's right . . . give it to me. . . ." Davies looks up into the camera and the expression on his face needs no explaining: *Turn that fucking thing off.*

CUT TO:

Tanya, outside the house again, standing next to the porch steps. On the porch, two janitors are removing the broken bay window. A few jagged shards of glass fall out and shatter on the porch. Another man begins sweeping up the shards and dumping them into a plastic trash barrel.

Tanya says, "Experts tell us that violence never really

ends, that the healing process may never be completed, that some of the survivors will carry their pain for the rest of their lives."

A MONTAGE begins at this point, with Tanya's closing comments heard in VOICE-OVER:

The image, in slow motion, of police officers and EMTs moving sheet-covered and black-bagged bodies.

"People around here will say that the important thing is to remove as many physical traces of the violence as possible. Mop up the blood, gather the broken glass fragments into a bag and toss it in the trash, cover the scrapes, cuts, and stitches with bandages, then put your best face forward because it will make the unseen hurt easier to deal with."

The image of the sheet-covered bodies cross-fades into film of a memorial service held at Randy Hamilton's grade school. A small choir of children is gathered in front of a picture of Randy and begins to sing. Underneath Tanya's voice can now be heard a few dozen tiny voices softly singing "Let There Be Peace on Earth."

"But what of that 'unseen hurt'? A bruise will fade, a cut will get better, a scar can be taken off with surgery. Cedar Hill must now concern itself with finding a way to heal the scars that aren't so obvious."

The image of the children's choir dissolves into film of Mary Alice Hubert standing in the middle of the chaos outside the Leonard house on the night of the shootings. She is bathed in swirling lights and holds both of her hands pressed against her mouth. Her eyes seem unnaturally wide and are shimmering with tears. Police and EMTs scurry around her but none stops to offer help. As the choir sings, "To take each moment and live each moment in peace e-tern-al-ly," she drops slowly to her knees and lowers her head as if in prayer.

Tanya's voice-over continues: "Maybe tears will help. Maybe grieving in the open will somehow lessen the grip that the pain has on this community. Though we may never know what drove Andy Leonard to commit his horrible crime, the resonances of his slaughter remain."

Mary Alice dissolves into the image of Russell Brennert kneeling before the stain on the foyer wall. He is touching the dried blood with the index finger of his left hand.

The children's choir is building to the end of the song as Tanya says, "Perhaps Cedar Hill can find some brief comfort in these lines from a poem by German lyric poet Rainer Maria Rilke: 'Who weeps now anywhere in the world, without cause weeps in the world, weeps over me.'"

The screen fills with the image of Jackson Davies embracing Russell as sobs rack his body. Davies glares up at the camera, then closes his eyes and lowers his face. Kissing the top of Russell's head. This images freezes as the children finish singing their hymn.

Tanya's voice once more; soft and low, no singsong mode this time, no inflection whatsoever: "For tonight, who weeps anywhere in the world, weeps for Cedar Hill and its wounds that may never heal.

"Tanya Claymore, Channel 9 News."

I turned the classroom lights back on, checked the time, and gestured for one of my students (from the AV club who'd helped bring the equipment over that morning) to rewind the tape and turn off the television.

Someone asked, "Did you get that in Cedar Hill?"

I shook my head. "No. My parents have had that for almost as long as I've been alive. I saw it for the first time two years ago, the same night they told me how I'd come to be orphaned. That was a fun dinner."

A couple of them almost laughed but didn't quite make it.

The AV student handed back the tape and took his seat at the same moment a girl in one of the back rows raised her hand.

"They left some of that out in the movie."

I nodded my head but said nothing.

"Do you know what happened to all those people after . . . *after*?"

"Why?"

She shrugged. "I dunno . . . it's just that, well, stuff like that's been all over the news about what happened Friday night, y'know? I mean, none of it's been, like, as . . . *thoughtful* as that was—" She seemed pleased with herself for finding the exact right word to characterize the Claymore tape. "—but when I was watching it, I started wondering if maybe ten or twenty years from now someone'll see the stories about Friday night and wonder what happened to *us*." Her brow furrowed. "Does that make sense?"

"It absolutely does."

She stared at me a moment longer, looked at the girl sitting to her left, then back at me. It was only as she spoke again that I realized I hadn't answered her original question.

"So . . . what happened to all those people?"

I looked at the clock once more out of habit; usually by this time they were gone to their first classes of the day and a different batch of faces had taken their place. "Are all of you good for your word? Remember, you promised me we'd try to talk about what happened Friday night if I—"

I was cut off by their muttered uniform agreement.

"Okay. Yes, I know what happened to most of those people. I sometimes wish I didn't, but there's not a lot I can do about that." I held up the tape. "If I remember correctly, the movie ends with a recreation of this news report, doesn't it?"

They assured me that it did. I believed them.

"Interesting things, movies and their endings." I tossed the tape back into my briefcase and considered for a moment taking out the second video I'd brought along. "A great movie director named Orson Welles once said, 'If you want a happy ending, be careful where you decide to stop the story.' I always thought that was a very clever way of seeing it."

The same girl asked, "Why? I don't get it."

"Because the ending of every human being's story is the same: they die. Since that's not exactly a rah-rah feel-good way to leave an audience . . ." I deliberately left the sentence unfinished to see if she'd make the connection on her own.

"Oh." She thought about it for a moment, then both her face and voice brightened as it sank in. "*Oh!* I *get* it. You're right—that's kinda cool."

"Welles was a *very* cool guy. His story ended a few decades ago, I'm sad to say."

"You still haven't told us anything we didn't already know." This from a boy in semispiked hair who was displaying his sensitivity to the current situation by wearing a T-shirt displaying the bloody logo of a once-popular death-metal band that currently was enjoying something of a comeback. He was either monstrously coldhearted or fancied himself something of an iconoclast—providing he even knew what the word meant. "You're going on about how important it is that we talk about things but you won't do the same. How are we supposed to fuckin' trust you if—"

"Ah-ah," I said, waving a finger in the air like some scolding mother out of a '50s sitcom. "I'll give you a 'damn' and a 'hell' and even raise you a 'shit,' but it stops at that, understood? The Big Bad Words are reserved only for the story."

He considered this, then gave a short, sharp nod. "Works for me."

"I'm not trying to detour around anything, okay? But some of this stuff gets even more personal."

"Like having one of your friends murdered isn't?"

A breath. "Point taken."

A girl near the front spoke up. "My brother graduated from here two years ago. He was in your Study of the Contemporary American Novel class. He said that"— she looked away for a moment, obviously feeling uncomfortable over whatever she was about to say—"that you had some kind of serious meltdown in class one day and that you had to take some time off."

"The school board and continued health of my bank account agreed that was best for all concerned, yes."

"Did that have anything to do with Cedar Hill?"

"It had everything to do with it. I just didn't know it at the time."

"What happened to cause you to . . . y'know . . . ?"

"I started seeing ghosts." I almost added: *And they're right here with us, standing in the back of the room. Now everyone turn around and say hello because 'boo' just isn't as funny to them as it used to be.*

The girl who'd asked the question was blank-faced and wide-eyed. "Are you kidding?"

"That would require a sense of humor, and as any student who's taken one of my classes will tell you, I don't have one of my own, so I have to rent."

That got a laugh; color me bemused.

I leaned against the front of my desk and took in their suddenly anxious faces. I don't know that I've ever felt as self-conscious as I did at that moment. There are times, rare though they be, when a dreadful knowledge hits you with the force of a hammer to the kneecaps: that you, as a teacher, might actually be doing something to shape your students' lives. It only shows itself as remarkable later on; when you're actually there in the moment, it feels like you're going to implode from the pressure: *Isn't stuff like this what parents are for?*

I rubbed my eyes and exhaled. I was about to either hang or redeem myself; regardless of the outcome, odds were I was going to be much talked about come this time tomorrow.

Death-Metal spoke up again: "So are you gonna tell us, or what?"

Sure, I thought. *And maybe we'll even speak of other ghosts and buried things and a lost circus and a great, grotesque, horribly magnificent honest-to-God monster that still walks the woods at night because it's lonely and scared and pissed off and most of the time can't tell the three things apart.*

"The offer to write any of you a pass for study hall still stands if you find you can't . . . well, listen anymore. With that said . . .

"If a happy ending depends on where you choose to stop the story," I said, "it matters just as much where you decide to start it. This one starts with ghosts.

"Don't say I didn't warn you."

PART TWO

HOME BEFORE DARK

"There is a grey thing that lives in the tree-tops
None knows the horror of its sight
Save those who meet death in the wilderness
But one is enabled to see
To see branches moving at its passing
To hear at time the wail of black laughter
And to come often upon mystic places
Places where the thing has just been."
—Stephen Crane, "There Is A Grey Thing . . ."

"What seest thou else
In the dark backward and abysm of time?"
—Shakespeare, *The Tempest*

CHAPTER ONE

The thing sitting to the right of the bed wore the shape of humanness but it was no longer human, assuming it ever had been; it was stooped and twisted and decayed and gave off the stench of rotting meat. Its hands were misshapen, with bloated, blackened fingers, most of which looked more like talons with their overlong, splintered nails caked with something foul beneath. Much of its flesh was hidden under dirty bandages made from shredded cloth, sheets or towels that had been filthy and stiff before they'd been used for this purpose; what flesh was visible was fish-belly pale and covered in tumors, red at the edges, black at the center. One all but veiled the right side of its face like a caul, thinning out just enough over the eye that the pupil could be glimpsed when it turned toward the moonlight; the rest of the caul thickened at the forehead, ending in a rocklike cluster at its brow. Its good eye stared out from behind the bandages covering the left side of its face and wrapped tightly all the way around its neck.

It saw that I was awake, and for a moment it managed to work its ruined lips into the semblance of a smile, shiny black liquid dribbling from the corners of its mouth and spilling down, further soaking the now-seeping bandages. It leaned into the diffused moonlight as its hideous smile widened, revealing ruined gums and yellowed teeth that curled backward like hooks. Lifting one hand, it pointed at me, hesitantly at first, as if it weren't sure I was the one it sought, but as I sat up in bed and leaned toward the light, its body stiffened with recognition and it began wagging its finger at me—*yes, yes, I'm in the right place; it's you!* It worked its malformed tongue around the inside of its mouth, trying to rasp out words. All that emerged were the sounds of someone being forced to gag down something thick and wet.

"Are we finally going to get to whatever it is you want tonight?" I asked it.

It stopped trying to speak and rose from the chair. The rest of the makeshift bandages encircled its torso from just below the neck to the waistline of its thread-bare trousers. As it moved, the moldy long coat it wore billowed as the air-conditioning came on and cool air pushed up from the floor vents, disturbing a few of the looser bandages, causing them to slip and reveal the terrible lesions, abscesses, and blistering eruptions of the sickness spreading underneath. Its legs were bowed, one much shorter than the other, and it shambled toward my side of the bed using an antique umbrella for a cane. There was a surprising amount of grace in the way it moved, swaying slightly to the left, then to the right, each time sliding one foot smoothly across the carpeting to find purchase before swaying again; a ballet for the broken one.

It was never the dream that bothered me—I'd been having the same dream (my first recurrent one) for weeks now, and while it was troublesome in its own way, it was simply a warm-up act for the main attraction that was now dancing its way toward me. There had been no pattern to the thing's visits over the past weeks; sometimes it was there, sometimes it wasn't. But these last five nights, it had been there every time.

I took a deep breath and looked up just as it reached my side of the bed. It raised its right hand, spreading its fingers as much as it could, and swung straight down, clawing my face from forehead to neck. There was no pain, there never was. Nor was there ever any change in what happened next; I lifted my hands and covered my face. I peeked out through the spaces between my fingers, watching as the thing stood there and with its free hand made a throat-cutting gesture across its own neck, back and forth, back and forth, the speed increasing with its own internal frenzy. It threw back its head and opened its mouth in a scream that never came; instead, there was only that gagging, desperate choking noise. Usually this lasted ten or fifteen seconds before the thing simply snapped out like a doused candle flame. Tonight was a little different; tonight it lasted much longer. And tonight was different in another way, as well; tonight, there was pain—but not in my face, in my left side, like an intense stitch some runners gets when deciding to try that last extra mile.

I winced, pulling my hands away from my face and blinking against the pain. The thing was now gone, as I knew it would be. So tonight was a little different. Tonight, he hung around a bit longer. Tonight, there was a bit of pain. And tonight—

—tonight my hands came away from my face smeared with something dark and warm.

Yvonne rolled over, half opening her eyes, and pulled in a deep breath. "Oh, God, honey—did you fart? That *smell* . . ."

"Sorry," I said.

" 'S'okay."

I sat very still, waiting for her to fall back asleep. While waiting, I turned toward the other bedroom window, the one in which you can sometimes see your reflection in the middle of the night, if it's dark enough. Tonight more than filled the bill.

My face was lacerated, a sliced mass of meat streaked with black tears. I moved to get out of bed but the pain in my left side was having none of it. I sat there, wrapped in my own arms, rocking back and forth until the pain decided to pass. I knew not to trust what the reflection showed me; the Broken One had a way of altering reflections. The pain in my side, however, was real, and I trusted in that. I always trusted in pain. It seemed foolish to do otherwise.

"Thanks a lot, pal," I whispered to the darkness.

CHAPTER TWO

This is what stays with me for the longest from the dream:

"I don't know," he said. "I don't much feel. . . ."

"Me, neither."

"Really? I thought it was just me."

Standing in front of the bathroom mirror, cold water still dripping from my unharmed face, I realized that the words made no more sense to me now than they had when I'd awakened from the dream to find the Broken One (as I'd come to think of him) waiting patiently. There was, I sensed, a connection between the two. ("Well, *duh*," as one of my students might say.)

I grabbed a hand towel from the rack and pressed it against my face, rubbing at my flesh and the water until it felt as if both were being soaked into the fibers. The image of the black liquid spilling from the Broken One's mouth and sopping the bandages projected itself for a moment against the back of my eyes, but just as quickly dissolved. I stood like that for a moment, breathing strained, face hidden, hands trembling, then slowly pulled the towel down to just below the bridge of my nose, revealing only my eyes to the reflection that stared back at me.

A few minutes ago, when I'd finally tried to climb out

of bed without disturbing Yvonne, she'd reached out and gently grasped my elbow. "Same dream, Mr. Farty-Pants?" The Broken One's smell still lingered in the room. I smiled at her in the darkness and nodded, then leaned down and kissed her cheek. I told her that she shouldn't waste her energy worrying about me. She moved closer, snuggling her head against my chest, and whispered, "You're going to have to go back there sometime. Why not do it now, while all of that information is still fresh? I wish you would. Find a way to end it. Talk to people, ask questions, do whatever you have to do so you can forgive yourself for having survived. It's poisoning you. It's *been* poisoning you ever since your parents showed you what was in those boxes. At least think about it, all right? If you won't do it for yourself, do it for Patricia and me. Do it before something cracks and it all comes spilling out, ugly and incoherent."

"What an odd way to put it," I said.

"I suppose, but that's how I feel. There's a storm brewing in you, Geoff, and if it hits, it'll be terrible. I think you know that as well as I do. I—what? You've got the strangest look on your face suddenly. What is it?"

"It's weird, you know? I mean, it's not as if I didn't *know* I was adopted. Mom and Dad told me that when I was—what?—nine years old? I had some trouble with it at first, always wondering why my birth parents gave me up, but I never pressed for details. It was hard enough for Mom and Dad just to tell me about the adoption. Oh, they'd give me bits and pieces whenever I asked for something specific—like whether or not my birth parents were still alive, things like that—but I never asked them for the whole story."

Yvonne squeezed my hand. "Why do you suppose they waited until now?"

I shrugged. "My guess is because of Dad's heart attack. Scared the bejeezus out of him."

"Yeah, but at least he's quit smoking now. He's watching his diet and exercising more. He'll live to be ninety."

"I hope so. Still . . . I think it scared him enough to . . . I don't know . . . *come clean* with me about everything—everything that he and Mom *know*, anyway."

"And tell you just enough to tell you almost nothing at all."

Without having to ask, I knew that both Yvonne and I were thinking about the contents of the boxes Mom and Dad had given to me; the cards, the letters, the newspaper clippings, the videotapes, about everything that connected them and, just as importantly, the missing threads, the absent correlations.

"They told me all they could. Christ, Yvonne, it's been over *thirty-five years* since it happened. Even back then, there was no way they could find out everything. What chance do I have *now*?"

"There's only one way to know for sure—and you're bound to find out *something*."

"And if I don't?"

She pulled herself closer to me. "At least you'll have *tried*, and that will have to be enough."

Looking into the bloodshot eyes that glared back at me from the mirror, I realized that she was right. I was flailing, unanchored, because the true history was missing. I wondered if that history would be of any use now. Didn't *everyone* need to fill in the gaps at some point in their life? I was a high-school English teacher, for chrissakes. If anyone should know the value of history, it ought to be me. Every moment I spent in that classroom was geared toward making students understand the necessity of using art, music, and language to carry the

Now into the Yet To Come so as to give human memory in all of its frailty some form of permanence. How else could you measure the worth of your life when you woke one day to realize more of it was behind you than ahead?

I'd known for a while now that my true history was still out there someplace; fragmented though it might be, it was still *mine*, and no one else could claim it, no one else could give it form, no one else could value it the way it needed to be valued. If I was going to do it, I had to do it soon. Most of the people were already dead and those who weren't were getting on in years. If I waited too long, the fragments might slip through their aging mental filters, and what remained of the facts would either be lost forever or reshaped into something other than the experiences—the ordered, necessary, unavoidable *truths*—they represented. Was I willing to take that risk when this was, I knew damned well, the *only* chance I was ever going to have?

I tried convincing myself that all of this free-floating disquiet was because of the book. Ever since childhood I'd loved storytelling and storytellers, would sit up nights reading tales of werewolves and witches, vampires and ghosts, lonely souls and adventurers, charlatans and thugs and the gallant heroes who always triumphed in the end. By the time I was eight years old I knew that the rest of my life would somehow be about stories; their telling, their teaching, their creation. Now, thirty-five years later, one of my fondest dreams was about to achieve a kind of reconciliation: my first book—a collection of short stories as yet untitled—was scheduled to be released early next year. I had none of the high hopes of many writers, no delusions of best-sellerdom and standing-room-only lectures and hectic book tours; the advance was small, as was the publisher, a "specialty press," the print run would be limited to 500 copies, trade paperback, but it would be enough. For weeks now I'd been avoiding sending in the final revised manuscript—not because it was bad (it wasn't—at least I didn't think so), but because something was . . . missing.

"*I don't know,*" *he said.* "*I don't much feel. . . .*"

"*Me, neither.*"

"*Really? I thought it was just me.*"

Maybe that's what the dream was really about—my anxiety over the book. And it occurred to me now that maybe the Broken One sprang from the same source. I knew damned well he wasn't real—not in the sense of genuine corporeality. (The lingering smell in the room was undoubtedly because I *had* passed gas without being aware of it.) He was some kind of manifestation connected with my anxiety over the book, and that anxiety, instead of announcing itself with just one irritating symptom, decided to be born as two; one for my sleep, one for my just-barely-awake world. (Isn't self-deluding self-analysis wonderful, especially when you can fall back on the easy happy horseshit you learned in quote Advanced Psychology unquote your senior year in high school?) All because of the book.

If the publisher were going to bring it out on schedule, I had less than three weeks to turn in the final polish—providing I could find the right piece with which to close the collection. There was *one* piece I had, but . . . I just didn't know. *Maybe you should go back and read it,* I thought. Maybe looking at those few pages of words on paper would show me what was lacking in the whole—which thus far wasn't nearly as good as the sum of its parts.

But that was just blowing smoke and I knew it; this was still about history—*missing* history. Empty spaces where the lost fragments should be, spaces filled with guesses and metaphors and exaggerations and often outright lies until the whole thing was transformed into myth.

Everyone has their fragments, a certain piece of time, some specific moment that was so intense, that had so deeply affected them, that every minute detail was forever chiseled in their memory; and perhaps sometimes the power of that moment was so overwhelming that they had to share it. If they were lucky and Chaos had its back turned at that instant, this person with whom they shared their fragment would remember it—and thus in a way the one who had shared it, as well. A fragment passed from keeper to keeper: "Remember this for me after I'm gone." Moment to memory to scroll, page, canvas or stone; permanence: History.

I lowered the towel, unveiling the rest of my face, and looked into the reflection, past the eyes, past the skull beneath the skin, past the veins and blood and gray matter until it seemed I was staring into the ancient heart of some holy mystery—the answer to which had been, until this moment, just out of reach.

Chapter Three

Understand: I wrote the following after I'd had the dream for the third time—unchanged, unaltered, every detail unnerving in its clarity. I wrote it down because a part of me thought it might make for a good closing story for the collection—it was just odd and (hopefully) eerie enough to do the job, but I still hadn't decided whether or not to use it.

The Broken One first appeared to me the night after I wrote this.

And one more thing: I wrote this *weeks* before I knew the names of any of Andy Leonard's victims, or the circumstances under which they'd died.

As I sat down at my desk and brought up the file on my computer screen, I read the first few lines, saw the names, and was suddenly so unnerved I not only didn't want to go back to Cedar Hill, I didn't even want to leave our *house* again.

Because if I didn't know the names, or the circumstances, then how in the hell . . . ?

There should have been more left once the children were gone, more than just empty bedrooms, broken toys discovered in the backs of closets, the occasional pair of gym socks or panty hose found hiding under furniture, collecting dust like the little ones used to collect dolls or model cars.

There should have been more, but Irv and Miriam quickly discovered otherwise. The children were gone and they were alone for the first time in thirty years. Their conversations were short; too short. Their eyes didn't meet as much as they once had. Irv cleared his throat a lot in order to break the silence and often read the same newspaper page three times in a row because he couldn't think of anything else to do. Miriam kept telling herself there was a ton of laundry and cleaning to do because she was used to working from morning till bedtime, but the truth was that hardly any of it needed doing. Except for the stains, of course. So many *stains*, and neither she nor Irv could figure out what they were or how they'd gotten there.

Not now.

Now that the children had left.

Always smiling, never any tears as they hauled themselves and their stuff out the door.

All over.

All Gone.

Bye-bye.

Irv tried taking up a hobby, but found he hadn't the patience for anything that demanded he sit still for more than twenty minutes at a time.

Miriam joined a card-playing club, but the women in the group were always talking about their own children and how proud they were of them and took care not to ask Miriam about hers because it was common knowledge that Miriam's children never wrote or visited and seldom called. She quit going after three weeks. The other women were too obviously being courteous to her.

Irv spent a couple of days working on the spray stain

that arced on the wall in the entryway almost all the way to the ceiling. Regular cleaner didn't work, and his lungs couldn't take the stronger industrial stuff, so he opted instead to repaint the entryway. That took him three days, and when he'd finished, the stain was still there.

"Huh. Now ain't that something."

And so they were alone for the first time in thirty years, not knowing what to do or say because they'd rarely spared any thought for themselves; the children had been their pleasure and their purpose.

The rooms of the house should have grown larger but they didn't. Irv took to opening the windows even in cold weather; the place was too stuffy. Miriam took to watching television in the mornings before working on her latest cross-stitch project for an hour; then she cleaned for two hours before preparing lunch, then it was her daily walk around the neighborhood before it was time to start dinner; later, after the dishes were washed and put away (a task both she and Irv performed, taking as much time as possible) she would return to the television and watch her evening programs until sleep claimed her.

Then one afternoon, struck by a now-rare desire to rearrange one of the old rooms, Irv discovered something from his days as a younger man. He showed it to Miriam.

For the rest of that afternoon and well into the evening they sat at the kitchen table recalling all the old memories they'd shared many times before, never embellishing them for each would know if the other was fibbing, and it should have been a fine time for them, talking about the old days while eating popcorn and drinking coffee (Miriam) and beer (Irv was a devout Schlitz man), but their words rang hollow, their eyes met too rarely, and when Irv reached over to take Miriam's hand it was more the gesture of a drowning man clutching at a life preserver than a loving husband trying to take comfort in his wife's touch.

At last, after refilling her coffee cup and fetching another beer for her husband, Miriam cleared her throat and said, "Why don't they ever call or write or visit?"

"I don't know," said Irv.

Then, and only then, did their eyes meet and stay fixed.

"I was a good mother, wasn't I?"

"You were grand. A wonderful mother. You really were."

"I mean we never . . . we never let them go without, did we?"

"Whatta you mean by that?" His face said that he'd been thinking the same thing, but since she'd mentioned it first, the responsibility of talking about it was hers.

"I just keep thinking about some things, you know? Like that prom dress I made for Beth."

"It was a beautiful dress. I remember how hard you worked on it."

"But she didn't like it, remember? She said it didn't match her favorite shoes."

"Well, we got her a new pair, didn't we? And them matched the dress all right. I thought she looked lovely."

Miriam dug a cigarette out of her purse and lit up. Even though he was trying to get her to quit, Irv didn't say anything.

"What is it?" asked Miriam.

"I was just thinking that cigarette smoke don't smell half bad. Makes me wished I smoked a pipe or something."

"We could always go out to the shopping center to-morrow and look in that new smoke shop. I'll bet they got real nice pipes in there. We could pick one out."

"Place's pretty expensive, from what I hear."

"I suppose, but you'd be getting a good pipe for the money. You could even maybe start yourself a little col-lection. We can afford it, hon, really we can. We could even get you one of them wood display cases so you can put them all out and then . . ." She sat staring at her hus-band, her mouth working to form sounds, words, sen-tences; all that came out was cigarette smoke.

"We could always go to the movies or something," said Irv.

"Could you sit still that long?"

"I don't know. I suppose I could give it a try."

Miriam found the movie listings in the paper and called the theater to check on show times and prices.

"Seven dollars apiece?" said Irv.

"That's what they said."

"Christ! Fourteen dollars to see a movie! We can't af-ford that—I mean, not that and dinner, too. Ain't a proper movie night without stopping for dinner while you're out."

Miriam put a hand on his shoulder. "Once every couple of weeks wouldn't be so bad, would it? We don't have to go to a fancy place to eat, just some hamburgers or some-thing."

"I don't know. I don't got any real nice clothes—you know, nothing that you'd wear out on a date." He was staring at the stains all over the kitchen.

Miriam followed the direction of his gaze and stared at other nearby stains. "We could always go out and buy you some new clothes."

"I don't know," he said. "I don't much feel. . . ."

"Me, neither."

"Really? I thought it was just me."

"Nope."

They sat in silence for a little while longer as the night drifted in around them.

There was no way to give it voice. There was no way one of them could look at the other and say, *We did it all for them. All the work, all the worrying, paying the bills and keeping the house up, it was all for the kids. Never for us. I love you, hon, I really do, but we lost each other somewhere along the way. Sometime in there when we weren't looking we stopped being Irv and Miriam and became* their parents. *And now what? I love them with all my heart but they ain't part of us anymore, not really. I don't think it's because they're ashamed of us or anything—I'm sure they still love us and all—but they got families of their own now. They're not our children anymore, they're Chet and Jessica and Elizabeth. And they're not here. It's just us now and we let ourselves slip away in there someplace. We're not what we wanted to be when we were young. When they left they took their parents with them and left* us *in their place, and we don't know much about these people, not anymore.*

Because there were no children left to care for. They'd hauled themselves and all their stuff out the door.

All over.

All gone.

Bye-bye.

Except for the stains, of course. So many *stains*, and neither she nor Irv could figure out what they were or how they'd gotten there. And so many of the stains had these small, hard bits stuck in them; some so deeply they actually went into the wall.

Soon, when the kitchen became so dark they almost

couldn't see, they rose and went into the living room and sat very near one another on the sofa. Irv placed the keepsake from his youth on the floor by his feet and lovingly put his arm around Miriam. Breathing slowly, she put her head against his shoulder, one of her aged hands dropping down to hold both of his.

"Will they ever visit?" she asked, knowing what they were going to do.

"I think so. I think they're coming right now."

They sat in silence as the shadows of night came into the room and made themselves at home.

"Do you hear them?" said Miriam, smiling.

"Yes, I do. See there, hon? They didn't forget us."

"They're not ashamed of us, are they?"

"Nosiree," said Irv. "Listen to them talk. They're proud of their workin' folks."

"Never a king's castle, but a good home."

"A fine home. Damn fine. They never wanted for a thing."

Miriam touched her husband's cheek. "That's on account of you bein' such a good, hard worker. Always providing for us."

"I did my best."

"Your best was just fine, it was." She smiled, eyes wide, and pointed in front of them. "Look, there's Chet."

"My God," said Irv. "Look at what a fine man he's become. So strong and sure of himself."

"You always said that he had a good head on his shoulders."

"They all did. I told them that."

"Oh my, there's Jessica and her husband and—look! Oh, they brought the *baby* with them! Isn't he beautiful?"

"Do you think he knows we're his grandma and grandpa?"

"Of course he does. Look at him giggle at your big hands."

"Yeah, and he's—aw, did you hear that? Jessie said they named him after my dad. They call him Joseph."

"And there's Beth with the twins!"

"Makes you proud, don't it?" said Irv.

"It wasn't all for nothing."

And time stood still for them for a little while, as it will for everyone at least once in a lifetime, if only at the end.

But soon the visit was over. The children left, hauling themselves and their families out the door.

"All over," whispered Irv.

"All gone," said Miriam.

"Bye-bye," said both to the darkness.

Irv leaned over and kissed Miriam.

"I love you," she said to him. "What a fine family."

"Yeah. I guess maybe it was worth losing us, after all. They're a fine bunch. But I still miss them."

Miriam hugged him. "We mustn't harp on things, hon. The children are safe and happy and they love us and remember us. You heard for yourself."

"They make a body proud."

"Isn't our new grandson wonderful?" she whispered in his ear, pressing herself close to him.

"I love you so much," said Irv. "I've given you a good life, haven't I?"

"A woman would be foolish to ask for one better."

"We'll babysit Joseph, won't we?"

"You bet."

"Here he is now, all fussy and hungry."

"I should change his diaper, don't you think?"

"Hell, yes! Look at him kicking up his legs."

"That giggle!"

"Oh, *now* he wants to chew on my finger."

"He'll outgrow that."

And he did.

"Graduating college," said Irv. "Didn't think I'd ever live to see the day *one* of my grandkids graduated college, let alone all of 'em."

"And Joseph is so handsome in his cap and gown."

"A heartbreaker."

"Just like his grandpa."

"A good life," said Irv.

"A fine life," said Miriam, her hand reaching down to brush against Irv's keepsake. "Your father gave that to you, you say?"

"Yeah. He loved to go hunting."

"You miss him, don't you?"

"That I do. That I do."

Miriam kissed his cheek as the glare of a car's headlight beams filled the living room. The engine clattered as the ignition was turned off.

"We should go now," said Miriam. "The children will be expecting us for a visit."

"Okay," said Irv, digging two shells out of his pocket.

They held hands as they walked upstairs to their bedroom, but before vanishing into the darkness they turned and looked at their home, each remembering some moment from their family's life together.

But that was done now.

All over.

All gone.

Bye-bye.

Even the stains left.

As they rounded the landing and started up the second,

darker flight of stairs, the lock on the front door jiggled, then turned. The door opened and a harried-looking young man in a business suit entered, fumbled around until he found the light switch, and turned on the overhead lights.

A young couple with a little girl of four or five came in behind him, wide-eyed and grinning as they looked from one spacious empty room to the next.

"This is *so* perfect," said the young woman.

"I knew you'd love it," replied her husband.

"It's so *big. . . .*" whispered the little girl, awestruck.

"Yeah," said the young man in the suit. "This's a great house, all right. We've had it on the market for over a year now. A lot of us down at the agency are surprised that no one's made a firm offer on it until now. And I'm glad to say that everything here is in solid working order."

The young woman placed a hand against her protruding belly. "It's going to be perfect for our family."

"Of course it will," said her husband, putting his arm around her.

"The perfect family home," said the young man in the suit. "What a wonderful way to begin."

CHAPTER FOUR

I was less than ten minutes into my Contemporary American Novel class the next morning when that pinching pain in my left side returned, and my arm started trembling. I didn't know what was causing it and could not get it to stop; a steady, rhythmic twitch that sharpened and then ebbed with the stitch in my side. I hoped my students wouldn't notice. I decided to stay behind the small desktop podium just in case.

". . . You've noticed by this time how much Miss Amelia and Cousin Lymon have come to depend on each other for the support and affection denied them by others. Admittedly, Miss Amelia isn't at first the most likable person—"

"I thought she was a real bitch," mumbled one of the students. The rest of the class tried unsuccessfully to suppress their laughter.

"A little indelicate, but well put, nonetheless," I said, smiling myself. "She's a bitter, lonely woman who will not allow anyone to get close to her, except now her hunchback cousin. And though Cousin Lymon is almost immediately popular with the townspeople, Miss Amelia sees in him something the others don't. Anyone care to tell me what they think that might be?"

Silence.

"C'mon. There's no right or wrong answer to the question. Anyone?"

A few students looked at their desks, others cleared their throats. It was one of those moments, equal parts tension and apathy, that so many teachers endure every day. I had long ago resigned myself to riding out such moments with as much grace and humor as I could.

(*"I don't know," he said. "I don't much feel. . . ."*
"Me, neither."
"Really? I thought it was just me.")

The words blossomed in my mind unexpectedly, and with their arrival the pain in my side became a small shard of glass stuck under a rib, and the twitch in my arm became a constant shaking. I looked down at my hand and saw it shudder, then involuntarily jerk outward, as if I were trying to snap away a cluster of blowflies.

I blinked and pressed my arm against my side. "No takers?"

There weren't.

"Okay; I'll toss out an idea and you tell me what you think of it. Maybe what Miss Amelia sees in Cousin Lymon is the physical embodiment of what she imagines her own soul to be; twisted, misunderstood, outwardly repulsive, but buried deep inside is a decency and a grace and a love that have been looking for a way to express themselves for a long, long time. How's that grab you?"

The students would not look at the front of the room.

I exhaled, gripping my arm—*why in hell won't it stop?*—and thought again of the dream, of the two ghosts sitting on the couch, looking at other ghosts who couldn't see them. Maybe I *should* take Yvonne's advice and go back to Cedar Hill, check things out—for all the good it would do. Maybe I'd ask the Broken One for his advice tonight. He struck me as one who wouldn't squander words.

I blinked against the softly pulsating aura forming at the periphery of my vision; the surefire beginnings of a cluster headache.

The shaking in my arm worsened, as did the pain in my side. Were I in an ER and asked by a resident, I would have rated the pain at about a six, six and a half.

"Or maybe what she sees in him is a chance to redeem herself in her own eyes for her failed marriage to Marvin Macy. McCullers does spend some time early on hinting that the marriage was brutal and bitter and left Miss Amelia somehow deformed of spirit."

The pain was throbbing against the inside of my skull; the hiss of pumping pistons, the clanking of steel, brass and tight compression, glittering shards of pain that reflected against my eyes like sunspots on chrome. I took a deep breath. This wasn't like the other headaches, the others had never come on this fast. *Keep talking*, I told myself.

"Okay, then. Remember that passage about the liquor Miss Amelia serves to her customers? McCullers talks about the 'special quality' it has." I looked down at my copy of the novel, flipped back a few pages until I found the passage (one of my favorites from the book), then began reading: " 'It is known that if a message is written with lemon juice on a clean sheet of paper, there will be no sign of it. But if the paper is held for a moment to the fire then the letters turn brown and the meaning becomes clear. Imagine that the whiskey is the fire and the message is that which is known only in the soul of a man—then the worth of Miss Amelia's liquor can be understood.' "

—and there were Mom and Dad, coming downstairs with two bulging cardboard boxes held together with duct tape and a section of clothesline, and I knew from the look on Mom's face that whatever was inside those boxes was going to change some part of my life forever—

—get on with it.

"Damn, people, that's writing! That single passage is one of the most incredible I've ever read—not only because of the brilliance of McCullers's metaphor, but because that particular metaphor serves to underscore everything that happens throughout the rest of the story. Yes, maybe it is a good thing that 'the message' that lies hidden 'in the soul of a man' can be brought out by her liquor, but that same liquor, as we later find, can also bring out the worst in a person; all the bitterness and hatred and self-destructiveness that drove Miss Amelia away from everyone in the first place. Yet here, at the start of the story, this woman who for years has been a thorn in everyone's side suddenly, because of the appearance of this hunchbacked dwarf, begins to show a part of herself no one suspected existed. Don't you see? Cousin Lymon is 'the fire' that makes the meaning of Miss Amelia's 'message' clear—that she is as lonely and as frightened and as capable of tenderness and love as everyone else. Which is why the ending is such a goddamn tragedy." Someone gasped at my profanity, but I didn't care. I closed the book and stretched my back, then—my resolution shadowboxing with the spasms in my arm and the increasing power of the headache—moved from behind the podium to be nearer to the students.

"That's what's so exciting about fiction like this, folks! It works on so many different levels. On one level, McCullers is telling us about this glum little town and the dispirited woman who runs its café, but on another level she's warning the reader that dwelling on bitterness and personal failure is pointless because it only renders you incapable of recognizing happiness and peace of mind when it's within your grasp."

The paper touched fire and the words became clear: "*It's poisoning you. It's been poisoning you ever since your parents showed you what was in those boxes. At least think about it, all right? If you won't do it for yourself, do it for the rest of us. Do it before something cracks and it all comes spilling out, ugly and incoherent.*"

"I know," I said to the class, "that a lot of you have to wonder why the hell we bother teaching you some of this shit. What possible use are you going to have for geometry or assonance or metaphors or enjambment or . . . or whatever later on in life? I thought the same thing when I was in high school. The trick is to realize early on that you have to look for the message hidden in everything. You have to touch that paper to your own personal fire and know that—" The pain in my head and the shuddering of my arm seemed to fuse together in my chest. For a moment I feared that I might be having a heart attack, God knows I was sweating enough . . . but my breathing was fine, just fine.

The students sat unmoving, their gazes fixed on me.

I squinted, realizing just how long it had been since I'd held their attention like this.

"—you'll know that you're not apart from the world around you or the people in it. You'll be able to make yourself—your 'meaning,' as it were—clear to those who are your friends or wives or husbands or lovers, and you won't have to worry about becoming someone like Miss Amelia, so lonely and bitter and broken that you'll nail boards all over your windows and never venture out into the world for fear of being hurt by it." While speaking, I'd managed to reach into my pocket and pop the cap off my emergency medicine bottle. I found the Percocet by its shape, turned away from the class as I put the book on my desk, and quickly dry swallowed the pill.

I turned back to the class. A group of people, ghostly people, each more diaphanous than the one before, were standing at the back of the room behind the students. Most of them were strangers, but there were two people, holding hands, a husband and a wife, who seemed somehow familiar, and it took a second for their faces to register but soon enough—

—*Will they ever visit?*

—*I think so. I think they're coming right now.*

(*All over. All gone. Bye-bye.*)

—I recognized them as the characters from my dream. Oh, goody.

"Now, if you think," I said to the class, "that . . ."

The ghosts flickered in place, each one becoming in an instant a ruined, bloody version of itself; some were doubled forward, holes in backs of heads turning faces into dangling, shattered masks; some were thrown in the opposite direction, backs arched with pain, faces mangled by terror and shock, features streaked with black tears, dark stains spreading out from the center of chests; still others slumped with bodies and heads to one side or another, some were now on the floor, faceup, facedown, face gone, all of them stained, so many stains, pooling on the floor, trickling forward—

(*There's a storm brewing inside you, Geoff, and if it hits, it'll be terrible.*)

—the shaking grew so strong that I thought my arm might jerk right out of its socket.

"Uh, like . . . like I was saying, if you think that . . ."

Another flicker, and the ghosts were their old selves

again; staring, all at attention and looking so full of . . .
purpose.

I clutched my trembling arm against my side and held
it there with my steady hand. To the students, it must
have looked like I was having a stroke.

*(Now me and your mom, we've been talking about things
since I got out of the hospital, and we decided it's best we tell
you everything we know about what happened before we adopted you . . . .)*

I blinked, felt a shudder ripple upward from the base
of my spine, and looked once more at the back of the
room.

Everything yawed before me; now the faces of the students changed, becoming flat and one-dimensional, fluttering against the breeze, collapsing inward with
sick-making dry sounds, bits and pieces of flesh crum-
bling off and spinning away into a twisting back cloud
where the flickering ghosts waited, sometimes whole,
sometimes shattered and bloody and broken. . . .

I rubbed my eyes, then shook my head once. "Um . . .
did anyone happen to read any of the pieces in the science section of last Sunday's paper?"

Silence. The ghosts continued staring, continued
flickering.

"There was an article about the remains of a mammoth found in upstate Ohio. The article compared the
discovery to the one that was made on the banks of the
Beresovka River in Siberia around 1902. Both mammoths were frozen solid, but the thing is, both of them
were so well preserved that the buttercups they had been
nibbling on were still in their mouths. I don't know if
any of you know anything about gardening—my wife,
she's a major gardening enthusiast—me, I was born with

a black thumb. Anyway, a knowledgeable gardener will tell you that buttercups, like sedges and grass, thrive on alternating rain and sunlight, usually in temperatures around seventy-six degrees in a moist, warm climate." I leaned against the desk. A droplet of sweat rolled down my nose; I wondered if it were leaving a black streak in its wake. The pain in my head was intensifying with a vengeance.

The students continued to metamorphose; shimmering figures, translucent and ghostly, shifting, becoming mere base sketches of human beings with featureless oval heads atop puppet-hollow torsos, dim figures in the background of some massive painting that was drawing me inside—

—*keep going, don't let it win*—

"Now, consider a couple of things. Buttercups have a certain chemical makeup that, if you eat them, puts something in your system that acts as a natural antifreeze—but even that can't prevent dehydration when something is frozen by slow degrees. In order for those buttercups and that mammoth to be so well preserved, to be frozen that deeply *without* dehydration, the temperature would have to have dropped from around seventy-five degrees to at least one-hundred-and-fifty degrees below zero *in a matter of seconds!* The cold had to have descended on that mammoth so fast that its lungs immediately froze and its blood turned to ice. One moment it's eating a quiet summertime lunch, and the next thing you know—*wham!*—it's frozen where it stood."

I realized that my voice must have gotten quite loud because more than a few of the students looked nervous—a few downright scared—but the storm was loose and I couldn't stop.

"Don't you see? *Something happened* then, something scientists can't fully explain even today, and if they don't know what caused it, then they have no way to tell if or when it might happen *again*. At any given second we could all be slammed into the fucking deep freeze and I'll bet most of us in this room spent at least six minutes this morning trying to decide what to wear!"

The Broken One, his bandages looking even worse than last night, was now here, dancing among the ghosts, making that throat-slitting gesture back and forth across his neck as his head jerked from side to side.

Mayday, Mayday. . . .

"if there's . . . I mean . . . d-do . . . do you . . ."

I didn't even realize that I'd begun crying.

". . . do you think that mammoth *knew* what was happening when the ice came crashing down on its head? Was it afraid? I mean, yeah, sure, experts tell us that animals don't have any real sense of mortality, not like you and I are supposed to have, they don't think in abstract terms like 'love' and 'joy' and 'hope,' or all the rest of it . . . maybe that makes them the *lucky* ones, huh? But let's just suppose for a moment that experts are all full of shit and that animals *do* possess that capacity for abstract thought, okay? Then ask yourself this: in its last millisecond of life did that mammoth suddenly know how to feel regret for all the things it hadn't yet done? Or maybe its race memory dictated that this fragment of history had reached its end and it was time to become a ghost—because that's what it is to us now. Eventually, we all become ghosts— oh, sure, maybe there's a glitch in the universe somewhere and a few of us don't die when we're supposed to and end up as specters haunting our own lives, but we're still just ghosts-in-training, piles of carbon destined to be future fossils. Someone should have told that to Miss Amelia, or whispered it into the frozen ears of that mammoth."

I stared at the grotesque vaudeville in the back of the room. The students were normal again, fully corporeal, three-dimensional human bodies. The ghosts still flickered, but now in a steady, unbroken pattern; ruined, unruined; ruined, unruined. And the Broken One, standing front and center of all of them, the circus ringmaster in the middle of the middle row of desks, was in a frenzy, his hand slashing back and forth across his throat so fast it was little more than a blur.

"You know, the high school in the place where I was born, Cedar Hill, has the third lowest graduation requirements of any school in the state. As far as the school board there is concerned, the students are just marking time, waiting to swap their diplomas for a factory timecard or a place on the unemployment line. In a way, it's a town full of Miss Amelias and frozen mammoths. Sometimes I wonder how I managed to get out of there alive." Those last words suddenly struck me as hysterically funny, and I damn near gave myself a hernia trying not to laugh.

Something snapped inside of me—*physically*, as if I'd just torn a muscle—and a fear like I'd never known spread through my body, dragging wire hooks against the inside of my skin, but that was only the start; I felt my knees starting to buckle and fought to remain standing but the sensation was damn-near overpowering, I was next to nothing against it, and then I felt something looming overhead, just out of sight, something huge, vast, bigger than me, bigger than the room, bigger than the whole goddamned planet and we were all buried in its shadow as it plummeted toward us and I wanted to look up but my head wouldn't move and I wanted to breathe but the air was so *cold* and I knew that in a moment I'd be lying there a crushed and frozen bloody pulp on the frozen ground of the frozen world because whatever was coming was about to slam on top of me and there was nothing I could do except stand here and wait—

—and now the Broken One was shaking—*throwing*— his head from side to side, his throat-slicing hand remaining a blur to him, to one delirious, in ecstasy, flinging snot and spit and blood all over the room, the floor, the desks, onto the students who sat unnoticing of the globs and ribbons of blood that streaked their faces, who didn't so much as blink when a string of it landed across their eyes or a wad of it spattered against their cheeks and just as quickly became tumors that grew and seeped, devouring their features, filling themselves, becoming almost luminescent with joy as cells and tissue were chewed away—

—singing, the Broken One was singing, in a voice not clogged or choking, but one that rang like bells, one composed of several children's voices, a nonsense tune of *Oh, my quiver is once again empty/and that just will not do/will not do/will not do/My quiver is empty/and that just will not do* as he continued to flail and spray and sing while the flickering ghosts moved toward him, into him, filling him, becoming him as he, in turn, became something else, a large, hunched creature of white mottled flesh that turned toward me and reached out with impossibly long, muscular arms ending in skeletal hands with quadruple-jointed fingers, and because I couldn't accept it as a whole, because to look directly at it would mean accepting it, the rest of it fragmented into a rapid series of impressions: of wide, compacted nostrils leaking black oil; of puckered, scarlike knots where eyes should have been; of a mouth drawn downward, stretched wide to create a triangular maw of teeth, flesh, and black-red gums; of something flopping from its back, a huge growth, a growth that threw one of its arms over the thing's shoulder, its hand landing with a wet *slap!* as it pulled itself up, the area beneath *its* torso fused to its host's back by a thick, membranous band; of cold slick fingertips with jagged nails brushing against my cheek as I stumbled back against the desk—

—and just like *that*, it was gone; I was just a teacher standing in front of his class in a room where no ghosts stood in the back, where no broken phantom danced, where no monster reached forward. His students, their healthy faces now returned to them, sat staring, confused and worried and afraid, a few of them even close to tears.

I could not look at any of them. "I, uh . . . I'm sorry," I croaked. "I . . . uh . . . don't feel so well today . . . haven't been, been sleeping very much for the last week or so . . . don't know what it is. So . . . go on ahead and cut out early. Class dismissed."

The school nurse checked me out. I was running a temperature of 101. I called Yvonne to please come drive me home—things were getting very foggy and my center felt as if it were melting. Yvonne was there in fifteen minutes, but instead of taking me home, she took me to the ER. My temperature had spiked up a full degree. The attending ordered a series of shots and two IVs. Then I fell back into the hospital bed and slept for the next sixteen hours. I was in the hospital two nights, most of which I spent in various states of near-consciousness or near-unconsciousness. I remember at one point waking to find Patricia washing my arms and side with a warm, damp cloth while Yvonne slept in a nearby chair.

"Your snowflake's all pink and puffy," she whispered.

"It kinda . . . kinda hurts," I said. My throat was so dry it was painful. Patricia stopped her bathing duties and reached over to pour me a cup of water. Settling down near the head of the bed, she held the cup while I drank.

"No, Daddy—you have to *sip* it! You might burp if you don't."

"Says you."

"Sip, please?"

I sipped while she gently stroked my hair.

"The Graveyard People came by while you and Mommy were asleep."

The water stopped halfway to my throat and for a moment I almost choked, but then got hold of myself and finished swallowing. "*Who* came by?"

"The Graveyard People. They said they visited you at school? They saw how sick you got and they were all real worried. I told them you were doing good, that I was taking good care of you so Mommy could saw logs for a bit." She giggled at the memory. "They laughed when I said that, 'saw logs.' One of the men, he said that's what he used to call it when he was my age." Her attention shifted to my hair, which for the better part of a minute she tried to comb with her fingers into something presentable. "Nope," she said at last, shaking her head. "Gonna have to wash it. That's for sure."

"Honey, did . . . did they say anything else?"

"They said they were glad to see you were doing good. They were nice. Too bad they're all dead, huh?"

I stared at her for a moment. "Yes, yes it is."

"Shhh, now you go back to sleep, Daddy. I'll make sure to get your hands real clean."

Four days after I was released from the hospital (antibiotics and bed rest before I went anywhere), without ever having said *I told you so* (though I could tell from the look on her face she very much wanted to), Yvonne handed me a Triple-A TripTik with directions to Cedar Hill. I skimmed the thing—it only had three pages—and shook my head. "Ha—it's a *straight line*," I said. "Look at this—I just get on I-70 and follow my nose."

"I know," said Yvonne. "Wonder of wonder, miracle of miracles, directions with which even *you* can't screw up. At least until the third page." This said with a smile. She pulled the TripTik from my hands and flipped to the pocket-page in the back. "I made a reservation for you at the Marriott on the downtown square. I figure if you're going to establish a base of operations, you might as well be right smack in the middle of the city. The TripTik dumps you right in the hotel's parking lot. From there, God help us, you're on your own."

"'A base of operations'? Am I scouting things out for some sort of military coup? Ooh, hey, if that's the case, would you say, 'reconnoiter'?" I pulled her close to me and squeezed. "I'd *really* like to hear you say 'reconnoiter.'"

"Stop joking. I wasn't about to put you in some sleazy motel out by the mall or something."

"I appreciate this, honey. Thank you."

"You can thank me by making sure you take your medicine on time, Mr. Pneumonia, and not being gone for too long." She smiled again and shook her head. "You sure can't beat the timing on this, though. Only *you* would get this sick and then have to make a trip during spring break." She gave me a hug. "You haven't even left yet and already I miss your sorry ass."

A gasp from the bedroom doorway. "You said *ass*." Patricia was doing her best to look shocked and not as if she were about to burst out laughing.

"Yes, yes, I did," said Yvonne. "And I'm going to say it

again." She turned back to me and smacked the top of my head with the TripTik. "Ass!" Patricia lost it then, as did both Yvonne and I, and for the next minute or so we took turns shouting out variations on "ass"—"butt," "caboose," "derrière," Patricia even came out with "booty"— that sent all of us back into fits of laugher.

After it had passed and we were catching our breath, Patricia sat next to me on the bed and took hold of my hand. "You goin' on a trip, huh?"

"Yes, I am. I won't be gone long. I promise." This said to both her and Yvonne. "Three, four days, tops. I'll be back in time so that we can have a cookout this weekend."

"Hot dogs?" asked Patricia.

"*And* cheeseburgers. You know me—Daddy has to have his cheeseburgers."

"Can I flip?"

"You can flip."

"Well, all right, then." She kissed my cheek and scurried to her room, having just remembered some urgent kid appointment.

I sat on the side of the bed, staring at the doorway. After a few moments, Yvonne joined me, putting a hand on my shoulder. "You really think you'll only be gone for three or four days?"

I shrugged. "I really can't see it taking much longer than that, do you?"

She said nothing for several moments, only stared at me, expressionless. Taking a deep breath and squeezing my hand, she said: "Don't get me wrong, it would be great if that's all the longer it took I just . . . I just don't want you to feel like you have to hurry through this just so you can get back in here in time to burn hamburgers."

"I don't burn—wait, scratch that. I do. I do burn hamburgers. God, the *shame* of it all."

"Wandering off the highway, baby."

"I know." I thought about it for a few moments more, and then said: "Okay, I won't put a time limit on it—but I also won't disappoint Patricia. If things aren't finished in Cedar Hill, I'll come home for the weekend, head back there on Monday. My leave of absence will still have, what, ten days left?"

"Something like that, yes."

"So we'll go with my . . . my nontimetable for my nonplan. Fair enough?"

"Fair enough." She hugged me. Looking over her shoulder, I saw the antique umbrella that the Broken One had used during his last visit; it sat propped against the wall like Edmund Gwenn's Santa cane at the end of *Miracle of 34th Street*. Its being there should have surprised or even shocked me, but the truth is I would have been more startled if it *hadn't* been there. I wondered if Yvonne could see it at all, and then decided it didn't matter.

CHAPTER FIVE

There cannot exist in this or any other possible world a more mind-numbingly dreary, spirit-crushingly tedious, suck-out-your-soul *dull* stretch of highway than the one separating the front door of my home from the parking lot of the Marriott Hotel in downtown Cedar Hill: 116 miles of straight, flat, gray monotony occasionally interrupted by fleeting moments of ennui that serve to break up the empty miles between clusters of lifeless scenery. Every once in a while, I'd spot a cow. The highlight of the drive was a llama farm just outside of Columbus where the llamas—all three of them—stood with their heads resting on the top of the wooden fence, watching the traffic go by. I swear one of them was laughing at me.

I stopped for gas halfway between Columbus and Cedar Hill, at a mom-and-pop station that was located opposite a church graveyard (the same station where Bruce Dyson would stop two years later). I tried not to think too much about what was *in* the fuel I was pumping into my tank, but I had to admit that the station being directly across the road from a graveyard was perhaps the best visual metaphor for supply and demand that I'd encountered in a while.

Then it was back on the road. One hour down, one

hour and twelve minutes to go. A month. A lifetime. An epoch. And not a cow in sight. I was doomed.

Since I was driving the car that didn't have a CD player (boy, was that a mistake) I fiddled with the radio to see if I could find some music. What I found was an assortment of, A) static; B) county music; C) religious talk shows; and, D) religious talk shows that played country music when they weren't fading in and out of static. Doom, bleak and dark. I think I spent the second hour of the trip with one hand on the steering wheel and the other on the radio dial.

Eventually, the local Cedar Hill station, WCLT, began to creep through the white noise the closer I got to town. The station played an assortment of modern pop music interrupted every so often by news breaks and traffic updates. As soon as I drove past the WELCOME TO CEDAR HILL sign, the station came in clear as a bell just in time for the news break. After stories about the recent city council meetings and budget cuts and school bake sales, one story made me laugh out loud:

"Well, folks, it looks like we've got another animal sighting in town. In case you haven't been following this story, for the last couple of weeks there have been numerous prank reports of some rather . . . well, *odd* and exotic animals spotted in and around Cedar Hill. Last week there was a lion reported near Black Hand Gorge, as well as a tiger in the woods surrounding Dawe's Arboretum. This week started with a report of a Kodiak bear lumbering through Moundbuilder's Park. But today's report takes the cake. Today, we have reports of—get this—a baby elephant—I'll say that again in case anyone is cleaning the wax out of their ears to make sure they heard me correctly—a *baby elephant* near the Twenty-first Street exit. So if you're heading in that direction, folks, make sure you don't run over Dumbo." The DJ laughed. "I'm sorry, but I *so* look forward to these reports. Is that a sad commentary on my life, or what?" He laughed again, and then played about a minute of Henry Mancini's "Baby Elephant Walk" before segueing into something by Willie Nelson.

Still laughing, I checked the TripTik and discovered, much to my delight, that I would be driving past the Twenty-first Street exit shortly. I'd have to keep an eye out for Dumbo; even if I didn't spot the little fellow, it was still going to make a funny story to tell Patricia when I got home.

Traffic began to slow, and in less than a mile came to a near standstill. I rolled down my window and looked out. There were emergency lights in the distance, and what looked like at least one car—a minivan—sitting at a bad angle in the middle of the four lanes. Terrific; I arrive in town just in time to watch everyone else rubberneck at a fender bender. I sat back and crept along. Traffic moved along slowly, everyone making sure to get a good look at whatever lay ahead, but my attention was suddenly drawn to a couple of frighteningly large black dogs wandering the side of the highway. Bull mastiffs, and not particularly friendly looking ones, at that. I hit the automatic door lock, just in case one of them rose up on two legs and decided to try and catch a ride with me. Don't ask me why I did this.

The line of traffic moved farther up, and it wasn't long before I saw the blood. God, there was a lot of blood smeared across the lanes, most of it in a straight line, as if someone had been struck by the minivan and then dragged several yards. I could smell the blistered rubber of the tires from when the vehicle hit its brakes and came to a skidding halt. I closed my eyes and shook my head. I did not want to see this. The police and sheriff's vehicles, along with the ambulance and fiery flares alongside the accident, told you in no uncertain terms that this was bad.

Traffic moved again, and despite my better instincts— I've never been one to gawk at other people's public misery—found myself looking.

An old man, dressed in what once was a nice pinstriped suit (now soaked in his blood), lay in the road, surrounded by police and EMTs. There was another man—whether or not he was the driver of the minivan, I couldn't tell— kneeling down next to the old guy (who was still alive somehow). The man who was kneeling was my age, maybe a little younger, and he was offering something to the old guy: a hat. But not just any kind of hat—a *bowler*, like that guy on *The Avengers* used to wear. I watched as the old man reached up and grabbed the other man's shirt, and then spit up what looked like the remaining half of his blood supply. I looked away, shaking. The two black bull mastiffs sat off to the side of the highway, side by side, staring at the scene. WELCOME TO CEDAR HILL, indeed. Where the hell was Dumbo when you needed him? I thought, for a moment, that I caught sight of something with wings darting behind some foliage when I looked to the side, but it must have been a trick of the light.

I didn't realize that traffic had started moving again until a sheriff's deputy knocked on my window and waved me on. I nodded at her and pressed on the accelerator. I couldn't get away from there fast enough. It took maybe three minutes to drive away from the scene but it felt like an hour. I knew damn well until the day I died I'd see that old man spitting up blood in my dreams. I wondered if the Broken One would ask me about it. It seemed the kind of thing that would fascinate him.

* * *

I arrived at the hotel about fifteen minutes later, still shaking from what I'd seen. I sat in the parking lot for several minutes until I had a grip on myself, then gathered up the shoulder bag containing all the official paperwork, newspaper articles, photos, cards, letters, and videotapes I'd brought along to prove I was who I claimed to be. After that it was a simple matter of grabbing my suitcase from the trunk of the car, locking up, and going in to register. The young lady behind the desk was bright, pretty, and friendly, welcoming me to the Cedar Hill Marriott and informing me that if I needed anything, all I had to do was call downstairs and they'd take care of it. Despite her perpetual smile, I couldn't help but feel there was something forced about her cheeriness. Maybe she'd had a fight with her boyfriend or girlfriend. Maybe she was called in to work this shift and had to cancel plans. Maybe it was none of my business. I took my card-key, thanked her, and boarded the elevator for the top floor.

Yvonne had booked a suite for me, and it was surprisingly spacious and homey. I unpacked my clothes and then sat on the bed and looked through everything that I'd stuffed into the shoulder bag. This had to be more than enough to prove who I was—or, rather, who I once was. I'd made several photocopies of the adoption papers, along with my original birth certificate. I was pretty sure that someone was going to demand proof, and I wanted to be prepared.

I checked the time. Yvonne would still be at work, so I called her there.

"Made it in one piece," I said.

"Was it a nice drive?"

"Boring as hell." I almost told her about the accident, but then thought, *What's the point?*

"Do you like the room?"

"You didn't tell me you'd booked a suite."

She laughed. "Is it fancy?"

"It's really nice, yes. Thank you."

"Nothing but the best for my man. So—what's your first move?"

"A shower. Then I thought I'd go to city hall and see if they can direct me to the old records." I rubbed my eyes and sighed. "Tell you the truth, after that, I'm winging it."

"Which is to say you have no plan."

"Which is to say I have no plan."

"That's my Geoff."

"Oh, give me a break! I'm not *that* disorganized."

"Looked at your home office lately?"

"So now we're going to talk about my lack of housekeeping skills?"

Yvonne laughed. "You know I'm kidding, baby. You sound . . . you sound fried already. Is everything all right?"

"Well, let's see. I'm recovering from pneumonia and a nervous meltdown, the drive was lousy, I'm hungry, I need to use the bathroom, I don't know anyone here aside from the girl at the front desk, I miss you and Patricia so much I want to come home right now, and worst of all, I think it's quite possible that I didn't bring enough underwear."

Once again, Yvonne laughed. "What a drama-llama you are."

"Oh, hey, that reminds me—I passed a llama farm on the way here."

"You're joking?"

"One does not joke about llamas. Llamas are a serious matter."

She sighed somewhat theatrically. "Oh, *you*. Go take your shower and get something to eat. Call me back tonight and let me know what happens at city hall, okay?"

"Definitely."

"Promise?"

"Promise. I love you."

"You'd better. By the way, I love you, too."

I hung up and sat there for a few moments, letting the events of the day sink in. I crossed over to the window and opened the curtains. My suite was at the front of the hotel, so I had a pretty decent view of part of downtown; I could see the courthouse, several shops, the Midland Theatre . . . but no restaurants besides a fast-food place. After I showered and changed, I'd ask the young woman at the desk if she could recommend someplace where I could get a decent meal.

I felt a chill trickle down the back of my neck, the kind you get when you realize that you're no longer alone. I took a deep breath and nearly coughed from the stench. *Oh, Jesus, no, it couldn't possibly be—*

I turned around and saw the Broken One sitting in the chair at the writing desk. There was no pointing this time, no screeching or choking sound. When he opened his mouth to speak, no dark liquid spilled down his bandaged face and neck. His voice was thick, full of dirt.

"Welcome home," he said. His clothes were fresher, cleaner—not much, but a definite improvement over the ragged, soiled, maggot-infested rags he usually wore. Even his bandages looked fresher, far less stained and sodden, this time covering his entire torso so that none of the seeping sickness eating away at his body could be seen.

I shook my head, wanting to say, *You're not here, you're not real*, but I couldn't get my voice to work.

"Why?" he said, as if I'd spoken aloud. "Just because I'm here during the day?" He reached over and picked up the empty plastic ice bucket and tossed it at me. "Catch!"

I did, and felt the slick coldness from his fingers. I dropped it at once and staggered back toward the window.

"Now how do you suppose I could do that if I *weren't* really here?"

I began shaking, still trying to speak, to deny his existence.

He waved his hand, silencing me. "Stop. Just . . . stop. You don't have the time to piss away trying to rationalize whether or not I actually exist. Just listen. I'm going to be fucking with you over the next few days. I don't want to, I *have* to. It's not something that I take any particular pleasure in, but . . . your being here, your very presence, has set long-dormant things in motion. The old guy on the highway? That was because of you. Not that it's your *fault*, okay? So don't go putting yourself on the rack over him. He's not from around here—he slipped in through a . . . for the time being let's call it a doorway that's been opened because of your presence. There's a lot you don't know, a lot that needs to be made known to you, but not yet, and a good bit of it not by me.

"Just understand that you've started it, and you have to finish it. I'm here to make sure you *do* finish it, got it? And in case you're wondering about the way I look . . . in a way, I came from here, just like you. The farther away from Cedar Hill you are, the more I decay and the longer it takes me to assume physical form. But you're home now, and I'm feeling better, and I *like* feeling better, Joseph—or Geoff. To me, you'll always be Joseph Hamilton.

"Oh, by the way—don't even *think* about leaving before you finish what you came here to do. It won't be just me that will do everything in its power to stop you—and you can bank on this, pal: you *do not want* to meet the other thing that's helped to call you here. Not the most genial of sorts. Low affability factor. Questionable hygiene practices. *Scary* motherfucker, is what I'm saying."

I opened my mouth to speak but still the choking sound crawled out of my throat; if I could have spoken, I would have asked him: *What other thing?*

"You'll know soon enough," he said. "Okay, my friend, you've got a lot to do, I suggest you best get to it." And with that, he was gone: sitting there one moment, an empty chair the next. Even his smell vanished. But the ice bucket lay at my feet, glistening from where he'd touched it.

I ran into the bathroom, dropped to my knees, and vomited into the toilet. After the third round—dry heaves by then—I leaned forward and rested my head against the cool porcelain. Everything inside and outside of me was trembling. Flushing the toilet, I rose to my feet, opened my travel kit, and removed the bottles of medicine, taking a Zoloft. I sat on the edge of the bathtub for several minutes, and then gathered what was left of my wits to do what I'd originally intended: take a shower.

Nerves, I told myself. *He has to be a hallucination of some sort brought on by nerves. Christ knows you haven't exactly been the picture of stable mental health these days.*

There. That did the trick. Sometimes a delusion is the best coping mechanism in the world, especially if you *know* it's a delusion and can train yourself to forget about that little fact for a while.

I adjusted the temperature of the water until it was as hot as I could stand, and then stood under the spray for a good five minutes before I picked up the soap and shampoo. It felt good, the heat, the suds, even the smell of the shampoo was soothing, something real, something banal and everyday, grounding me in the here and now, in *reality*, goddammit.

Turning off the water, I took a deep breath, feeling much better, and then opened the curtain and stepped out into the steam-filled bathroom. I grabbed a towel, wiped off my face, did a quick once-over on my hair, and then reached out to wipe off the mirror so I could see to shave. My hand stopped midway when I saw

(. . . *What other thing?—You'll know soon enough* . . .)

the single word written there:

Hoopsticks.

CHAPTER SIX

The young lady at the front desk—LORI, according to her name badge—whose cheerfulness seemed even more forced than before, provided me with a map of the downtown square, and suggested that since the hotel restaurant was closed until four P.M. I should try a place called the Sparta that was located only a few blocks away. The map was obviously designed with visitors and tourists in mind, because everything was well marked and easy to follow. I was standing in the lobby studying the map when I heard Lori give out with a single, quiet sob.

One of these days I'm going to have to learn how to mind my own business. Seriously; it will be my undoing.

She was wiping her eyes as she watched a small television set behind the desk, and I suppose my motivation for going back over there was only half altruistic; I desperately wanted something to take my mind off of the Broken One's visit, as well as the cryptic word he'd written on my mirror. I walked to the desk and leaned over. "Lori?"

She started at the sound of my voice, wiped her eyes again, and donned that too-cheery smile once more as she rose from her chair and came over. "Is there . . . is there something else I can do for you, Mr. Conover?"

I stared at her reddened and glassy eyes. "I was going

to ask you the same question. Can I . . . can I help in any way?"

For a moment she looked as if she were going to shrug it off, but then the smile disappeared and her expression became a thing of heartbreak. "I'm sorry, it's just"—she looked over at the small television set—"two little girls disappeared from here about six days ago and they just . . . they just found one of them." Her voice cracked on the words "found one of them" and she wiped her eyes again. I didn't have to ask whether or not the little girl was alive.

"I'm so sorry," I said. "Did you know her?"

"Oh, no, no, not at all. It's just . . . it's so *sad*, you know? A lot of folks and businesses around town, they tied kites to their roofs or flagpoles or the tops of buildings— didn't you see all the kites on your way in?"

"I, uh . . . no, I didn't." Which was odd, because I'd been a kite freak when I was a kid. Still am, truth be told.

Lori pointed to the hotel entrance. "They're all over the place; you'll see them when go to the Sparta. People have got them up all over town. We've been having some nice wind, so a lot of them, they're still up in the air. You'll see some when you walk over to the Sparta. Ashley—that was her name—she liked to fly kites. I mean, her and her sister, Sharon—she's the other little girl who's still missing. It was one their favorite things to do. The news, it always said that in the stories."

"How old was she?"

"Six. Sharon's only four."

"Christ Almighty."

"She was so *little*, you know? And the police, they're not . . . they're not saying how she was killed, and when they won't talk about something like that, you know it must have been pretty awful. So I was crying. I apologize."

I resisted the impulse to reach over and squeeze her hand. "You don't need to apologize for this. If someone didn't cry over something like this, I wouldn't want anything to do with them, would you?"

She didn't have to think about it. "No, I wouldn't. Not at all. Thank you for asking me if . . . well, you know. It was very sweet of you. Thanks."

I couldn't think of anything else to say—good God, what *can* you say about something like this?—so I simply nodded my head and walked outside, examining the map. Then I looked up, and damn if she hadn't been right; there seemed to be kites everywhere: tied to flagpoles, attached to railings atop buildings, several had their strings affixed to benches around the courthouse or to tree limbs. Star kites, red box kites, glider kites, small fish kites, several colorful, complex butterfly kites, and a few rounded-head Tonkin kites, as well. It looked as if all of them had a photograph attached to them, and I didn't have to be close to any of them to know who was in those photographs. One kite in particular—this one attached to the top of the courthouse clock—was exceptionally stunning; larger than any of the others by far, it was an eight-point star constructed of strip wood, fretwork nails, plywood, and unbleached greaseproof paper; two frames, one diamond-shaped, the other a simple cross attached to opposing miter joints, formed the eight corners of the star, while a trio of balancing cups attached to the three highest corners by bracing strings created updrafts of air, giving further lift to its delicate form. Each set of corners was decorated in a different color of tinfoil—red, blue, bright green, gold—which, when reflecting the sunlight, turned the star into a flying prism, made all the grander by the unbelievably bright square of thin, silver tinfoil in its center. Light from the silver centerpiece glittered downward in waves, bounced off the upward inclination of the lowest wing corner at the angle of positive dihedral, and gave the whole scene an otherworldly feel. All of the kites blurred for a moment, and I reached up to rub something from my eye, wishing poor little six-year-old Ashley peace. As morbid as it may sound, I hoped that she died quickly and painlessly, not in terror and agony, crying out for Mommy or Daddy or anyone at all to come and save her because she was alone and scared and it hurt *so much*. . . .

Something shiny flashed in my peripheral vision, sunlight off brass, and I turned to see something box-shaped vanish atop the roof of a building. Once again, I could have sworn I caught a glimpse of wings, mothlike wings . . . and something like a camera.

You're tired and getting morbid because of it. Big surprise there, eh?

I stopped myself from going any further down that trail of thought, shook it off as best I could, and consulted the map, telling myself, *Think about something else.*

Let them find Sharon alive, please? The poor girl. I wondered if she'd had to witness the murder of her sister, had to hear her screams and cower in the darkness, terrified that she was going to be next and weeping for the loss of Ashley and all the things they'd never do together, all the tenderness they'd never share, the birthdays and Christmases never to be, all of the kites they'd never fly. Christ. She was the same age as Patricia, and I couldn't even begin to imagine the horror that Patricia would feel if—

—stop it. Think about something else.

(. . . *your being here, your very presence, has set long-dormant things in motion* . . .)

Dear God, was my presence somehow responsible for—?

Stop it. *Stop* it. *Stop it right now.* You're losing it again. The map, look at the fucking map. Can't lose it if you're looking at the fucking map. So look. Do it. Do it now.

The Sparta was clearly marked. I just needed to cross the street, go past the Midland Theatre, cross at the end of that street, make a left, then a right at the first corner. So simple even I couldn't screw it up—which, to my surprise, I didn't.

The Sparta itself was one of the warmest, most homey restaurants I've ever seen; a long, old-fashioned, all-wood soda counter took up the right half of the front (complete with an impressive large double-broiler grill behind it where all the food was cooked), while an equally long glass candy display case took up the other side. A sign— probably as old as me—boasted that all candy sold here was made by hand. There was a row of chocolate-and-caramel bars that made my blood sugar rise just by looking at them, and I promised myself to buy some to take home this coming weekend; if I didn't, neither Yvonne nor Patricia would forgive me.

The back half of the restaurant was filled with polished, dark wooden booths on either side, and when I sat down the first thing I noticed were the mirrors; the inside wall of each booth was a mirror from floor to ceiling. Sitting down at the first empty booth I found (the place was filling up for the lunch rush) I looked at my reflection sitting beside me, and then caught a glimpse in my mirror reflected in the mirror of the booth on the other side of the restaurant; for a moment, I sat staring at the reflection of me staring into a mirror where the reflection of me staring into a mirror stared out from the mirror in *that* reflection while another, smaller version of me stared out from an even smaller reflection of another mirror . . . an endless succession of Geoff Conovers staring out from inside reflections of countless mirrors in innumerable worlds where all of them were stressed-out and hungry. I wondered if any of *them* had a Broken One in their lives and, if not, perhaps they'd care to swap places for a little while.

"Don't think I've seen your face in here before," said the waitress, an older woman—sixty, sixty-two—who my dad would have described as a "sturdy-looking gal." Her name tag identified her as MILLIE. Millie had the most beautiful gray hair I'd ever seen, evenly streaked by thin lines of black hair that weren't quite yet ready to surrender their hue.

"This is my first time here," I said.

Her eyes the color of cobalt widened at this. "*Really? Just got into town today?*"

"As a matter of fact, yes."

She pulled a pencil that was more of stub from behind her left ear and removed an order pad from the pocket of her apron. "We ain't had many visitors here—well, not until the last week." When she said this, she glanced over my head toward the counter. At the time I thought nothing of it. Millie licked the tip of her pencil—something I'd never seen a waiter or waitress do in real life—tapped it once against the surface of the order pad, and gave me a wide, bright smile. "What can I get for you, darlin'?"

Although I'd picked up the menu from behind the napkin dispenser as soon as I sat down, I hadn't yet looked at it. I opened it, skimmed the items, and asked, "Do you have liver and onions?"

"Sure do—but if you don't mind me making a suggestion, if this is your first time here, you *have* to try our cheeseburger. Best you've ever had or it's free."

"Wow, that's a brave sales pitch. Okay, then, sold. Two cheeseburgers, lettuce and onion only, fries, a Pepsi, and a small fruit salad."

Mille was once again looking at something past me, near the counter. Her face was a slab of granite. "Got it." She finished writing the order, looked at me, and—voilà!—the radiant smile returned. "This won't take but four or five minutes at most. Sylvia—she's our cook—she's going to be thrilled that someone new is about to try her cheeseburgers for the first time. Oh, hey—do you want her to grill the buns?"

"Sounds fantastic."

Millie winked at me, but even her smile and friendly manner couldn't stop the single tear that formed in that eye and began to slide down her cheek. "Be right up," she said, and all but sprinted away.

I pulled my shoulder bag over and began to open it when I had a chilly sensation that reminded me too much of what I'd felt back in the hotel room right before my uninvited guest had shown up. I froze for only a second, then pulled out one of the files. It wasn't the one I'd wanted—in fact, I suddenly couldn't *remember* what I'd intended to get.

I laid the file on the table and opened it. The top page contained names and phone numbers of people who might have some information, or who could at the very least point me in the right direction. I flipped over the first page and stretched my back. The chill remained with me. And the crowded restaurant had quieted somewhat; nothing dramatic—it wasn't as if every customer in the place had just stopped talking—but the volume of the conversations buzzing through the air had definitely been turned down a level or two.

Looking up, I saw that several people on both sides of

the restaurant were looking over toward the counter, and those customers who sat with their backs to the counter were turning around at sometimes awkward angles to look for themselves. I followed suit.

There was a thirty-inch flat-screen television mounted over the corner of the counter closest to the back half of the restaurant. The set was on, and even though the sound wasn't turned up, there was no mistaking what had caught Millie's eye earlier, and what had nearly everyone else's attention now.

Across the bottom of the screen, in oversize and dramatically colored font, the words MISSING CEDAR HILL GIRL, 6, FOUND DEAD. SISTER, 4, STILL MISSING. Above the words, in high-definition color, with the word *LIVE* in the upper right hand of the screen, a small, black-bagged body was loaded onto a gurney and then strapped in place by two burly men wearing black jackets (each with the word CORONER printed in bright yellow across the back), who then proceeded to maneuver the gurney and its grim contents up a small incline covered in tangled vines that reached to their ankles. Police and sheriff's officers could be seen searching the area as two members of what had to be a CSU team packed up their evidence and gear and followed the body. After a moment, the camera pulled back to reveal some generic Handsome Male Reporter standing off to the side, microphone in hand, talking into the camera as the screen split in half: Handsome on the right side, Serious-Looking Female Reporter asking questions from the safety of the news desk on the left.

I didn't want to watch anymore and began to turn away, but then saw that Millie and Sylvia were staring at me. Millie noticed that I'd noticed and so lifted her hand, giving a small wave and even smaller smile. Her faintly red, slightly puffy eyes betrayed that she'd cried a little more since leaving my booth but had made fast work of it. I looked up at the television again, then back at her, shaking my head, letting her know that I found this just as terrible and heartbreaking as did everyone else. Save for the monster who'd killed little Ashley.

Sylvia, the cook, stood with her arms—roughly the same size and thickness as those of a wrestler's—folded across her ample bosom. She was a good twelve inches taller and ten years older than Millie, was built like a walk-in freezer, kept her hair buried underneath a thick hairnet that clung to her skull with the force of a medieval torture device, and looked as if she'd enjoy nothing better than come out from behind that counter and clean my clock. There was not only wariness and suspicion in those steely eyes, there was an unmasked *disgust*.

Millie leaned over and whispered something to her, and Sylvia waved her away, turning back to the grills and flipping what looked to be about a dozen burgers with such speed and skill that for a moment, I swear, her hands became a blur. Then she stepped to the far end of the counter and picked up the phone.

Turning back, I saw that several restaurant patrons were sneaking glances at me and trying to appear as if they were looking somewhere else. Slowly, the volume of conversation rose back up to a normal level. I sat staring at the opened file on the table, feeling the surreptitious gazes of everyone around me. *Stop being paranoid. It's not that big of a place. Everyone probably knows everyone else—if not by name, then at least by sight. Millie knew right away that you weren't from around here. And stop making this about* you, *Mr. Narcissus.*

As if to make that last thought less abstract, I looked

once more at my reflection sitting next to me, then tried focusing on the endless series of reflections-within-reflections cast in the mirror of the booth on the opposite side. I was so lost in this amusement that I almost didn't see Millie walk up to my booth and sit down on the other side of the table. *What the—?*

I turned to face her, only to find that the seat across from me was empty. Rubbing my eyes, I closed the file and slipped it back into my shoulder bag, casting one last glance at the mirror as I did so. In the reflection, the Broken One sat across from me.

"Hi'ya," he said, lifting one of his hands and giving me a little finger wave. His hands looked fine now, washed clean, no sign of wounds, fingernails cleaned and clipped. The coat he wore was not the same one as earlier; in fact, it wasn't a *coat* at all, more of a light windbreaker, blue, and new-looking. A clean gray shirt underneath covered most of the bandages encircling his torso, though now his entire face was wrapped, leaving openings for his eyes, nostrils, and mouth. The job looked to have been done by a pro this time because the overlaps were nearly seamless. And the areas of his face where the clusters of large tumors should have been were smaller and a bit smoother, though a few bulges and small stains still remained.

"Interesting thing, mirrors," he said. "Did you know that on *this* side of a mirror—this mirror, any damn mirror, really—there's an inverse world? Hand to God, I shit you not. An inverse world where the insane go sane and bones crawl out of graves and grow flesh and welcome the nursing home wheelchair—after all, they're on their way *back in*, not out. The sun rises in the west in the evening, which confused the hell out of me first time I saw it. People in love cry buckets because each passing

twenty-four hours makes them a day younger, and they know that soon childhood is going rob them of all they've known together, all they've shared, the pleasure of each other's bodies. It would all be sad except that, over here, sadness is joy. It's very confusing . . . but never *boring*, I'll give it that. I try not to linger here when I come this way, so you'll pardon me if I stop waxing mawkish."

"Is this what you meant with that 'I'm going to be fucking with you' line? That you'll be randomly popping in to deliver these portentous little tidbits? The shock factor is rapidly losing its luster, pal."

He silenced me with a wave of his hand. "Don't talk, you'll draw attention to yourself—and speaking of, try staring at our reflections a little less, would you? Something tells me that if Millie were to come back here and catch you talking to your reflection, things might—oh, how to put this?—go slightly awry. Oh, hey, I want to show you something." He reached into the left pocket of his windbreaker and removed a hat—a tan English Ivy cap, to be specific. He looked out toward the restaurant— which, from his point of view, must have meant he was looking at *his* reflection—and, using both hands, put the cap on his head and adjusted it until it was at an angle that pleased him. "Ta-da!" he said, parting his arms in front of him. "Do I look like a smart and sophisticated man-about-town, or what?"

"It's very nice," I said.

"Well, at least wait until you taste everything," said Millie, setting down the platter of cheeseburgers and fries, then the Pepsi and fruit salad. "I'll make sure to tell Sylvia that you said everything looked nice, though. She'll get a kick out of that."

She couldn't maintain eye contact. Her hands would not remain still (she was either messing with her hair, her order pad, or her apron), and she kept glancing in the direction of Sylvia and the counter. There was definitely something wrong. Both her manner and her smile made me anxious; combine this with the bad vibes Sylvia had all but shotgunned at my face, and it was Plan B time. Plan B, which had just come to me, consisted of this: run away.

I reached in my pocket and pulled out a twenty. "Millie, I hate to ask you to do this, but could you take all of this back and fix it up to go? I didn't realize the time, and I've got to be somewhere in about fifteen minutes." I handed her the twenty. "Will this cover the food and your tip?"

She stared at the bill. "Hon, this'll cover the food and leave something like ten dollars."

"Keep it. You have a nice smile, and I needed to see a nice smile today."

She blushed, and for a moment whatever wall she'd been trying to erect ceased construction. "That is so *sweet* of you, hon, but I can't take all that."

I smiled. "I'll bet you could if you really tried."

She laughed, then playfully smacked my shoulder. "I'll meet you up by the door in two minutes. Thanks again. Sure hope you'll come back sometime when you can sit for a while and enjoy your food."

"I will come back, Millie. Promise."

She took my food back to the counter. I did a quick once-over to make sure I hadn't dropped anything, and began sliding out of the booth when the Broken One said: "Didn't mean to scare you off."

"Yeah, right."

"Seriously. It's just that I forgot to give you something." He pulled a key ring from his pocket and placed it on the table on his side of the mirror. "You're going to

need this. I'm not sure *when* exactly, but you will need it."
There was a single key on the ring. "Just don't take it off
and mix it in with your own keys. If you want to attach
the ring to yours, that's okay, but don't take the key off."

I looked at his bandaged reflection. "What am I supposed to do, just reach through, clap if I believe in fair-
ies, chant a mantra, what?"

He took off his cap and laid it next to the key ring.
The stain under that area of the cap was spreading. He
reached up and felt the spot, and pulled away two fingers
with bright blood on their tips. "Shit. I'll ruin the cap if
I don't watch it."

I don't know why I said what I next did. "It *is* a nice
cap." And with that, I slipped out of the booth and made
my way to the front of the restaurant. The candy counter
beckoned, but it was going to have to wait. My left side
was throbbing, breathing was difficult, I was sweating
like crazy (either a migraine or a panic attack was on the
way; my guess was the latter), and I could feel Sylvia's
gaze boring into the back of my skull like a lobotomist's
drill.

"Here you go, hon," said Millie, coming from behind
the cash register on the candy-counter side. She handed
me a thick brown paper bag and a cold can of Pepsi. "I
couldn't find the right kind of lids for the pop cups, so I
figured you maybe wouldn't mind a can."

"Not at all." I took them from her and thanked her
again for the good service, and was just beginning to push
open the door when another waitress called out, "Hey,
mister! *Mister!* Millie, would you stop him, please?"

Millie grabbed my elbow. "Hang on, darlin'. Seems
you left something at your table. Wait right here. I'll get
it for you, your hands are full."

It took her maybe fifteen seconds to meet the other

waitress in the middle of the aisle and come back. The whole time Millie was gone, Sylvia never once stopped glowering at me. This time, I stared right back at her, replaying four things in my memory: Millie's questions about my being new in town, the news report about Ashley's body, Sylvia making a phone call, and how nervous Millie had been when she delivered my food.

She called the cops. New face turning up in town the same day Ashley's body is found—of course *she called the cops. Look at that face. This is an angry and heartbroken woman looking for someone to blame.*

It didn't seem like that big of a leap in logic to assume that I was right. *Jesus, Millie, where are you?*

"Here you go," she said, startling me. "Whoa, there, steady as she goes. You okay?"

"Wha—? Oh, yes, thank you. I think I've got a migraine coming on."

"You need to eat is probably what it is. Where you staying?"

Without thinking, I told her.

"Oh, well that's not much of a walk, is it? And maybe the fresh air will do you some good."

"Hope so."

"But you need to be careful about leaving things like this. Sure is a nice one, though. Bet it cost a pretty penny." She handed me a tan English Ivy cap and a key ring with one key.

Chapter Seven

I wound up sitting next to a dead woman on a bench in front of the courthouse. We had a nice view of the Midland Theatre across the street. I thought about being courteous and offering her some of my lunch, but she seemed content to just sit there, her arm extended to toss a last handful of birdseed onto the lawn.

The dead woman's name was Henrietta Holcomb. She'd been the manager of the Courthouse Records Department from 1942 until her death in 2006 at the age of eighty-five. She left behind a husband, Daryl (who passed away the following year), five children, nine grandchildren, and three great-grandchildren. She liked needlepoint, Glenn Miller records, Mickey Spillane novels, and spending Sunday afternoons in spring and summer feeding birds in the park and watching children fly kites.

I knew all of this about Henrietta because the bronze plaque affixed to the bench offered the same information to anyone who was willing to stop long enough to read it; then all they had to do was look to the left and see the impressively detailed bronze sculpture of Henrietta sitting there, perpetually feeding the birds. The sculpture was a re-creation of a photograph taken by one of her children. *This was her*, I thought. *And this is all that's left of her*: The Henrietta Holcomb Memorial Bench.

She wasn't alone, though. Scattered around the court-house lawn and the downtown square were a dozen similar memorial benches, each with its own plaque (sometimes two) and its own bronze sculpture of someone who'd been important to the community. Before I left Cedar Hill I was going to walk around the square and read all the names, look into all of the faces, maybe even take photos of all of them, if they didn't mind.

I finished the last of my lunch and leaned back. Millie had been right. The Sparta made the best cheeseburgers I'd ever tasted. These were the cheeseburgers that all other cheeseburgers aspired to be. Cows munching grass on land halfway across the country prayed that they would be used for the meat in these cheeseburgers when their time came.

The early afternoon sun warmed my face, soothed my muscles, and for the first time since arriving here I felt relaxed. I closed my eyes and just sat there, enjoying the sun, the lingering taste of the food, and Henrietta's companionship. I hoped she was enjoying all of the kites. And that she didn't ask me why there so many of them, and downtown, at that.

Don't go there. We're relaxing, *remember?*

I put the tan cap on my head, angling it downward so that my eyes were covered, crossed my legs, crossed my arms, crossed "get food" off my list. I needed a few minutes to settle my nerves. This first excursion into Cedar Hill hadn't exactly been the most fortuitous. It was too bad Henrietta couldn't be allowed to speak to me for just one minute; I bet she'd know exactly where I needed to go, who I needed to talk to, and what I should ask for.

"You here to fix my television?"

Startled, I looked up to see an old man in an equally old charcoal gray suit standing a couple of feet away

from the front of the bench. His hands shook, he needed
a shave, and his chin shimmered with spit.

"Don't gawk at me like that," said the man. "I asked
you a question, son. You here to fix my television?"

"Uh . . . no, no I'm not."

He sneered. "Well, ain't that a pisser? I been on Henrietta here to get hold of someone for weeks. Henrietta,
there ain't nobody she don't know, nothing she can't look
up for you or tell you where to find it yourself. That
grand old gal practically *ran* this city at one point. She
told me that she'd have somebody here this week to fix
my TV. Can't watch my programs if the damned TV
don't work!" His voice had that eerie, hollow, echoing
quality that one hears from patients with advanced em-
physema, lung cancer, or some other terminal condition.
His eyes were wide—too wide—and covered in a glaze
that suggested what once sparkled in there had long ago
faded away, or was in the process of fading. He had dif-
ficulty maintaining eye contact—not because of timidity
or nervousness, though; it looked as if he didn't have
complete control of the movements.

I remembered the last year Yvonne's father was alive,
how the Alzheimer's had chipped away at the man he was
bit by bit, leaving less of him with each new morning.
During those periods of lucidity that became less fre-
quent as the weeks wore on, he sometimes called Alzheimer's the "leaking faucet." We'd been visiting him
during one of his good weeks, and made plans to go out
for dinner and a movie. He went back to get his jacket
and tie from the closet and what should have taken two
minutes at most dragged on for nearly ten. I went back to
see if there was a problem and found him standing in
front of the closet, staring at the clothes hanging there.
He looked at me and began to cry. "I can't go to the

movies," he said. "It's . . . I mean . . ." He pointed to his head. "I can't follow them, I can't keep track of what happens from one scene to the next. Sometimes I think I've got it, and then . . . it drips out of the leaking faucet and goes down the drain and . . ." He wiped his eyes, then looked in the closet. "Was I supposed to be getting something? I can't . . . hey, Geoff? Are we getting ready to leave or are we just getting back?" He never really recovered from that night. In the last few weeks of his life, he'd begun to display symptoms not unlike those the old man before me was exhibiting, not the least of which was his voice becoming more hollow, an echo of a thing rather than the thing itself.

I looked at the old fellow once more, and felt something in me deflate just a little.

The deep, discolored lines that had burrowed into his features were all too clear, souvenirs from a life that had been too long and too hard, filled with too many disappointments and heartbreaks, a life now measured not in years or months but weeks or days, because that was all his damaged, dying brain could hold on to. You could almost see Death pausing to savor the moment and admire the agonizing poetry of its handiwork, and then move on with a whispered promise to return in a while.

He looked at me for a moment, helpless. "I can't watch my programs anymore. What'm I supposed to do?"

"I'm sure that Henrietta will get someone out here real soon."

The old man stuck out his chin and defiantly adjusted his tie, tightening its frayed knot with palsied hands. "They told you to say that, didn't they?"

"Who?"

"The Vapor Children. They hide in my coffee or my hot cocoa. They get out through the steam that comes off the top. I see their faces—they think I don't because the vapor is always swirling around, but I see them. I don't see a lot of things real clear these days, but them I see. And they don't much like me. They'd enjoy nothing better than to see me not have my TV. Well, don't you try it. Don't you be trying to take away my television, you hear me?"

"I won't take your television. I promise."

He nodded. "They think I'm the one who told on Katie Lynn. Well, I didn't. I oughtta not to be punished for that. I mean, sure, everybody saw how bad the cut on her face was, that it needed stitches and all, but I saw her fall off her bike, all right? *I saw her.* Her daddy didn't beat her like she said. She just said that so all the kids'd feel sorry for her. Everyone picked on her, y'know? She smelled kinda ripe and always wore them old dirty clothes. Shameful, it was." A tear slipped out of his eye and ran down his cheek, dangled at the corner of his mouth, then tumbled onto his chin. "I loved her, though, really, I did. Once you got past feelin' sorry for her, she was kinda sweet. Do anything for you, she would. A *sweet* girl. Terrible thing, don't you think? Her daddy touching her like he did, then beating her up all the time so she wouldn't tell, making her say that she fell off her bike. I saw him pound on her." He made a fist and swung it down toward an invisible target near his hip. "Just hammered on her like she weren't supposed to feel a thing. Poor girl. She made me promise I'd tell folks I saw her fall off her bike. Poor girl. She was sweet. Do anything for you. I felt sorry for her. Them dirty clothes all the time. She used to help me on my paper route and tell me stories that she made up—and they was clever ones, to boot. Dragons going shopping at the bakery, factories where the machines came to life and did all the work for you, elephants dancing the ballet. I got to know her on account of them stories, and she was pretty when you got to know her. She gave me my first kiss. Her lips tasted like fresh strawberries. And her in them dirty clothes. I loved her. She's dead now, almost forty years. He pushed her down the stairs and she"—his voice cracked on the next word— "*smashed* her head against the radiator and then she went away. She was only ten. I miss her something terrible. I wish I'd've married her, that she'd've lived that long. I'd've treated her tender, y'know? But I never told her I loved her. Don't think anyone ever did. Someone should've loved her and told her so. Now I can only see her on the TV and it's all broke." He clamped his mouth closed, his rheumy eyes releasing a few more tears. His body swayed a little to the left; then he shuddered, snapping himself from his wistful reverie. "You here to fix my television? I got it right here. Just a little portable thing." He held up his hand, fingers and thumb curved into a crescent as if grasping a handle.

I felt something in my chest wither even further. The storms continue to come. The nights only grow darker. What use was there, then, for tenderness? Swaddled in this darkness, a word of mercy within a word of despair, unable to speak either one, proffering deeds to oblivion and love to the prosperity of the grave: this old man; this harsh light; this frozen woman feeding birds while kites twirled in the air.

"Let me take a look at it," I said.

The old man meandered over. "You be careful. This's the only one I've got and I can't afford to replace it. Probably can't afford your prices, either, but we'll work something out."

I stared at the empty spot on the bench where the TV was setting. "This one'll be on the house."

"Best get to it, then," said the old man, looking on his wrist at a watch that wasn't there. "Almost time for my programs."

I gave him a half smile, nodded once, then reached into my shoulder bag for a small nail-clipper that I used as a screwdriver to repair the loose antenna in the back of the set, hoping that my pitiful pantomime matched up to whatever he imagined the shape of the television to be.

"Nice set," I said, squinting at the complicated detail work as I removed the back panel and replaced one of the electronic chips.

The old man watched, glistening-eyed and anxious.

A twist here, a tightening there, then replace the back panel; I gave the antenna a jiggle to make sure it was securely in place, then turned the set around and asked the old man to try it now.

"Hey, you do good work," he said, his smile still haunted by the ghost of the handsome devil he must have been in his younger days. He picked up the small television—which now, in a blink, was as corporeal as both him and me—and turned it on.

I was still trying to pull another breath into my lungs and keep my heart from squirting out through my rib cage. There was no rationalizing this one. I had not blinked, not looked away, not squinted because of the sunlight suddenly reflecting against something shiny. I'd seen it happen. One second, nothing there; the next, he was lifting a small portable television set off the bench and turning it on.

"Picture's clear as a bell. Thanks, son. You're a good boy. Yessir."

I felt half removed from my body, but managed to pull in that second breath and say: "My pleasure, sir. My very great pleasure."

He shuffled across the lawn toward the sidewalk. "She ought to be on pretty soon. I miss her, y'know? Poor little thing. Do anything for you. Kids shouldn't've picked on her so much. That's all she ever knew, people picking on her...." He turned his back to me, walked away, rounded the next corner, and was gone. I almost followed him. I hadn't asked his name, and I found myself wanting to know.

But the *television* . . .

"How in the hell . . . ?" I said aloud.

"This is Cedar Hill," said a voice from behind. "Weird shit happens here. Get used to it."

I turned to face a man who could have easily passed for either Grigori Rasputin or Charles Manson, except that this man's eyes, while undeniably intense and mesmerizing, were also kind. His wavy, shoulder-length dark hair was speckled with gray, as was his sharply trimmed beard, and only served to make his startling bluish gray eyes stand out all the more. He wore blue jeans and a black, short-sleeved, banded-collar shirt with a thin strip of material placed over the neck that created a solid white collar all the way around, signifying him as a member of the clergy. I immediately felt bad for having thought he resembled either of the Great Psychos.

He pointed toward the street corner the old man had just rounded. "You know what's always bugged me? Nowhere in the Bible—oddly enough, a book with which I have some passing familiarity—are there any beatitudes for the lost or the lonely. The poor, the hungry, the meek, the persecuted, the cheese-makers, blah-blah-blah. But nowhere does it say that the lost or the lonely are blessed. I like to think they are. Don't flee screaming, I'm not going to hand you a pamphlet and claim that I can save your soul. I can barely claim to save money at the grocery store, and I clip coupons like you wouldn't believe." He smiled. "Sorry about the minihomily." He held out his hand and I stood.

"Nice to meet you, Father."

He laughed. "It's 'Reverend,' actually. I run the Open Shelter on East Main. Just over the bridge and few blocks down in Coffin County." He shook my hand.

"In *where*?"

"Coffin County. I *knew* you weren't from around here. Folks call it that because there used to be a fairly large casket factory in the area. It burned to the ground in the late 1960s and took most of the buildings on the surrounding four blocks with it. The area never recovered. It's not the best part of town, to couch it as a euphemism, but I get free use of the building and can usually talk someone qualified into making repairs for cheap. And you are . . . ?"

"Joseph—um, sorry—Geoff Conover." I shook his hand again.

"You sure about that?" he said. "Don't answer 'yes' unless you're willing to make the commitment."

Now *I* laughed. "Yes, I'm sure." I looked back at the street corner. "You saw what happened here, didn't you, Reverend?"

"You bet."

"The TV?"

"The little portable one that appeared out of thin air, *that* television? Yes."

"How did—hang on. Do you know his name?"

The Reverend shook his head. "I'm not sure anyone in town *does* know it. He's been a semiregular at the shelter for years and he hasn't even picked up a nickname. If you met my staff, you'd know they're big on assigning nicknames to *everyone*. But that old fellow? Not for him.

Watch out for the birds." He gently took hold of my arm and moved me to the left of the bench. About half a dozen pigeons were gathered on the grass near the sculpture, gobbling up the birdseed scattered there.

"Henrietta's nothing if not covert," said the Reverend.

I grabbed up my shoulder bag and began walking away. "Okay, Reverend, this just officially got a little . . . irritating."

"Not 'weird'?"

"You have no idea what the past couple of weeks have been like, let alone the past couple of hours since I arrived here. 'Weird' doesn't quite pack the punch it used to."

He began following me across the courthouse lawn. "Please don't go—at least, not like this. You're irritated, okay, I get that. Maybe I can help. What brings you here, anyway?"

I stopped and turned to face him. "What makes you think something *brought* me here? Maybe I'm just passing through, maybe I'm on vacation and came here for a visit. Maybe it's none of your business."

He stood beside me, hands in pockets, looking over at the Midland. "First of all, if you were only 'passing through,' that's exactly what you'd have done—just driven though and kept on going. Cedar Hill is a place most people see only in their rearview mirrors, or if they're on their way to someplace more interesting and have to stop for gas. Second, no one comes here *for* a vacation, they get away *from* here for that. Third and last, *you* were the one who said 'since I arrived here.' The word 'arrived' implies that this was your intended destination, and people who have an intended destination usually have one for a specific reason or reasons, so I'll ask again—what brings you here?"

I stared at him for a moment, then shook my head and laughed. "I'll bet you think that's clever, don't you, that little Sherlock Holmesian demonstration in deductive reasoning?"

"Actually, yes, yes I do."

"The TV and the birdseed, Reverend. How were either of those things possible? And please don't give me that 'This is Cedar Hill where weird shit happens' line again."

"Fair enough." He looked past me for a moment. "I'm guessing you're staying over at the Marriott, right?"

I heard a car pull up and park behind us but thought nothing of it. "Yes."

"May I call you there this evening?"

"I don't see what—"

He looked straight into my eyes, his gaze nailing me to the spot. "I can probably answer most of your questions, Geoff, because I'm the only person here who literally knows or is known by everyone in town—if not by name, then by sight. Not much happens here that I'm not aware of, so the person you need as your sidekick right now is me. Skip the city hall visit, they installed a new computer network a couple of weeks ago and still haven't figured out how things work, so you'd only get the bum's rush. Just know that I can help you and I will help you. But as far as the TV and the birdseed go . . . the being you think of as the Broken One told you the truth. Your presence here *has* set long-dormant things in motion and—and you want to know how I know this, don't you?"

I almost couldn't find the word. ". . . y-yes . . ."

"Then tell me it's all right for me to call you this evening. I keep my word, Geoff. Say it's all right."

I nodded.

"Excellent." He looked over my shoulder and grinned at someone approaching us. "Hello, Ted."

"Reverend," came the reply. "Everything still on for cards this week?"

"You've got six dollars of my grocery money I need to win back—what do *you* think?" He looked at me. "I also can't save money at the store because our sheriff here keeps taking it from me."

"Right, blame me because you suck at poker. Go ahead, you will anyway, we both know it."

The Reverend put a hand on my shoulder and said, "I'm going to act as the Cedar Hill Bureau of Tourism for you, my new friend. Allow me to introduce you to Sheriff Ted Jackson. I suspect he may cheat at cards, but let's not spoil the moment with a less-than-flattering first impression."

So I'd been right—Sylvia had called the authorities, though I wondered why she'd called the sheriff instead of the police. I offered my hand, hoping he wouldn't slap a cuff on it. "Nice to meet you, Sheriff."

He gave me a halfhearted smile and shook my hand. "Likewise, Mr. . . . ?"

"Conover," said the Reverend. "Geoff Conover."

I looked back and forth between them and decided to take a chance. "It's the name my parents gave me after the adoption. For the first thirteen months of my life I was Joseph Hamilton. I was born here."

"Is that right?" said Jackson. "Don't take this the wrong way, Mr. Conover, but if I asked you to prove that, could you?"

I lifted my shoulder bag. "I sure could, Sheriff."

"I'm afraid I'm going to have to ask you to do just that."

"Do it at the Hangman," said the Reverend.

Jackson blinked and looked at him. "*What?* Why should I—? Oh, look, do me a favor, Reverend. I had a lousy night, a lousier morning, and I suspect the rest of the day isn't going to be making my highlight reel. I knew it before my feet hit the floor."

The Reverend's expression softened into something much more serious. "I heard about the Millhauser girl. I'm so sorry, Ted."

Jackson gave a sad nod and looked up at some of the kites in view. "Makes me sick."

"Will there be another search party to look for her sister?" I asked.

Jackson stared at me. "How long have you been in town?"

"A few hours, maybe less."

"Then how could you know *anything* about—?"

"There was a live newsbreak on television a little bit ago. It showed Ashley's body being moved from the crime scene."

Jackson winced. "Did they have her in a body bag or was she covered with a sheet? Please tell me it was a bag."

"It was a bag."

He stared at me a moment longer, and then nodded. "Well, that's something, anyway. If it'd been just a sheet, it could come loose and fall in places, slip away. Some folks would love to catch a glimpse of one of her hands, a foot, some of her hair. Makes for some nice dramatic footage on the six o'clock news." He nodded again. "Can't happen in a body bag, not with those zippers. Nothing 'accidentally' slipping out of place there. Newspeople will have to get their gruesome video and photos at some other goddamn site of pain and misery." He rubbed his eyes and pushed back his hat. "Want to swap jobs for the next couple of days, Reverend? Dumb question, I know, forget I said anything."

The Reverend walked over and put a hand on Jackson's shoulder. "Did you work the search?"

"From six last night until about four thirty this morning. Ashley was found around nine fifteen."

"You haven't actually signed in for duty yet, have you?"

Jackson shook his head. "I'm not going in until four, when the second search party heads out. I'd planned on sleeping in a little bit, but then Sylvia called me from the Sparta." He pointed at me. "That woman did not take a shine to you, Mr. Conover. Sylvia may be a nib-shit who reads too many tabloids and thinks the absolute worst of damn near anybody when she first meets them, but you can't get *too* upset with her over this. A stranger acting a little nervous shows up in her restaurant just a few hours after the body of a little girl's been found. I think under the circumstances—and by 'circumstances,' I mean that your timing bites—you see where I'm going with this?"

I nodded. "I kind of suspected that she'd called someone. May I ask—why did she call you instead of the police?"

Jackson sighed. "Because she's my aunt, and she's the only blood relation I have left. Because I have dinner with her every Sunday night and she spends half of it telling me ways she thinks I could be running the department better. Because she loves me and I guess I love her—grand old grumpy broad that she is. And because she's convinced you had something to do with Ashley and Sharon Millhauser's disappearances. She will not give me peace until I've checked you out. So now do you understand why I have to ask you to prove you are who you say you are? Unofficially, of course."

I set down my bag and grabbed the top zipper. "Of course."

The Reverend cleared his throat. "Ted here usually grabs a quick bite out at the Hangman's Tavern right around this time. Lunch hour there runs from eleven A.M. to two P.M. A lot of folks from Cedar Hill head out that way."

Jackson grinned. "You *do* sound like some sort of tourist information guide."

The Reverend shrugged. "You have to admit, it's a friendlier atmosphere for questioning someone than that Lovecraftian crypt you call an interrogation room."

Jackson looked at me. "It used to be a storage room for old filing cabinets, janitorial equipment, things like that. And he's right—it's not the cheeriest place. Now that I think about it, it's kind of creepy, actually, even with the fluorescents on."

"Here," I said, handing copies of my birth certificate and adoption papers to the sheriff. I'd slipped them out of my shoulder bag while he and the Reverend were talking. "They're photocopies, but I can produce the originals if you want. Oh, that reminds me . . ." I pulled out my wallet and removed my driver's license, handing that over, as well.

Jackson examined everything while the Reverend stood peeking over his shoulder.

"Seems like proof enough to me," said the Reverend.

Jackson gave everything another look, then nodded his head and handed all of it back to me. "Same goes for me, Mr. Conover. Thanks for not being a prick about this." Jackson's eyes drifted to the right for a few moments as he thought about something. "Hamilton . . . Hamilton . . . Why does that sound familiar to me?"

"It's not exactly an uncommon name."

"I know, but . . . your birth parents, their names, Thomas and Jessica, that's why I asked. Something about their names rings a bell . . . Tom and Jessica Hamilton . . ." He thought for a few more moments, then sighed and shook his head. "Never mind, can't get it. I *must* be tired."

Deciding to try my luck, I said: "My birth mother's maiden name was Leonard. Her father's name was Irving—*Irv*, I guess most people called him. His wife's name was Miriam. Besides Jessica, they had three other children: Elizabeth, Chet, and Andy."

Jackson's head snapped up when I spoke the last name, his eyes wide. "Oh, *Christ* . . . Andy Leonard? *The* Andy Leonard?"

"Afraid so."

Jackson pushed back his hat a little farther, looked at the Reverend, began to say something to him, and then froze.

"Ted?" said the Reverend. "Ted, are you all right?"

Jackson spun back toward me. "Hamilton—*Joseph Hamilton! You* . . . oh, my—you were the little baby who—"

I nodded. "Yes. That was me."

"The only survivor of the Leonard Massacre. Wow." Jackson looked as if he didn't know whether or not to smile, so he just continued staring at me.

"Give our good sheriff a moment," said the Reverend. "A thought is forming, trying to hitch a ride on the next available synapse. Just wait, it'll find a way . . ."

Jackson snapped his fingers. "The Hangman!"

". . . and there it is."

"What's the deal with the Hangman?" I said.

"I need to take you there," said Jackson, turning away and starting toward his car. "You coming along, Reverend? You want to see this as much as I do."

"Sorry, Sheriff. I have to meet Sam and Timmy over at Main Hardware to pick up some drywall supplies. But you call me later and let me know how it goes. Take a picture with your cell phone."

"Your wish, etcetera, etcetera."

The Reverend gave him a salute, then pointed to me. "Remember what I said, Geoff. This is Cedar Hill—"

"—weird shit happens here," said Jackson and I simultaneously, then looked at one another. I grinned. Jackson just shook his head.

"Like I'm ever gonna forget *that*," he said, pulling out into traffic. Then: "Seat belt. I hate writing tickets for passengers. You might think I'm rude."

CHAPTER EIGHT

The Hangman's Tavern is located halfway between Cedar Hill and Buckeye Lake, and if I'd had to find the place on my own I would probably have gotten lost. Once you get off the highway there's a long stretch of county road that winds uphill for a couple of miles, surrounded on both sides by trees and thick foliage, with an occasional footpath or bike trail in between. The road to the Hangman was on the left near a crossroad past the two-mile mark. The first thing that drew my attention was the eight-foot T post a few yards off the main road—that, and the steel noose hanging from the side facing the entrance.

"I know," said Jackson, slowing as he drove past so I could get a good look. "The Klan was once pretty big in this area, especially during Prohibition and the civil rights movement. During Prohibition, Klan boys brought blacks out here to hang them, then go on down the road for a few drinks. That's how the place got its name. It's been in Grant's family for generations. His great-grandfather was Klan and built the tavern. Grant's father decided not to pursue membership in that particular boys' club, and Grant has no tolerance for people who look down their noses at someone else because of the color, or religion, or because they're poor, or . . . or whatever bullshit reason people come up with to hate others because they haven't got the brains God gave an ice cube."

The parking lot was two-thirds full, and music drifted out of one of the opened windows: "Dreams I'll Never See" by the Allman Brothers.

"Jukebox, one with honest-to-God vinyl forty-five rpm records," said Jackson, parking in one of four spots marked RESERVED PARKING: VIOLATORS WILL BE MADE TO SING KARAOKE.

"I take it this spot is yours?"

"He made me sing once. I enjoyed it. The people listening—not so much. So, yes, this is my space. The Reverend has one, as well; one is for Grant's van, and the other one's for Bill Emerson—you haven't met him yet, but that's his '68 Mustang right there. Bill's a detective with the Cedar Hill police. He didn't used to hang out with us all that much until about a year ago—that's when he lost his partner. Don't get me wrong, guy didn't die or anything like that, he just . . . disappeared. His name was Ben Littlejohn and he was a pretty decent guy himself. But four years ago, his wife—who was pregnant— was shot and killed during a store robbery. I guess from what Bill says, Ben felt guilty as hell because he was sick and Cheryl—that was his wife's name—she'd gone to the store that night to get him some cold medicine. The day of the third anniversary of her murder, Ben just up and vanished. No phone call, no note, nothing. Bill was depressed as hell for damn near a whole year. Spent most of his free time trying to track down Ben's whereabouts but . . . no luck. Finally, the Reverend dragged his ass out here one night so we could cheer him up some, and he's been a regular ever since. I tell you this so you don't make the mistake of asking him if he's got a partner.

You're going to ask him about anything personal, ask him about his car, got it?"

We both sat for a moment admiring the Mustang. Bill Emerson took exquisite care of his car; it looked as if it had come off the Detroit assembly line this morning. I wondered if he did it because he wanted to keep it in top condition so he could show it off to Ben Littlejohn, if and when the man ever returned.

"That is one sweet ride," I said.

Jackson nodded. "Classic muscle car, and Bill's the last guy you'd peg to drive a machine like that." He took his keys out of the ignition. "Come on."

"You're really not going to tell me what this is all about, are you?" I'd been trying to get him to give me at least a hint during the drive, but he'd remained tight-lipped.

"And spoil the surprise? Not in my nature."

As we neared the entrance, I saw that the field behind the tavern was a hilly, densely wooded area that spanned at least a mile, probably more. For the fourth time since arriving in town, I caught a glimpse of something box-shaped, and then something with wings, and then . . . what could only have been the hind legs of a wolf. These things disappeared into the trees as soon as they registered with me—and it was easy for them to disappear: the trees began to dip a hundred or so yards in, and continued to do so until any ground was no longer visible, only thick leaves and branches and heavy limbs. I shuddered at the thought of being a child lost in those woods at night—which, of course, brought my thoughts back to Sharon Millhauser and whether or not she was still alive. Dear Lord, please let her be okay. I wondered if Jackson would object to my volunteering to be on one of the search parties.

Just as we reached the doors, Jackson turned to me. "Listen, Mr. Conover. I'm pretty sure this will go well, but if it doesn't, I will apologize and get you out of here if you want."

"Not that you're trying to make me nervous or anything."

"Wouldn't dream of it." He gave me a quick wink that did little to ease the anxiety, pulled open the doors, and in we went.

There are places in this world that somehow immediately feel *right*, where you sense that you're welcome even before you've spoken to anyone. The interior of the Hangman had just such an air about it. Whatever anxiety I'd been feeling seemed to have stayed outside, and it could remain there as far as I was concerned. In here, I was safe. This was a protected place, and all who entered shared in that protection. It was a strange impression, this certainty that we were all protected from harm as long as we were under the Hangman's roof, but it would not go away. For a moment I could only stand just inside the doors, absorbing everything.

The interior was long and narrow, bar on the right, small round tables on the left, and a comfortably scuffed polished-wood dance floor in between. Set against the wall at the far end of the dance floor was a stage (for local bands and where parking violators were punished). An ancient but superbly functioning jukebox was playing off to the side, and as the record changed from the Allman Brothers to B.B. King I suspected the selections leaned heavily toward the blues. Fine by me. Gleaming brass horse rails braced the opposite wall and the bottom of the bar itself, while electric lanterns—anchored on thick wooden shelves just barely wide enough to hold them— kept an air of perpetual twilight inside. The place smelled of cigarettes, pipe tobacco, beer, hamburgers, and popcorn, all of the scents mixing with the lemon oil used to polish the stunning mahogany bar.

Jackson and I sat at the bar, where the stools were surprisingly comfortable and the marble top was free of any nicks, gouges, or scratches. A waitress with beautiful red hair was not so much going from table to table as she was *gliding*. She couldn't have been much younger than me, but she moved with the grace and skill of someone who'd been waiting tables all of her life, and who'd turned her routine into something like a ballet. A bell rang in the kitchen and a voice called, *"Order up!"* The waitress danced by us, gave Jackson a little wave, and disappeared into the kitchen through the saloon-style swinging wooden doors.

"That's Laura," said Jackson. "She used to just work weekends, but the last year or so business has really picked up, so Grant brought her on full-time. Plus they're an item, *finally*." He pulled over a bowl of popcorn and helped himself to a handful. "If Grant hadn't finally worked up the nerve to ask her out, I was about ready to ask her out for him. Those two had been making doe eyes at each other for so long it was getting kind of sickening. You tell either of them I said that and I'll ticket you for disturbing the peace. *Mine*, specifically."

A man in his midforties came up through a trapdoor behind the bar carrying a couple of bottles of liquor. With a nod to Jackson, he kicked the trapdoor closed and placed the bottles among the impressive four-shelf display that ran half the length of the bar. Giving his hands a quick wash, he grabbed a towel from beside the sink, dried them, then placed the towel over his shoulder and turned to us.

"Hey, Ted. The usual?" He was already sliding a glass from the overhead rack.

"Can you ask Randy to go a little easy on the salt and pepper today? And make it medium-well." Jackson looked at me. "I'm guessing you're not hungry."

"As wonderful as your aunt's cheeseburgers were, I could still eat." I looked at the man behind the bar. "You got any pie?"

"Are you allergic to pecans?"

"No."

"Then we have pie." He nodded at Jackson as he stepped closer to me. "He's rude, and I'm Grant McCullers."

"My pleasure," I said, shaking his hand. That's when I noticed his left hand; it looked more like a gnarled claw than anything else. Grant caught me looking at it and held it up. "Arthritis, big-time."

"I'm sorry," I said, feeling myself blush from embarrassment. "I didn't mean to . . . to stare like that."

"Don't worry about it. The staring never bothers me. It's when people go out of their way to act like they *didn't* notice it that pisses me off. Whipped cream? Not the canned stuff, homemade."

"*What?*"

"On your pecan pie. Whipped cream?"

"Oh, um . . . yes, sure, that sounds good. Can I have a glass of water and a cup of coffee?"

"Same for me," said Jackson.

Grant, using only his right hand and working with remarkable speed and dexterity, filled our drink orders in about forty seconds, and then went to catch Laura as she came back out of the kitchen.

Laura wrote our orders on her notepad, looked in my

direction, then gave Grant a quick kiss on the cheek and pushed open the kitchen doors, shouting, "Oh, Chef Patterson! The sheriff is here. . . ." Her laugh was a clear and musical thing.

Grant joined us after taking care of refills for the six or seven other people seated around the bar. "So, Mr. Conover—"

"Geoff, please. Call me Geoff." I looked at Jackson. "That goes for you, too."

Jackson waved his acknowledgment because his mouth was full of popcorn.

"This man can put away more popcorn in three hours than most people can eat in a month," said Grant, grabbing the nearly empty bowl and refilling it from the popcorn machine. "But do I complain?"

"As often as possible," replied Jackson, snatching the bowl from Grant. "Tell him the cover charge already, why don't you?"

"I thought you would have warned him."

"Nope."

Grant freshened my water and added a wedge of lime. "You seem a like a lime guy, am I right?"

"As a matter of fact." I raised my glass to him.

"Are you new in town or just passing through?"

"I'm here for a visit."

"Any idea how long?"

"At least five days, maybe a week, maybe more."

Grant considered this. "Okay, I'm going to make an exception for you because Ted asked me to tell you about the Hangman's one-time cover charge, even though it's usually just for regulars. But if you're going to be here at least a week, that's good enough for me. Besides, we don't get that many new faces, so it gives me a chance to make sure my spiel hasn't gotten rusty." He took a step back and pointed up at a long, *long* shelf that ran above the entire length of the bar, a shelf filled with an odd but eye-catching assortment of objects; knickknacks, books as well as comic books, curios, bric-a-brac, small household and kitchen items, and a few pieces that appeared to be nothing more than junk. It was impossible to take in everything at a single glance, but I did find myself lingering for a few moments on some of the more intriguing pieces: a handmade model of a lighthouse, complete with an ancient-looking clipper ship crashed upon the shore beneath; an old harmonica; a workman's cap stained with oil; an old leaflet advertising a traveling carnival; a small grotesque figure, carved from wood, with stumps for legs, long arms, ridiculously large hands, and a moon-shaped head that boasted two deep chasms where eyes should have been, no nose, and the too-wide rictus grin of a mummified corpse; beside it, in a chipped frame with a spider-web crack in the center of the glass, the yellowing front page of a newspaper with the headline FIRE ENGULFS OLD TOWNE EAST; a beautiful gold urn used for holding a loved one's ashes; and a few inches away from that, sitting upright as if it were a cello, was the highly polished broken neck of an acoustic guitar. There must have been fifty, sixty items or more along the length of that shelf.

"So," said Grant. "What do you think?"

"*That* is incredibly cool. *Strange*, but cool. What does all of that stuff have to do with the cover charge?"

Grant grabbed a small step stool and climbed up to retrieve the statue of the lighthouse and clipper ship, setting it on the bar between Jackson and me.

"Oh, man," said the sheriff, wiping his hands on a napkin and picking up the model with great care. "It's been *years* since I've seen this thing up close. It's still as beautiful as I remember it."

Grant nodded. "The detail work is amazing."

"You know, I almost kept this thing for myself." Jackson placed it back on the bar. "I hung on to it for a while after Carol left, but between her leaving and Jim disappearing like he did . . ." He let the sentence trail off.

"Captain Jim," said Grant, touching the top of the lighthouse and letting his hand rest there. "Jim and his late wife, Gloria—called 'Glory,'—the love of his every life, in this world or any other."

"It's my story," said Jackson, taking something that looked like a ticket stub from the rigging of the main mast. "Remember the rules, Grant. The person who brought the story in here is the one who tells it."

"You feel like telling it to our new friend here?"

Jackson slipped the ticket stub back into the ship's rigging and turned to me. "Seems only fair. There're things about it that might be useful to you later on. Besides, it was my bright idea to bring you here and put you on the spot, so I ought to be willing to be put in the same position, as well.

"This happened a while back, when Joe McGuire, God rest his soul, was sheriff and I was still a deputy with the department. Some days it seems like yesterday, other days it's easy for me to believe that it all happened to some other guy, a different Ted Jackson, in another world, another time. . . ."

Grant rapped his knuckles against the bar. "Stop waxing nostalgic or I swear to God, I will warm up that karaoke machine and make you sing 'The Piña Colada Song' *and* 'Piano Man.'"

"You *would*, too, wouldn't you?"

"Try me."

Jackson threw some popcorn at him. My sense of the Hangman being a protected place, a safe haven, returned.

Jackson no longer seemed to be carrying the weight of the world on his shoulders. I had no doubt that Ashley and Sharon Millhauser were still very much at the forefront of his thoughts, but at least here, for now, he could allow himself a reprieve without self-recrimination.

"I'll start it the way we start all stories in here," he said. "Once upon a time . . ."

CHAPTER NINE

... there was a fifty-six-year-old merchant seaman named John Larousse who was traveling to San Francisco where a possible job with a fishing fleet waited. He boarded a bus in Topeka, Kansas, and transferred to another in St. Louis. Between the two points he noticed that the final destination on his ticket was marked Los Angeles, not San Francisco. The L.A. route would take him south through Texas and Arizona, but he needed a northern route through the West to stop in Salt Lake City so he could empty an old bank account to pay for the rest of his travels in case the job didn't come through. Jim explained to the teller in St. Louis what the problem was, but there was nothing that could be done for him until he reached Amarillo; once there he was given a new ticket on a different bus line that was going toward Denver. He got on the bus, assuming the bus lines would take care of his luggage, and slept until he reached Colorado.

The most important part of his trip was not getting the job but fulfilling a promise he'd made to his wife, Gloria, when she was in a hospice in Kansas, dying of cancer.

Gloria Larousse had only seen the sea three times in her life—one that was plagued by illnesses that left her unable to do much traveling—or anything else, for that matter—and she depended on her husband to bring the sea home to her. Jim gladly filled her room with the sea's souvenirs, from multicolored shells to oddly shaped bits of driftwood and stones so long-tossed by the tides that their surfaces were as smooth and clear as glass. He made sure that his every voyage brought home with it stories and keepsakes with which he could fill his wife's days and dreams, always holding her hand and brushing back her thinning hair so her eyes were never far from his gaze, until it was time to pack up his seabag, which had belonged to his father and his father before him, and head out on the waters again to find more treasures and tales for the woman who waited faithfully.

Jim Larousse had promised Gloria that he would scatter her ashes in the Pacific Ocean.

Her ashes—sealed in a gold container because gold was her favorite color, the color of a true sunrise, she'd said—along with his personal records, rating slips, and recommendations from previous employers, were in his seabag, which he'd been told was too large for a carry-on.

When Jim got off the bus in Denver, his seabag was gone. So were all of his work records, his personal effects, and his wife's ashes. There was no way he could keep his promise to her.

He tried to locate the bag, but . . . no luck. He called the main offices of both bus lines but neither was able to track down his missing luggage. His problem had been passed on to the line's Lost and Found offices, and he gave them his new mailing address.

He used the money he got in Salt Lake City to buy a bus ticket to Ohio, where one of his cousins owned a restaurant. It left him nearly broke. His cousin gave him a job washing dishes for six dollars an hour and that, at least, managed to pay for his cheap room at the Taft Hotel, as well as two meals a day.

Three times a week he would walk from the Taft to the Cedar Hill bus terminal, ticket stub in hand, to check for the bag. The bus lines had programmed his move to Ohio into their computers so the bag—if it hadn't been lost completely, or stolen—would eventually find its way to Cedar Hill, if all went well.

Days became weeks; weeks became months. Five months and three weeks. Bus line officials informed Jim that if the bag did not turn up in another seven to ten days, odds were it never would.

And his promise to his wife would forever be a lie.

At least that's how he saw it.

The nights became sleepless, the days little more than bright blurs that kept him in motion until the sun set and it was time to walk again to the tiny bus depot to be either laughed at or treated with indifference, to take his place among the other denizens of the night streets who were lost but didn't know it, who were dying but couldn't feel it, who were all waiting for something they knew would never come but refused to admit it, his only comfort the ticket stub in his pocket that told him not to lose hope, she was out there someplace, she had to be, and maybe she knew this wasn't his fault, that he was doing everything a good and loving husband was supposed to do, but that didn't stop him from wondering very late at night when sleep wouldn't come if he'd made the promise to her because he loved her, or if he'd done it to clear his conscience of all the things he'd wanted to say to her, all the things he'd wanted to do for her in life but never got around to.

Jim Larousse began to go a little mad. In conversation, he talked rarely of anything but the sea's smell and how his wife loved it, how its smell on him brought the salt air to her and helped her imagine that she could breathe it so deeply, bragging about how fine she felt listening to the breakers crash against the cliffs, or the clanging of the buoys, or the lonely keening of ships' horns sounding at midnight for the lighthouse keeper to show them the way. Jim himself had once been a lighthouse keeper, and when he wasn't talking about his wife or the smell of the sea, he talked about the majesty and nobility of the lighthouse and those whose duty was to stand watch over the waters.

If you talked with him often enough, and if he'd had enough Crown Royal to loosen his tongue sufficiently, he'd tell you where he kept his precious ticket stub when he wasn't waiting at the bus station, how he built a small model clipper ship out of bits of found wood and tissue paper, some tiny struts, and a chunk of balsa out of which he carved the hull; he'd tell you about the model's display stand, how he put that together using pieces of discarded crates dug out of the trash behind the restaurant and assortments of rocks and stones to create the faux cliffs; he'd tell you about the small lighthouse he built from a model kit he bought for three dollars at a flea market, and how, on those nights he's too tired to make the trek to the bus station, he'd take the ticket stub and place it atop one of the masts, amidst the yards, booms, and rigging, and how it looked like a mighty sail up there, one that is bright in the beam of the lighthouse beacon, which keeps his ship on course, regardless of the weather.

"We were always gonna find us a lighthouse, Glory and me," he'd say. "There's dozens—hell, maybe even hundreds—of 'em abandoned all up and down both coasts. We were going to find one that needed fixing up—that way we'd get it for a song, you know? Something with a tower like a French castle, with a spiral staircase inside. Glory, she'd've liked that right down to the ground."

Then he'd take out the necklace he always carried, one that looked like something a child would make, seashells and little stones strung together, souvenirs from the sea cluttered together on a strand of knitting thread. Rumor has it that one night some drunk tried to take that necklace from Captain Jim's hand—just to look at it, mind you, not to steal it. The guy left with a broken nose.

Haunting the Hangman only on a semiregular basis, I'd heard about Captain Jim but had never actually met him. My visits to the tavern were restricted to Tuesdays and Thursdays, between five and eight P.M., depending on which shift Sheriff McGuire had assigned me that week. I'm a deputy, have been for the past six years. For a while Joe—Sheriff McGuire—had assigned me only day shift so I could be home in the evenings with my wife, Carol, who was expecting our first child. "I know it sounds old-fashioned and sexist as hell," he said to me, "but a man ought to be around to help out when his wife is in the family way . . . and I cannot believe I said 'family way.' Tell anyone else and I'll stick you with graveyard."

Carol miscarried halfway through her fourth month, and things between us didn't exactly sour, but she made it clear to me that it might be best for a while if I took a later shift. Since her sister was now staying with us to keep Carol company . . . I guess there are some intimate sadnesses women can only speak of with other women . . . anyway, I asked Joe if I could have evening shift for a while, and he agreed. Which is how I came to be at the Hangman on the night I first met Captain Jim.

I'd finished around eleven thirty, changed into my street clothes—yeah, we really call them that—and was just putting the keys into the ignition of my car when I realized that I didn't want to go home. Any other time, I'd feel terrible about that, but Carol and her sister would either be asleep already or watching a movie or just sitting on the couch talking . . . the point is my company wouldn't much be missed, so I decided to head out here. I'd never been here in the evening before.

I don't claim to be an expert on the workings of the female psyche, but lately it seemed that Carol thought she was the only one in the marriage who felt the regret, the emptiness, the disappointment and grief at having lost a child. I'd tried to talk to her about it, but between the changes her body was going through and her sister constantly running interference, my existence in our home was . . . redundant. There were times I'd wanted to shout at the two of them that, yes, I knew Carol was in pain, but she wasn't the one who'd had to take apart the crib and box it up along with the bassinet and blankets and bottles and baby clothes and everything else we'd bought, haul it all back to the store, and then stand there and try to smile and be pleasant while the sales clerk who *knew* couldn't keep the pity from her eyes . . . but saying things like that seemed selfish and hurtful. If the only way I could show her that I loved her and wanted to honor her feelings was to keep my distance and remain silent, then that is what I would do. There would be time to try again.

I walked in here at five minutes until midnight. The place wasn't exactly packed, but there were more than enough people there to keep Grant adequately happy.

I took a seat at the bar—where we're sitting right now, come to think of it—and noticed that more people than usual were clustered around that small area back there where you shoot darts. I ordered a Pepsi and started gobbling up the popcorn. Grant's father had some secret recipe for flavoring the butter with subtle spices that turns each handful into an exotic taste of faraway lands. First time I told that to Grant, he grinned at me and said, "So you turn wistful as your thirties begin packing their bags, and my popcorn is the catalyst for your flights of fancy. I can die a fulfilled human being."

Grant served me just as the cluster of dartboard enthusiasts burst out laughing and someone I couldn't see shouted something in a tone of voice that suggested they were becoming agitated. I hoped no one was starting a ruckus because I wasn't in the mood.

"How're you doing these days?" Grant asked.

"Could complain but it wouldn't do any good."

"Carol still not talking to you?"

"Not much. I write memos and give them to her sister."

"Sorry, man."

"Thanks."

"Should I ask how goes the fight against the insidious forces of evil trying to overtake the streets of Cedar Hill or do we just get to the intellectual highlight of the evening with the first round of 'Rock, Paper, Scissors'?"

I shook my head and laughed. "Do you always talk like a character from a Ray Bradbury story?"

"Actually I was going for Rod Serling, but excuse me for trying to break the monotony with some crackling and literate conversation."

I lifted my glass and silently toasted him.

"Seriously, man, you okay?"

I shrugged. "Don't quite know what to do with myself at night lately."

"Well, now that you've finally gotten a taste of the nonstop fun and frolic that is the Hangman after dark, you could come here more often. It'd be nice if you actually bought a sandwich or something instead of just eating all my popcorn. You know, an impulse purchase to help keep me out of the poorhouse."

"Fine. Make me a BLT."

"Kitchen's closed."

"You're an evil man."

"Yeah, I get a lot of complaints about that."

The noise by the dartboard got louder, and Grant shouted, "Hey! Keep it civil, okay? You guys sound like an army in full rout."

Someone waved a placating hand. Grant finished racking the overhead glasses, massaged his bad hand, and leaned on the bar. "Tell you what. I'll see if I can whip up a club sandwich and fries if you'll do a favor for me."

"Make it onion rings instead of fries and you got a deal."

"Done." He gestured toward the crowd. "Captain Jim's here tonight, and he's in worse than his customary bad shape. I know he doesn't have enough to take a cab back to the Taft, and I'm sure as hell not gonna let him try to walk back to town, so do you think that you could—?"

"—sure thing. One less body in the drunk tank tonight." I craned to get a better look at the patrons sitting within the cluster, hoping to catch a glimpse of the legendary captain. "How the hell does he get around, anyway?"

"Most everybody knows Jim, so it's easy for him to bum rides out here. Usually I drive him back myself, but there's a Mitchum movie on Night Owl Theater at two that I want to catch and my VCR's on strike."

"Which movie?"

"*Farewell, My Lovely.*"

"Ah, Mitchum as the ultimate Philip Marlowe. I understand completely."

Grant squeezed my arm. "I knew if anyone would, it'd be you."

"I'm not sure if that's a good thing or not."

"Let's call it a good thing and we'll both sleep easier." He retreated to the kitchen. I ate two more handfuls of popcorn, then picked up my drink and walked over toward the Dartboard Brigade. Three guys dressed in denim and sporting John Deere hats were taking their turns, while another group of guys—some of whom I recognized as mechanics from the Buckeye Lake truck stop—occupied two of the four tables.

Captain Jim sat alone at the fourth table, two empty pitchers of beer, an empty mug, and three equally empty cocktail glasses spread out before him like an audience while he held court.

In his hand was a fourth glass, its ice melting into the scotch, turning it the color of weak iced tea.

He wasn't so old as to be thought ancient—I knew he wasn't quite yet sixty—but the shriveled damage to his face was a long time at home. The perpetual twilight glow from the lanterns seemed a welcomed companion to him; it hung about his shoulders almost exaltedly, soot and ash on the coat of a chimney sweep. He wore a small knitted wool cap with the edge rolled tightly at the tops of his ears. He was mumbling to himself and gesturing with the glass in his hand. A bit of the liquor slopped over the side and spattered the tabletop. He pulled off his cap, revealing a head covered in thick, startlingly silver hair. "I might be drunk," he said to himself, "but that's no excuse for untidiness." He used his cap to mop up the spill, stuffed it into one of the pockets of the waist-length, tattered blue sailor's coat he wore, then sighed and stared down at the floor.

I've dealt with my share of drunks—the violent ones,

the sloppy ones, the maudlin, pissy, angry, self-pitying ones—and over the years I've learned to place a barrier between them and too much of my sympathy. People are entitled to drink as little or as much as they want, I make no moral judgments, but when their drinking turns into public drunkenness and I have to step in, it's not advisable to let compassion get in the way of performing one's duty. So I've gotten really good at distancing my emotions when confronted with a drunk. Which is why I was surprised at how quickly and strongly I felt so . . . deeply sorry for him.

It was his voice more than anything else. His voice was the sound of an empty house when the door was opened, or an empty bed in the middle of the night, or an empty crib that never knew an occupant; dead leaves skittering dryly across a cold autumn sidewalk; the low, mournful whistling of the wind as it passed through the branches of bare trees; it was a sound so completely, totally, irrevocably *alone* that hearing it just in a whisper's instant made you long for the warmth and safety of home and hearth . . . even if your company there was superfluous, at least you weren't as alone as *that sound*.

I moved in closer, making it appear that I was interested in the dart game, but in truth I was drawn to Jim's voice as he talked to the floor and the table, the boards, empty pitchers, and glasses. The man had a captive audience.

"They say the first ones were probably built by the Phoenicians or the Greeks. The port of Rodas was once guarded by a statue of Helios, *El Coloso*, they called him, standing taller than any of the ancient gods. Held a fire in his outstretched hand for all the ships to see. Egyptians had one in the port of Alexandria, built by Sostratos of Knidos, did'ya know that? Wouldn't lie to you.

Sailors say its light can still be seen some nights, even though the structure's long gone. I've been there. I've been in all the places where the ghosts of the towers live, yessir. Along the Mediterranean coast where the Romans used to have them, the Atlantic coasts of Spain and France, up to the English Channel. You know, I once even stood at the top of the Tower of Hercules in La Coruña. *It* was built in the first century—AD, that is . . . probably to guide Spanish ships sailing to Ireland. It's still there. In the beginning they were all just piles of stones with wood fires burning at the top. Fires in towers, fires in the heart, all guiding you home. And to think it all started a night thousands of years ago when someone stood on the shore and looked out to the sea and thought, 'I'm going to build a tower whose firelight will be seen by those lonely travelers on the waters far away. Perhaps when they see it, they will come for a visit. A visit from the waters would be splendid.' All from a pile of stones." He looked up at one of the empty pitchers on his table. "In the end that's what they all go back to . . . just piles of stones scattered along the shore, waiting for the tide to come in and pull them into the water. But for a while, oh Lord! . . . for a while, they stand there in majesty, don't they? We'd've been happy there, her tending the rooms, me tending to the lights and foghorn. . . ." He began to sway in his seat, and for a moment I thought he was going to fall off his chair, but he blinked, seemed to realize he was losing it, and quickly righted himself.

His gaze met mine. He lifted his glass in salute.

"Wouldn't happen to be from the bus station, would you?"

"Afraid not."

"Ah, well." He brought the glass to his lips and held it there, not drinking. "Doesn't hurt a fellow to ask." He downed the rest of the scotch in one quick swallow. "I know you." He grinned. "You're the Man, Johnny Law."

"You forgot 'the fuzz.'"

He waved that one away. "Dumbass nickname, that one."

I introduced myself and shook his hand. Even his grip felt lonely.

He patted down his pockets until he found a slightly crumpled cigarette pack from which he managed to pull one slightly crumpled cigarette. "Glory used to get on me something fierce about my smoking. I quit for a while. Then one day a few weeks ago I just had a craving. You ever have that happen to you? Just wake up one morning and suddenly have a craving for something that you know isn't any damn good for you but you just got to have it?"

I shook my head.

"Well, you're young." He lit the cigarette, pulled on it, and let the smoke curl around his jaw as he slowly exhaled. "Ought to find yourself a vice of some sort. Keeps you sane when nothing answers the sound of your voice in the middle of the night."

I gestured at all the empties. "This your vice, is it?"

"I prefer to think of myself as an athlete in training. For the Olympic elbow-bending team."

"I'll have to remember that one."

He studied my face. "You here in an official capacity?"

"Yes and no."

"So I am doomed, after all."

"Still cheerful, I see," said Grant, coming up to the table and setting down a plate stacked with onion rings.

"Where's my club sandwich?" I said.

"I only got one hand, in case you haven't noticed." Then, to Jim: "I see you've met your ride home."

"Oh, I see. Too busy for your best customer tonight."

"Got a Mitchum movie tonight, Jim. Sorry. But you'll be safe with the deputy here. Can't afford to have anything happen to my best customer, can I? Who'd give the place a touch of color?"

"Is that what I am? Color?" He shook his head and looked at me. "That's what happens when you live long enough. You get colorful."

"Great line. Strother Martin in *Butch Cassidy and the Sundance Kid*."

Jim looked at me, then at Grant. "I see you found another guy for your act. Allow me to offer my heartiest congratulations."

Grant laughed, squeezed Jim's shoulder affectionately, then retreated for my sandwich.

"I appreciate your kindness."

I shrugged. "My pleasure."

"I wouldn't be so quick with that one," he said.

It was close to two thirty in the morning by the time I unlocked the door to Jim's room at the Taft. Despite the city's efforts to renovate the area in which the hotel was located, the Taft remains a depressing and slightly decrepit monolith of a building. In its heyday it had seen the likes of heavyweight boxing champions, famous artists, and three presidents; now it was just another in a long line of ruined places where the damaged, the despondent and the discarded, the lost and the shabby come when they reach the end of their rope and life offers no alternative but to crawl into the shadows of poverty and just give up.

"Nice room," I said to Jim as he turned on the only light, which hung down from a chain in the middle of the ceiling.

"Liar. But thank you."

Star and meteorological charts were scattered all around the room, which didn't surprise me—a sailor like Jim would have an understandable interest in such things—but what threw me were the opened books on physics and chaos theory, all of them with dog-eared pages.

I handed him his key and was trying to come up with a courteous way to ask about the books when I looked over at his bedside table and saw the model of the clipper ship, the ersatz beach, and the model lighthouse.

"That's quite something," I said.

"It's not done yet. I still need to finish carving out the figures." He looked at the display, then to me. "Myself and my Glory. Gonna show her the magic—Gloria, my wife."

"Yes, I know—I mean, I've heard about what . . . I mean—"

"It's all right. I realize that I am a popular subject of barroom conversation. Colorful character that I am."

"I meant no offense."

"I inferred none. Please, have a seat."

The only chair in the room was an old recliner whose stuffing had long since given up the ghost. I did not so much sit as sink. Jim reached into his pocket and removed a tarnished silver flask.

"A little nightcap, if you don't mind."

"Go right ahead."

He pulled down a couple of swallows from the bottle, sat on the edge of his bed, and stared at the display of ship and lighthouse.

"It looks almost as if you're recreating some sort of scene from a movie or book," I finally said.

"Close." Another swig. "It's part of my dream—the one that comes to me when I'm deep in my cups." He held up the flask. "If Glory was here, she'd tan my hide for partaking of the demon rum."

"I thought you drank Crown Royal."

"I was speaking in terms better suited to a colorful local character." Another sip; then he sat back against the chipped headboard. "So why isn't an upstanding fellow such as yourself home with his family?"

"I, um . . . had my shift changed recently and I'm a little agitated most nights once shift ends. Makes my wife nervous and I don't like to keep her awake."

"Ah."

"She's not been very well lately," I said, "and I—" The rest of the words retreated back down my throat. There was no reason for me to explain anything to this man with the voice that sounded like a cold and sunless shore.

"So you've heard about my wife?" he asked.

"Some. I'm very sorry she was so sick for so long."

Before I could say anything else, he began telling me about Gloria. He spoke as if he were composing a poem to be written down for the ages yet to come; the way she laughed, the delicate tapering of her fingers, the way she played rhapsodies on their piano, the frailness of body that could not cripple the strength of spirit, her temper that could flare bright and hot as any sudden fire, the way she would always place one hand over her heart when she laughed while holding the other straight out—just in case the mirth became too much and she died laughing, the softness of her breath against his neck at night, the velvet cradle of her hair, her sigh, her whisper, the way she always chewed on her lower lip when reading; all of this he wove into a rich tapestry before my mind's eye until, at last, I felt as if Gloria Larousse were sitting there in the room with us.

"You must miss her very much," I said when he finished.

"I do. She was the love I was meant to find. She was also grand company. Absolutely grand." He reached into another of his coat's pockets and removed the famous necklace. "See this stone in the center? This shiny black one?"

"Yes."

"I found this on the shore near the port of Rodas. An old, old, *old* man there swore up and down that this very stone was part of the rock that formed the flame which the statue of Helios held above its head. He told me of a local legend that claimed if this stone were tossed into the waters by a true soul of the sea, it would light their way home.

"Gloria put this stone in the center of her necklace. There are thirty-three pieces strung together here, driftwood, shells, stones . . . thirty-three pieces from thirty-three different places around this globe. And in the center, Helios's magical flame. It's part of my dream, as well."

"The same one with the ship and the lighthouse?"

"Have I mentioned any other? No need to answer that, it was a rhetorical question."

"I figured."

"Bright fellow. How proud your wife must be."

I know he meant it in a good-natured, joking way, but something in it stung me.

To get my mind away from that particular dark corner, I asked: "So, what happens in this dream of yours, if you don't mind me asking?"

He rose from the bed and began pacing as he spoke,

all the while rolling the necklace between his hands as if he were thinking of attempting a cat's cradle with it.

"At the very start, I'm standing on a beach in Florida. Glory always wanted to see Florida, so in my dream I've gone down there for her, and I'm at the *very spot* where Ponce de Leon landed in 1513, hoping it was the city of Bimini where he could find the fountain of youth; and as I'm standing there, I can see all the way to St. Augustine, overrun with the old and sick who wait in the salt air and sunshine for death to embrace them. I open my mouth to call out—don't know who I'm going to call out to or what I'm going to say, but it don't matter, because that's when the sea gives up its dead. They bob to the surface, all of these bloated bodies, some of them are skeletons, some are still, you know, in the process of falling apart because the fish haven't finished feeding. They've got these . . . *black* chasms where their eyes used to be, and there's seaweed spilling out of those chasms, and their mouths—if they still got mouths left. Some of 'em, their jaws are gone, torn away. Damned frightful sight, it is.

"And then I realize that all of them are moving in close to shore and coming right at me. All of the fish in the sea, as well; all of them so near, trembling and staring up at me with their odd and cold eyes—because by now, you see, I'm standing high above it all on a cliff and I'm saying, 'Show me the magic,' and when I look down I see that it's not a cliff at all, but the observation deck of a lighthouse that, even as I am trying to understand how, is rising out of the ground like some great titan awakening from a thousand years of slumber. And before me the dead of the sea make room for the great clipper ship that is coming toward my light. The ship moves closer to shore, and when it can't come any closer, when the rocks below become too jagged and treacherous for its hull to chance, the dead and the fish swim beneath it and carry the ship on their backs as they crawl onto land. They bring the ship close, closer, until the crow's nest of its central mast is level with the observation deck. And she's there, my Glory, in the nest. Her hand reaches out toward me and I try to take hold of her, to help her step over the rail and into my arms, and then . . ." He shrugged.

"You wake up."

"Nothing quite so dramatic. Then the Loch Ness monster sticks its head above the surface, looks around, decides not to take part in this silliness, and submerges once again."

"You're kidding?"

"I'm kidding. The truth is, the dream just stops there. Her hand, so close to mine. At least, that's how it stopped last time." He pocketed the necklace and grabbed up the flask. "The thing is, the last several weeks, the drunker I am when I fall asleep, the closer the ship comes, the nearer her hand grows. So I . . . well, I think you're a clever enough fellow to figure the rest out, aren't you?" He reached out and grabbed up one of the books on physics, flipped to a previously marked page, and asked: "You ever hear the term 'syzygy'?"

"Can't say I have, no."

"Huh. You know they got themselves that weather lab over at Ohio State University?"

"Yeah . . . ?"

"Well—and you can believe this or not—but I've been over there. Several times, in fact. Been over to the radio telescope, too. Damned impressive stuff."

"I'll bet."

He rubbed his eyes, seemed to consider something, then said: "I know folks think I'm crazy. I know they grin when they call me Captain Jim. And I know that you're probably gonna repeat this to everyone over at the Hangman and you'll all get a good laugh out of it, but I'm gonna tell you something I haven't told anyone else."

"Why haven't you told anyone else?"

He pointed to my hand. "Look at you. Young married fellow, shiny wedding ring on your hand, and here you are in a shabby-assed room with some crazy old man instead of on your way home to the wife. My guess is she don't much want you around these days—I know, I know, it's none of my business, I'm just guessing here . . . but I'm also right, ain't I?"

"How did you—?"

"It's the eyes."

"Something in a person's eyes tells you that they're having trouble at home?"

He grinned. "No. It's nothing *in* the eyes. It's something that's not there anymore, something that's gone. You get old enough, you'll understand. Anyway, that's why I'm gonna tell you about . . . about what I'm gonna tell you. Right now, you and me, we're kinda the same in a way. We both of us love women who ain't there for us in one way or the other. I think you got a good face, a kind one. And I think maybe a young married fellow with a kind face and a wife that don't want him around will understand how I'm feeling—how I've *been* feeling for a long time now.

"I miss my Glory, like I said. But I got this here stone, you see, from Helios's fire, and I know more myths and tales about the sea than anyone you'll ever meet, and I've been over to the university. They laugh and grin at me over there, too . . . but they also indulge me. They show me how their expensive equipment works, and they humor a crazy old man when he asks them a crazy-old-man question.

"I have memorized the heavens, boy, the position of the stars, the movement of the planets, the timing of the constellations, the patterns of the tides and the phases of the moon. I know a thing or two about meteorology. I've used compasses and barometers, sling psychrometers and aerovane indicators, light duration transmitters and radiosonde receivers. I can recite the variables of convection, tropopause, and jet stream patterns in my sleep. I can read any topography map you throw down in front of me and predict with a 76 percent certainty the migration patterns of over two dozen species of birds. People think all I do is wash dishes, go to the bus station, and drink myself silly. But I've been *working*, boy, you understand? Studying things. *Planning.*"

"For what?" I asked, genuinely interested; for a crazy old man, he was pretty compelling.

"Syzygy," he replied. "It happens when all the planets in this galaxy are in perfect alignment. It's happened before in our lifetimes, but do you know when it's gonna happen next? Well, okay, technically it's happening as we speak, the planets are all moving into position, but the alignment itself—the moment when high tide arrives and the moon reaches its zenith and the tidal forces vary in approximation with the inverse cube of the moon's distance from the Earth—*that's* going to happen in less'n twenty-four hours!"

I remembered having read something about that in the science section of last Sunday's paper and only understanding every other word of the experts' explanations; I'd shown it to Carol in hopes of sparking some

sort of response from her, but, as usual, her sister Gina
had waved me away with one of her you're-only-making-
things-worse expressions.

"So it's happening tomorrow night," I said. "So?"

"I got . . . I got me this stone, see?"

"From Helios's flame, yes, I remember."

He sighed and shook his head. "Didn't you ever read
anything about the gods of the sea when you were in
school? How the alignment of the planets and the pattern of the tides and . . . and all the rest of it, how they
can call the gods back to Earth?"

"I went to a Catholic school. The nuns weren't big on
pluralizing the word 'God.'"

He closed his hand around the necklace. "I have kept
part of Helios's light alive for him, and tomorrow night,
he's gonna reward me. He's gonna show me the magic."

I felt so sorry for him. The loss of his wife, and the
subsequent loss of her ashes, had truly driven him mad.
I'd heard about how crazy he was, but I don't think I really believed it until that moment. Then the deputy in
me came forward and I started looking around the room
for weapons—a gun, a knife, anything he might be able
to use to hurt himself or others. The madness in his eyes
actually scared me.

"I know that look," he said. "And you don't need to
worry yourself none. I'm not about to hurt myself or
anyone else. I finally got something to look forward to.
Why the hell would I want to shuffle off the old mortal
coil *now*?"

I thanked him for the company and left for home.

As the fount and origin of life, water is naturally connected with woman; Aphrodite was born of the sea, the
fountain is one of the emblems of the Virgin Mary, and

in the Kabbalah the Sefirah Binah is called the Mother, the Throne, the Great Sea. Modern magic links it with Chaos and the stars. It has always been associated with the moon and with light, both of which are constantly altering because of their 'flow,' changing shape, location, and purpose, as does anything that is intertwined with the core configuration of life. Some mythologies connect water and the moon with the depths of the mind, the unconscious, where the waters of Chaos are also the waters of potential life. "Perform no operation till all be made water," says the Book of Genesis; and so the vessel, the believer, this man of flesh and loneliness must himself be reduced to the liquid state of watery primeval Chaos before "philosophical mercury"—the miracle of physical existence from the sea—can surge forth to create a new material or condition. Or in the case of Captain Jim and the stone from Helios's fire, create both material and condition.

Yes, I've done a lot of reading and thinking since the night Captain Jim showed me the magic. I've mastered a lot of solitary pursuits. Luckily I have Grant and the Reverend and about half a dozen other people who keep me from falling too far into myself, but I'm wandering off the highway, sorry.

I walked through the back door of home a little after four in the morning. I saw it leaning against the sugar bowl on the kitchen table. The note was short and to the point, I'll give her that:

> *Gina asked me to fly back to Oregon with her. She thinks I might feel better if I got away from Ohio for a while. The walls closing in and all that. I'm sorry that we snuck out like we did, but Gina thought you might cause a*

*scene. I do love you. I'll call you when we get in—just
remember there's a three-hour time difference.*

I sat by the phone until ten thirty. She didn't call. I
knew Gina would convince her to wait until I left for work
before dialing the number.

I was pulling out of the driveway at three thirty when
I heard the phone ringing. The machine picked up on
the third ring.

I wish I could tell you that my shift that night was so
crammed full of portents that a man would had to have
been clinically brain-dead not to catch on, but in truth it
was—for the most part—one of the most supremely dull
shifts I'd ever worked. Traffic citations. Telling some
kids to keep the noise of their party down to a loud roar.
Keeping an eye out for a lost dog, which I found, safe and
sound, much to the owner's relief. Writing it down would
have bored the letters off a diary's page.

I kept thinking back to what Captain Jim had told me,
and whenever he or his rantings crossed my mind, which
was more and more frequently as the night wore on, I'd
roll down the window of the cruiser—it was a wonderful, clear night, temperature holding steady at sixty-eight
degrees—and look up at the stars. Forget what he said
about chaos and the stars; to my mind, the heavens
looked peaceful and all in order. Unlike my life. But that
was for later, when I had to face a house devoid of voices,
laughter, or the sound of a child sleeping in its crib.

It was getting close to eleven fifteen. I'd just checked
the weather for the area—clear and warm, with a 0 percent chance of rain, the forecast coming straight from
the National Weather Service, thank you very much—

when the radio squawked and the dispatcher told me to give Grant a call. Official business. So I had no qualms about using the car phone.

"It's me, Grant."

"Oh, Ted, thanks for calling right back, man. Look, it's Jim. He's really—and I mean *really*—in bad shape."

"Drunk?"

"Hell, yes, but that isn't the problem. Drunk I can handle. He was going on about something called siz . . . sizee . . ."

"Syzygy?"

A pause. "How the hell'd you know that?"

"My still waters run deep. So what happened?"

"He was almost out of control, man. I threatened to throw him out—and you know I *never* do that. He bummed a ride from a trucker heading up by Buckeye Lake. They left here about ten minutes ago. I tried to get him to stay, but he was hell-bent."

Something cold in my stomach. "Did he say *where* by the lake he was going?" Creation of material and condition: I think I knew what Grant was going to tell me before the fourth word was out of his mouth.

"He asked the guy to drop him off near the old fishing pier. Said something about getting himself one of the boats and rowing his ass to—"

"Cholera Island?"

"You got it."

"*Son of a bitch!*" I slammed down the phone, cussing myself up one side and down the other. All his talk of lighthouses. All his talk of the sea and his dream and Glory and Helios's light and the gods being called back to Earth by alignments and patterns and—

—I hit the siren, fired up the visibar lights, and floored

the cruiser. A crazy old drunk in a rowboat in the middle of the lake at midnight. Oh, yeah, no potential for disaster there.

In the early days of Cedar Hill when the Welsh, Scotch, and Irish immigrants worked alongside the Delaware and Wyandot Indians to establish safe shipping lanes through places such as Black Hand Gorge, the Narrows, and Buckeye Lake, it was decided that a beacon of some sort needed to be erected.

Two miles out from the shores of Buckeye Lake there's an isolated island that's maybe ten, twelve miles in circumference. Perfect for a lighthouse. Construction began in April of 1805, but was halted in June that same year when a devastating epidemic of cholera swept through the county. People were dying so fast and in such great numbers that bodies had to be collected in express wagons every eight hours. People were dying faster than healthy men could be found to bury them. In a last, desperate attempt to calm a rapidly panicking population, a group of Delaware Indians—who would soon die from their good deed—offered to take some of the rapidly accumulating bodies across the water to the deserted island and bury them by the tower's foundation. Something like five hundred bodies were buried there, and remain under the soil to this day. About a hundred years later the island was purchased from the county by the Licking Valley Boaters' Association, the foundation was given a fresh layer of cement, and on top of it was built the Licking Valley Yacht and Boaters' Club house; three stories of luxury and privacy where the members never stop to think that they're sitting on top of half a thousand dead bodies, or that their little paradise is called "Cholera Island" by the locals—most of whom will never be able to afford to set foot on its docks, let alone see the inside of the manorlike clubhouse.

Jim would have no trouble getting a rowboat from the pier; dozens of them were available year-round for the fishermen who rented the small bungalows. The waters of the lake were usually calm, but this late at night he might very well plow over some teenagers out for some midnight skinny-dipping.

I checked my watch. Given a steady speed of sixty-five to seventy, the trucker was probably dropping Jim off near the pier road right about now. Tack on another three minutes to walk up to the bungalows and docks, a minute or two more to untie one of the boats, climb in, and start rowing, and I had about five minutes. I'd make it.

And that's when the storm hit.

As simplistic and melodramatic as that may sound, it doesn't come close to conveying how suddenly, powerfully, and overwhelmingly *fast* the weather changed; one moment I'm flying up I-70 toward Buckeye Lake and it's a clear, warm, starry night outside, and the next second—and I'm not exaggerating here, this has been documented if you care to check—the very next second—*WHAM!*—a downpour so torrential I couldn't see five feet in front of me. The wind hit the cruiser so hard—at forty-eight miles per hour, as it turned out—I almost went off the road. The rain became horizontal, and the thunder was so violent I thought for a moment someone had finally dropped the Bomb.

Perform no operation till all be made water.

It took me nearly twenty minutes to make what should have been an eight-minute drive. By the time I climbed out of the cruiser armed with the high-powered portable floodlight each sheriff's vehicle is equipped with, Jim was at least a quarter mile out. I could see him because the emergency lights of both the lake's pier and the island's docks had automatically come on when the first power surge occurred. He was a shadow atop foam and fury and there was nothing I could do in time to save him.

There was a break in the storm, a moment of odd, displaced silence, and I heard something that might have been the sound of an empty-house voice crying out, *"Show me the magic."*

The storm cracked and slashed and fractured and screamed; the water rose up and made gigantic frothing fists that slammed against his pitifully small boat but on he rowed; the snarling waves crashing over the pier hit me at my knees, more than once nearly knocking me over; lightning splintered through the darkness and the rain turned to hail that clattered and assailed anything it found waiting beneath. All along the pier I could see curtains being pulled back inside the bungalows as frightened fishermen stared out at the insane man in the rowboat who was struggling through a storm that wasn't supposed to be.

I grabbed a dock pole and held on, watching, helpless.

The water seemed to be pulsing, teeming with hundreds, *thousands*, of small objects. I managed to train the floodlight downward and saw what at first appeared to be countless gray stones bouncing across the surface.

And then the wind eased up, as did the rain and hail, and I saw that they were not stones at all, but fish. Thousands of fish, all of them moving forward in deliberate, perfectly lined groups, synchronized swimmers, their cold eyes directed toward the crazy old man in the rowboat who was now standing up, twirling something over his head. A last cry, and he released the necklace; it flew out, caught an updraft, sailed along like a majestic bird, and was swallowed by the water.

The fish moved toward him, the waters churned and the sky thundered, and then bodies rose from beneath the waters and joined the fish; bloated, sodden, decayed bodies, many still with flesh, some that were only seaweed-covered skeletons. With each strobelike flash of lightning I saw more decay, saw more liquefied flesh slough from their bodies and float like mold on the surface of the lake. They cried out as one, the sea's dead, and the sound was a deep, terrible *gargling*, as if all of them were trying to clear their lungs and throats of the water and muck that had been clogging them for so long.

The fish and the dead surrounded Jim's boat, clinging to its sides, and through the mist and rain and waves guided him toward Cholera Island as a ship—an ancient clipper ship, majestic and ghostly—moved through the fog and spray.

I stood there trembling. I had never seen a Wonder before.

Jim quickly ran to the base of the lighthouse as its ghost rose from the center of the clubhouse; the higher it rose, the more substantial its structure became and the more spectral that of the Yacht and Boaters' Club. Whenever the structure looked as if it might tumble to one side or the other, the bodies of the cholera victims clawed their way up through the mud and ages to keep it steady and strong.

I watched as Jim ran up the spiral stairs within the lighthouse, his shadow soaring by one of the small windows placed every seven feet straight up. I watched him emerge on the observation deck and turn on the great light. It was touched with gold on this night. His silhouette against it took my breath away.

As did the sight of the clipper ship moving in close to shore, then somehow seeming to float above the water, coming closer until the crow's nest of its central mast was mere feet from the rail where Jim stood.

I saw a thin and elegant woman reach out from the crow's nest, and I saw Jim reach toward her. I whispered to the storm-ravaged night, "Show him the magic," and the woman took his hand and moved toward him, moved through the nest and rail which separated her from him, and in a moment that I will never forget, they held one another in the great light from the stone tower, so noble and patient and faithful.

Carol never came back from Oregon. I can't honestly say I expected her to. There is some grief you can never recover from, and some people who will always remind you of that grief, no matter how much they love you and hope to make you smile again.

The storm that ripped through Cedar Hill and surrounding areas was a hot topic of discussion and debate for weeks; the National Weather Service radar had detected no storm activity anywhere near our area. There was—and remains—no rational explanation; we were hit by something that should not have been, but was, nonetheless.

The fish, the sea's dead, the cholera victims, the clipper ship, and the lighthouse were gone with the dawn, of course. Wonders like that have no use for the analytic light of day. The sublime remains merely that, and always just out of reach.

And so the vessel, the believer, the man of flesh and loneliness was himself reduced to the liquid state of watery primeval Chaos before the miracle of physical existence from the sea surged forth, creating a new material and condition so he might hold in his arms the woman who was, is, and always shall be the love he was meant to find.

I still think of Jim and his Glory every day. I don't know if I find hope or sadness in these thoughts, but they keep me company.

A few months after all of this happened, I got a call from Dale Warner, who works days at the Cedar Hill bus terminal.

"I got something here you might be interested in," he said.

It was Jim Larousse's seabag. Inside was the container that held his Glory's ashes. I rented a boat and scattered them near the shore of Cholera Island. I kept the container. It's quite lovely. I don't know if you spotted it or not, but it's one of the items up there on the shelf. I like that her urn and the lighthouse are together up there, because I know the truth about Captain Jim's drunken dream. And even if my own life never amounts to more than a footnote somewhere, even if I never find a woman who will love me as Glory loved her Jim, even if the sound of my voice becomes more like an empty room or dead leaves skittering across the autumn streets, I will always have his story, and I will always tell it as well as I can.

Chapter Ten

I sat in silence, not quite knowing what to say or if I should say anything at all. As fantastical as Jackson's story was, there was no doubt in my mind that every word of it was true. I'd seen enough improbable, unlikely, and outright unbelievable things over the past ten days to forever quell the rationalist in me. I wondered if I were ever going to feel comfortable in my world again, assuming it had ever *been* my world.

Jackson gave me a wistful smile and then turned his attention back to the popcorn and his water. I think telling the story had jarred a few things loose, and he was trying to put the items on his own inner shelf back in their proper places.

After a moment Grant squeezed Ted's forearm, then grabbed the step stool and returned the lighthouse to the shelf.

"Ted's the only one who tells that story," said Grant. "Everything you see up here has a story behind it, and only one person can tell it. Randy, our cook, he's the only one who tells the story of Mr. Hands—that's this ugly son of a bitch up by the newspaper. The guitar neck is a story a number of us could recount, but it really belongs to Sam, one of the Reverend's assistants at the

Open Shelter. Now the harmonica—that's my story. The tale of the carnival leaflet belongs to Linus."

"Who's Linus?"

As if on cue, the kitchen doors swung open, a low voice called out, *"Comin' through!"* and a tray of appetizers at exactly bar level floated by. When I say a "low" voice, I don't mean deep; I mean low as in near to the floor. Grant tried suppressing a laugh and didn't quite make it as the tray reached the end of the bar and floated out toward the tables. That's when the hunched, balding little man whose legs were missing below the knees coasted into view. He was moving via a makeshift cart built from two skateboards and a crate. His right arm held the tray above his head, while his left hand used a cane to both propel the cart forward and skillfully maneuver it around the perimeter of the table area. He came to a stop, made a smooth half turn, and all but slid the tray onto the table. Once the customers had taken their appetizers, he dropped the tray into a plastic magazine holder attached to the side of the crate, pulled a second cane from inside, and spun around, making his way back toward us.

Jackson tapped my arm and leaned over. *"That's* Linus," he said. "He's going to ask you to guess who he's named after, and for chrissakes, whatever you do—"

"No fair warning him," said Grant as Linus smoothly wheeled up near us.

"Ha!" he said, looking at my shoes. "Thought I spotted a new pair of loafers in the joint." He looked up at me. "The name's Linus." He offered a hand.

"Geoff Conover." I shook his hand. His grip was quite powerful—and why wouldn't it be? If you had to haul yourself around relying solely on upper-body strength, *of course* you'd have a grip like a vise. I was willing to bet he had some impressive arms and shoulders under that shirt, as well.

"Geoff's visiting Cedar Hill for maybe a week or so," said Grant. "I was just telling him about the shelf."

"Ah, the Mantel of Myth—that's what I'm calling it this week, anyway."

"Doesn't do anything for me," said Grant.

Jackson nodded. "Me neither."

"What about you?" said Linus, pressing the tip of a cane against my shoulder.

"I, uh . . . don't do well under pressure."

He considered this for a moment, then pulled the cane away. "I'll let you off the hook for now, seeing as how you're new and everything. Okay, I'm guessing that Stan and Ollie here were trying to warn you about me before I got over here, so I'll save these gasbags some effort.

"You want to be a regular here, the rules state that you go through me. After I give you the once-over and decide you look okay—you passed the initial inspection, just so you know—then there are three questions. Answer each of them correctly, you're in. Miss one, I bite you in the back of the knee and you must leave and never darken our towels again. First question: who do you think I'm named after?"

"Easy—Humphrey Bogart's character in *Sabrina*."

All three of them stared at me in surprise.

Linus glared at Grant and Jackson. "You guys *told* him, didn't you?"

"No, they didn't," I said. "I just figured that 'Linus' isn't that common of a name, and since you seemed so convinced I was going to guess wrong, that meant you thought I was going to guess the kid with the blanket from the *Peanuts* cartoons, which is a bit obvious. And because we've never met before and I'm supposed to guess your namesake, that meant it had to be someone kind of popular. The only other Linus I know of that fits the bill is Bogey's character, so I went with that."

"You've met the Reverend, haven't you?"

"Yes." I was sorry he wasn't here; he might have gotten a kick out seeing me use his deduction trick on someone else.

Linus cracked his knuckles and rolled a little closer. "Okay, second question: if I say to you, Godzilla, Mothra, and Rodan, you would reply . . . ?"

"I would reply Ghidra—or, to be precise, *Ghidorah*."

Linus exhaled and slumped a little. "*Damn!* I almost always get the newbies with a Godzilla question."

"What's the third question?" I said.

"Easy: what's your story? You want to be a regular, the cover charge is a story. You got one?"

I looked at Jackson, who gestured for me to go on.

"Well, yes, I do. I think that's the reason the sheriff brought me here."

"Damn straight," said Jackson. Then, to Grant: "Is he here?"

"Two tables to the left of the stage."

Jackson looked back there. "Figures. The corner farthest from everything."

"Bill Emerson's with him. They've been sitting there for about an hour. They just finished their lunch about the same time you finished talking about Captain Jim."

Linus slapped a cane against the marble edge of the bar. "Let's grab a table!"

Jackson stood up and grabbed his water. "And I know just the one. C'mon, Geoff. There's someone who needs to hear this."

CHAPTER ELEVEN

The two men sitting at the farthest table were both a little shorter than average—five six, five seven—and were the type my dad would call "stocky." They appeared to be in their mid to late fifties, but something about the way they held themselves suggested that neither of them carried the embarrassing middle-aged paunch that afflicts so many guys who pass forty without checking either the bathroom scale or their waistline; in fact, both of them looked to be in solid physical condition.

I stood waiting for Jackson to make introductions, but none were forthcoming.

"Guys," he said to them, "I have a fellow here by the name of Geoff who's applied for temporary regular status. Since he answered Linus's first two questions correctly—"

"You're putting me on," said the man on the right.

"I never joke about someone besting Linus and his Three Questions of Doom."

The man on the right stood. "Allow me to shake your hand, good sir."

"But no introductions, not yet," said Jackson. "Oh, don't look at me like that, I have my reasons."

"Famous last words," replied the man. He looked as if he could have been a former professional boxer; everything about him was intensely square and tight and low to the ground. His thick, wavy hair was almost completely white and looked somewhat distinguished in a favorite-uncle kind of way. He sported a dense, bushy mustache, also near-totally white, and his face was sprinkled with numerous small pale scars. The only odd things about him were his hands; they should have been wide and heavy, as befitting a beefy fellow like this, but instead they were thin and delicate, an artist's or pianist's hands, with long, almost feminine fingers.

We pulled up extra chairs and everyone made room for everyone else. It was a little cramped, so another table was pulled over.

The second man pushed his chair back a foot or so that most of his face was hidden in shadow, but I could see that his jaw was clenched—in fact, his whole body seemed to stiffen as soon as the rest of us were in place. The anxiety that I'd thought had remained outside found a side entrance and once again made itself at home in the middle of my gut. I try not to judge anyone harshly upon first meeting—especially when the person in question has yet to so much as speak to me—but almost everything about him was triggering my Bad News alarm.

After some small talk between Jackson and the first man, Grant and Linus joined us, space was cleared for the food and so that I could place some files on the table, and then all conversation stopped as everyone looked at me.

I froze, suddenly having no idea where or how to begin. Just as I began experiencing that going-under-for-the-third-time feeling, Jackson threw me a lifeline.

"Geoff here was born in Cedar Hill," he said.

I smiled my thanks at him and opened the file containing my birth certificate and adoption papers. "Yes, I was. I was adopted when I was ten months old. My adoptive parents, Frank and Mary Conover, live in Dayton, so I've spent almost my entire life there. I, uh . . . I teach high-school English and Study of the Contemporary American Novel." I looked at the adoption papers, took a breath, and handed them to the man I now thought of as "the Boxer." "I don't know if this will ring any bells with any of you, but my birth name was Joseph Hamilton. My parents were Tom and Jessica Hamilton. Jessica's maiden name was Leonard. Her parents were—"

"—Irv and Miriam," said Bad News from his place in the shadows. His voice was rough and sandy, as if he gargled with Jack Daniel's four times a day; but more than the sound of his voice, it was the *tone* that I recognized, the hesitancy between each word that betrayed he already knew where the story was going.

I nodded in his direction. "Yes. Irv and Miriam. The grandparents I never knew. I came here to see if I could . . . if I could find out some of my family history. I've always wanted to know more about the Leonard family, but the only information I can find is on the Internet, and most of that is just about . . . well, I'm guessing all of you know what most of it's about."

Bad News pushed his chair back and rose to his feet so quickly that I jumped up, as well. His balance was more than a bit unsteady and my own legs felt as if the bones were still sitting in the chair. Everyone at the table was looking at Bad News, and then at me, back and forth, back and forth, as if we were two Western outlaws about to move out into the street and see who'd be left standing once the smoke cleared.

"Hey, listen," I said to him. "I don't want any trouble, it's just that the sheriff and the Reverend thought that one of you should hear what I had to say, and—"

"You don't have to explain yourself to me, Joseph," said Bad News, walking around his side of the table and then toward me. It was only when he rounded the head of the table and was looking straight at me that I felt the ground shift under my feet.

It didn't matter that his face was much more weathered and gaunt, that his cheeks were sunken, that he needed a shave, or that he'd developed crow's-feet you could spot from ten feet away; it didn't matter that his voice had become a rough, gravelly burlesque of the one I'd known for so many years, that his walk was now more of a guarded shuffle, or that his eyes seemed to have retreated as far back into their sockets as was physically possible, turning his gaze into a thing equal parts glimmer and shadow, floating above dark half circles, stars frozen at the event horizon of a black hole; nearly four decades, and none of this mattered a damn: I was looking, at long last, into the face of Russell Brennert.

"I used to make emergency diaper runs for your mother," he said. "I also used to help change your diaper—hell, sometimes I did it all by myself. I was always good at changing diapers. But you were a challenge. Even for a newborn, you shit *way* too much."

I blinked. "I have no response to that."

And we stared at each other.

Linus let fly with a sound that was half laugh, half snort. "Well, damn if this isn't the most touching reunion I've even seen. Makes a body want to openly weep manly tears." Grant smacked the side of his head, but not too hard.

Finally I managed to say, "Hi, Russell."

"Hello yourself, Joey—that's what we called you. 'Joe' sounded too much like some trucker's name, and 'Joseph' was just too hoity-toity. 'Joey'—that was the name of a dude who was your buddy, who you could hang out with. Guess I ought to call you 'Geoff' now, huh?"

"I've kind of gotten used to that name, yes."

Russell nodded. "Okay, then."

After a few more moments of awkward silence, the Boxer—who I now knew was Bill Emerson—said: "So what happens now? Do we wait for further instructions, do you guys take two giant steps, or what?"

I moved to shake Russell's hand, then opened my arms to embrace him, and then went back to offering only my hand because hugging him seemed presumptuous; at the same time, he opened his arms to embrace me, then offered only his hand, and, finally, grinning, threw his arms up in the air and shook his head.

Bill Emerson turned to Jackson. "I think I saw something like this in a Marx Brothers movie once."

We stepped toward one another and embraced. It felt so . . . forced, as if we were doing this because we felt like we *should* rather than because we wanted to. It lasted about five seconds; then we stood apart again.

"I never figured you'd ever come back here," said Russell. "I mean, when the Conovers brought you here after all the funerals, everyone wanted to hold you, you know? Get a look at the baby who was . . . spared. When it was finally my turn and I held you, you looked right at me and there was nothing there—you didn't recognize me, remember my touch, my voice."

"I was a baby."

"I know, but, still . . . I'd spent enough time with you before the murders that I'd hoped you might, y'know, remember something."

"I'm sorry."

"No reason to be, man. It was a shitty time for everyone."

"Would you . . . would you mind maybe talking to me about some of it? I really need to know some things."

"*Why?*"

"I honestly don't know, Russell. But lately I've been . . . I've been having trouble sleeping and concentrating and . . . and I've been seeing things."

"Now we get to it," said Grant, pushing out my chair with his foot and gesturing for me to sit back down. "You still haven't paid the cover charge, Geoff. One story, buddy. Now."

Russell and I took our seats again. I looked through the papers in the file and then closed it. The story contained in those documents was too well-known to everyone at this table. But I needed to tell them something, so I began with the only thing that came to mind.

"I've been seeing this . . . I guess he's some sort of ghost or spirit. I don't know his name, but I've come to call him 'the Broken One.' I have no idea what he looks like because his face is mostly covered in bandages, like something out of a mummy movie. He messes with my perception of the world, of reality. I don't think he means any harm, but he talks in riddles all the time. He appears mostly in reflections. Windows and mirrors so far, but I gotta tell you, there are times I'm afraid to look into the reflection in the back of a shiny spoon because I'm sure I'll see him behind me, upside-down and grinning. He appeared in my hotel room this morning, sitting in a chair.

"This isn't making a lot of sense, and I'm sorry. But he's been showing up at my home in Dayton, and he followed me here. He told me that he wasn't the only 'being' who summoned me to Cedar Hill. He said there was another 'thing'—his word. He told me that its name is Hoopsticks."

"Oh, *Christ*," said Emerson. "Not *him* again."

Everyone at the table looked as if they'd all been hit with a migraine at the same time.

"What is it?" I said. "Some local legend?"

Grant sighed. "You might call it that. There have been so goddamn many variations on who or what it's supposed to be, it's impossible to separate the facts from the bullshit. I'll give you the CliffsNotes version of the story—at least, the version I've known for most of my life. Hoopsticks is supposed to be some kind of demon—a giant, deformed monster that lives somewhere deep in the woods around here."

I felt something tighten in my gut, remembering the creature I'd hallucinated in class. "Deformed how?"

"A conjoined twin. His brother—*half* his brother, anyway—grows out of his back and is held upright by ropes of old belts or straps or something like that. There are some old-timers in town who will swear to you they've seen it up close and personal. The damn thing is kind of like Cedar Hill's version of Bigfoot or the Mothman."

"Do you believe it exists?"

Grant shook his head. "Further, deponent sayeth not."

"Oh, horseshit," said Linus.

"I believe it exists," said a voice behind me. I turned to see a man who was roughly my own age, dressed in a cook's hat and apron. If Russell Brennert's eyes were haunted, this guy's were damn near possessed by whatever memories lay behind their shine.

"Randy Patterson," said Grant, pointing at his cook. I turned and shook Randy's hand. He looked into my eyes with a directness that was unnerving.

"I'm guessing," he said to me, "that you've heard the Reverend's warning about Cedar Hill, weird shit, blah-blah-blah."

I nodded. "It might have come up once or twenty times, yes."

He laughed. "Did you notice how nobody batted an eye when you said you'd been seeing a ghost? That's because everyone here knows they exist. Just like monsters. I've seen a monster, Mr. Conover, and as far as I'm concerned, if one exists, then others do, too."

It took a moment for me to make the connection. "Mr. Hands, right?"

Randy nodded. "Yes. He—*it*—was something of a golem, I guess. I wasn't the one who gave it life. I was just one of the people it came after."

"I investigated the killings," said Bill Emerson. "Never made a goddamned bit of sense to me until Randy finally told me what happened to him. As crazy as his story sounded, I believed every word of it. You know that old Sherlock Homes line? 'When you eliminate the impossible, whatever remains, however improbable, must be the truth.' His story was exactly improbable enough to be the truth. I never wrote it down. The murders are still considered unsolved. God, that was a helluva time."

I looked at Randy. "Why did this thing want to kill you?"

"Because I accidentally killed my little sister when we were both kids." He said it so matter-of-factly that I at once knew this was a grief, a guilt, a burden that was so much a part of him that he probably wouldn't know how to function without its presence at the core of his being. I wanted to comfort him somehow but had no idea what to do, so I did nothing.

Randy grabbed a chair from another table and straddled it. "If you want, I'll tell you about it sometime while you're here. That statue of Mr. H up on the shelf? Linus here carved it."

Linus shrugged. "I used to sell them when I still worked the carnival circuit. I was billed as 'Thalidomide Man,' not that you'd have heard of me. The figures helped bring in extra money. Turns out, I gave one to Randy here when he was a little boy."

"He didn't remember until I told him all about Mr. H and Lucy Thompson—she's the lady who brought Mr. H to life. Like I said, long story there.

"But it's not Lucy that I meant to tell you about. See, I've been dreaming about Kylie—that was my sister's name. I've been dreaming about her and Mr. H again." He rubbed his eyes and adjusted his cook's hat. "I think about them a lot—every day, to tell you the truth—but I haven't dreamed about them and what happened in years. Then, a couple of weeks ago, the bad dreams started again."

"Is that why you've been so preoccupied lately?" said Grant.

"Yeah, sorry."

"Why the hell didn't you say something to me? I would've listened."

"Because you've already heard the fucking story two or three times, and I got nothing new to add except . . ." He looked at me. "This dude with the bandages, does he have, like, *tumors* anywhere?"

My mouth and throat went desert dry. "Yes."

"In the dreams, both Kylie and Mr. H have these really big, seeping tumors on their faces."

Ted Jackson and Grant McCullers looked at one another.

"The Mudman," said Grant. "I've been . . . I've been having dreams about the Mudman."

Jackson blanched. "Me, too."

"In your dreams, does it have these . . . these bleeding boils on its face?"

Jackson could only nod.

"What's the Mudman?" I asked.

"A thing—okay, okay, a *monster*—that we had dealings with a while ago," said Grant. "That busted guitar neck up on the shelf, that's from when we killed it."

"I still don't think we *killed* it," said Jackson. "Pumped a hundred bullets into the damn thing, but we didn't kill it. It just . . . well, it did what it came here to do, and then it left. That's a story I'm not in any hurry to tell or hear told again."

"Amen," said Grant.

Bill Emerson massaged the back of his neck and looked at the floor. "Okay, I am now officially . . . concerned."

Everyone stared at him. He looked up, tried to smile, didn't quite make it, and then reached into his jacket pocket for his wallet. "You're going to think all of us are batshit crazy, Geoff—may I call you Geoff?"

"Of course."

"Then you call me Bill, okay?" He took a deep breath and opened his wallet, sifting through its contents until he found a folded Polaroid photo. "This has got a crack down the center so part of the picture's a little mangled, but you'll get the idea." He started to hand it to me, then pulled back his hand before I could take it. "Can we all agree that, to paraphrase the old Buffalo Springfield song, there's something happening here that isn't exactly clear?"

"I'm amazed you even felt compelled to ask that question," said Jackson.

Emerson nodded. "Just checking." He took a drink of water, wiped his mustache, and cleared his throat. "A few years ago—hell, how long ago was it, Ted? Five, six years?"

"You talking about the time when Bob Londrigan lost his family?"

"Right around then, yeah."

Jackson nodded. "Five or six years ago sounds about right."

"Hey, guys," I said, "come on, will you? You're talking about stuff I know nothing about."

"Doesn't mean it isn't connected to what's going on with you and the Broken One," said Emerson. "Hear me out. About five or six years ago, there was this guy who was a pretty popular anchorman on the local news, Robert Londrigan. Halloween night, his wife goes into premature labor and it's . . . it's bad. Everything goes wrong and both she and the baby die. Londrigan, he somehow gets an attending to let him go down to the morgue to see their bodies, but he gets attacked by this guy with a mangled face who steals the body of his baby daughter. I never did find out what happened because Londrigan disappeared about two-thirds of the way through the investigation. My partner, Ben—he's, uh . . . he's not around here anymore, either—found out some stuff while Eunice and I were on vacation in London. This is weeks after the investigation was closed and labeled 'unsolved,' mind you." He waved a hand as if shooing away a circling insect. "It gets really complicated and bizarre, what happened with all that, but here's the thing: during the investigation, we get a call about the body of someone with a deformed face being found at the border to Coffin County beneath the East Main Street Bridge. Me, I figure it might be the guy who stole the body of Londrigan's daughter, so I hightail it over there. Pissing cold rain that night and there were all these mini mudslides, made it a pain to get down to the riverbank. This was the same night you guys had your dealings with the Mudman—did that ever occur to any of you?"

Both Jackson and Grant shook their heads. "Not until this minute," said Grant. "But—*Jesus*. No wonder it felt like the whole world was coming apart at the seams that evening. I remember the Reverend telling me about that photo you've got."

Emerson looked at the Polaroid again. "Nothing about that night felt good. It was as if we were all stuck in this waking nightmare—damn, that sounds melodramatic, doesn't it? Sorry. Okay, then; I get down there finally, and this guy, this body, he's seven feet tall if he's an inch, and even though his face is deformed, it doesn't match Londrigan's description of the guy who attacked him. But—well, here . . ." He handed over the photo. "Over the years, I've come to think of him as 'Homer,' because there's a section in *The Odyssey* about a being like him. Yes, I read too much."

I looked at the photo. Emerson was right: the guy had to have been almost seven feet tall—*over* seven feet, from the looks of it. He was naked and pale and dead, lying with limbs splayed in the mud and rain, covered in cuts and clumps of gritty detritus that had washed up from the river, one of those sickeningly typical poses of the diminished dead, grotesque and heartbreaking, but that wasn't what caused me to tremble.

He had only one eye socket, directly in the center of his forehead, where two separate eyeballs struggled to stay in place. His face had no nose; instead, there was a proboscislike appendage that looked like an uncircumcised penis growing from the center of his too-small forehead. His few teeth were yellow, jagged, backward hooks that looked so much like the Broken One's that I felt my blood pressure plummet from the abrupt rush of shock. Despite what the rational part of my mind was trying unsuccessfully to deny, I knew damn well that I was looking at a photograph of a dead Cyclops.

"Good God," I said, handing the photo back to Emerson. "That poor man."

"I know." He looked at the Polaroid once more before folding it and slipping it back into his wallet. "It just makes me want to die when I think about it. He had to have been so miserable—just *look* at him. His life was probably an unbroken string of lonely miseries that ended on the muddy, freezing banks of that river with no friend near to hold his hand or mark the moment of his passing or even shed a single tear or—ah, well, *shit*." He inhaled deeply and wiped at one of his eyes. "I'm turning into an old woman, I swear it.

"I spin this convoluted yet cheery yarn because, like the rest of you certifiable lunatics, I've been having my own dreams lately. They started about a week, ten days ago, in keeping with the group timetable, so I'm not the odd man out. In my dreams, Homer is still alive when I get there. He doesn't say anything, he's too sick, but he reaches up so that I can hold his hand. I know he's cold and lonely and scared, so I reach out to take his hand, but then all of these . . . *horrible* growths erupt all over his body. Red things with black centers that start bleeding, and I know that if I touch him, they'll spread up my arm like fire and consume me. And all the time, Homer's crying out in pain. The tumors—*God!*—they get so *big*. . . ." He closed his eyes for a moment and swallowed loudly. No more words were necessary.

The place had pretty much emptied out by now. How Laura had managed to take care of clearing the tables and working the cash register with no help, I couldn't imagine, but if she'd minded, it didn't show; Grant looked over at her and she gave him a soft, sweet smile, then blew him a kiss.

"Why didn't the Reverend come out with you guys?" asked Randy. "If there's one dude who can put the pieces of this puzzle together, it's him."

"'Pieces of this puzzle'?" said Linus. "Since when did you start talking like Hercule Poirot?"

"Since I started borrowing books from Bill—what the eff does it matter? We all know he knew damned well what would happen when Ted brought Geoff out here. He *knew* that we'd eventually end up comparing stories and all this shit'd start coming to the surface. So why isn't he here?"

"He told us that he, Sam, and Timmy had to pick up some stuff at the hardware store," said Jackson.

Randy huffed. "Yeah, right—since when has he ever gone along for grunt work like that? Sam and Timmy can handle pickups by themselves, he's got Ethel to run things at the shelter whenever he needs her to and ain't *nobody* gonna try and mess with that lady. You ask me—and I know you didn't, *Linus*, so save your breath—you ask me, he's up to something."

"I can ask him about it later," I said. "He's going to call me at the hotel tonight."

Randy stared at me for a moment, considered something, and then shook his head. "I don't know. With everything that's been happening around here lately it just seems odd to me that he'd bow out of what he knew was going to be an important . . . whatever in the hell this has been."

Jackson nodded. "I was thinking the same thing. The Reverend passes up a chance at one of your deluxe cheeseburgers, something's going on."

"You got that right, Sheriff."

Grant looked at his watch. "Well, whatever's going on, it doesn't excuse any of us from kitchen duty. Come on, you two, let's go assess the damage from lunch." He rose, with Randy and Linus following, and then turned back to the table and said: "Geoff, it's been a real pleasure meeting you, and I fully expect to see you in here a lot more before you leave. I will be disappointed if we don't get the chance to talk again."

"Same here," said Randy.

Linus looked at me for a moment before responding. "I guess you'll do."

"Praise from Caesar," said Bill Emerson.

Ted Jackson's cell phone went off. He pulled it from his pocket, looked at the number, and then quickly excused himself from the table. I felt something go cold in my stomach and at once thought: *It's Sharon Millhauser. She's dead, too.* I immediately hated myself for thinking such a thing.

"Dare I ask," said Bill Emerson, "what you think of our strange little burg, or is it too soon for you to have formed an opinion?"

"I think I like it. I think I like it very much. Don't get me wrong, I've been damn near a nervous wreck since the moment I got here, but this visit with all of you . . . I feel better. I think I like it here. Check back with me tomorrow."

Emerson tipped his water glass to me. "Will do." He checked his watch, then his cell phone and pager.

"No word yet?" asked Russell.

"Silly question, that."

Russell shrugged, then looked at me and grinned.

"What department are you, Bill?" I asked. "I mean, are you Robbery, or Homicide, or something else?"

He sighed. "I am whatever is needed at the time, Geoff. The Cedar Hill Police Department—not exactly a bastion of excess personnel—has exactly *two* full-time detectives, and until the new guy starts at the end of next month, I am both of them. The job is often frustrating, the hours are ungodly, but at least the pay stinks." He picked up his pager and glared at it as if he could will it to beep through sheer force of will.

"You've been very tactful," he said, "not asking me why it is I'm sitting on my butt in here instead of out investigating Ashley Millhauser's death."

"I figured it was none of my business."

He nodded. "Officially speaking, that's true. *Un*officially speaking, I am very tired and more than a little pissed off because the FBI has temporarily shut us out, and so I don't much give a shit about departmental regulations and protocol right now, so I'll tell you the same thing I told Russell here: I cannot do anything more until the FBI says it's all right for the department to come back in on the investigation. That's not going to happen until the coroner releases Ashley's body, and he can't do that until . . ." He looked over at Jackson, who was pacing back and forth while trying not to shout at whomever he was speaking with.

"Bill . . . ?" said Russell.

Emerson turned back to me. "It'll be made public soon enough. The coroner can't release her body because he doesn't have all of it yet. The cause of death was . . . sickeningly obvious to everyone on scene this morning, but there has to be an official determination. So I am, unwillingly, temporarily 'at liberty,' as the saying goes. Bear in mind, I've spared you all of the headache-inducing federal doublespeak that I had to endure. The only bright spot in this is that in their fervor to take over the investigation of Ashley Millhauser's disappearance and murder, they failed to hand over any orders specifically giving them jurisdiction over the investigation of *Sharon* Millhauser's disappearance. You don't know how much I'd love it if something would—"

Ted Jackson slapped a hand on Emerson's shoulder and squeezed. "Sorry, didn't mean to eavesdrop, but you and I have got the upper hand for now, Bill."

Jackson was smiling.

"What?" said Emerson.

"Sharon Millhauser turned up alive and unharmed near Moundbuilder's Park thirty minutes ago. One of my units spotted her near the south entrance. They didn't report it yet, and that call I just got came from a public pay phone. Right now, the feds have no idea that she's alive."

"Neither do her parents then, I gather."

"That's where you come in. You're driving the Red Dragon out there, it's unmarked. I was hoping you'd take the back way to their place and see if you couldn't, you know, get in to see them without drawing too much attention. If you can, bring them to the station. Use the underground garage entrance."

Emerson began gathering up his stuff as he rose to his feet. "Consider it done. You do know, don't you, that we're going to get in trouble for doing this without authorization?"

"*Fuck* proper authorization," said Jackson. "And fuck the mayor, the city council, the commissioner, the FBI, and anyone else who's going to get pissy about 'proper channels' and paperwork. Sharon's with an artist right now, giving her a description, and everyone on shift right now knows that I'll can the first person who dares breathe a word of this outside the station. We work this fast enough, Bill, and we'll have that piece of shit who killed Ashley in custody before anyone else even knows Sharon's alive." He looked at me, and then Russell.

"Geoff, I'm sorry, but I have to go. Russell, can you take him back to his hotel?"

"No problem. That's great goddamn news, you guys. Go. We'll keep it to ourselves."

I nodded. "You bet. I'm really glad she's alive."

Jackson gathered up his things and squeezed my shoulder. "You hang tight, buddy. I'll see you again later tonight." Jackson and Emerson stated toward the doors; then Emerson snapped his fingers and turned back.

"Russell, think you can give Barb a call in about half an hour and ask her to meet me at the sheriff's station?"

"I'll do it now, if you want." His cell phone was already in his hand.

"No!" said Jackson, a little too loudly. Then, softer: "Bill and I need time to get to where we need to be before she knows. She'll chew us out, but she'll also back us up all the way. Thirty minutes, okay?"

Russell put his cell phone back in his pocket. "I won't start the clock until you guys are out of the parking lot."

"Thanks." The two of them all but sprinted through the doors, something that was not lost on Grant and the rest of the Hangman's staff. It took Linus maybe three seconds to wheel himself over to us.

"What gives?"

Russell smiled. "Can't say."

"*Bull. Shit.* What gives?"

"We promised to keep it to ourselves," I said.

"Oh, my *God*," said Laura from behind the bar. "It's— oh, they found the other little girl, didn't they? Is she okay? Please tell me she's okay!" By now Randy had come out of the kitchen, having heard the commotion of the recent exits.

Laura leaned on the bar and fixed Russell with a wide, intense stare. "*Tell me* she's okay."

Russell, smiling wider than I'd yet seen him do, repeated, "We can't say."

It took only a moment, but when Laura realized what Russell *wasn't* saying, she smiled in return, then pulled on Grant's arm and kissed his cheek.

"This stays here," Grant shouted to everyone. "Until Bill or Ted says otherwise, we keep this to ourselves."

I laughed. I couldn't help it.

"What's so funny?" asked Russell.

"*Bill and Ted*. I didn't make the connection until just now."

"Whoa, dude," said Linus. "That is, like, *so* totally bogus."

"We've been kidding them about that for years," said Russell. "It'd be even funnier if either of them had actually seen one of the movies." He looked at his watch. "Okay, I'm starting the clock right now. Thirty minutes." He stood and gestured for me to do the same. "We got places to go."

"I don't want to go back to the hotel just yet."

"I had no intention of taking you there. We have some catching up to do, in case you'd forgotten. But I've got an errand to run first. It might be nice to have some company along for it. For once."

CHAPTER TWELVE

Russell knelt in front of Mary Alice Hubert's grave and brushed away some of the dirt and leaves with his gloved hand. At his side was a medium-size plastic carrier filled with cleaning supplies and handheld gardening tools he was using to attend to her gravestone. I stood a few feet off to the side holding the fresh flowers that he would put in the ground vase when everything was finished.

I don't know that I've ever seen someone tend to a grave with such delicate care; the way he used a toothbrush to scrub out any dirt that had gotten into the chiseled lettering, how he then sprayed the stone with cleaner and used a new polishing cloth to bring out the marble's luster, the precision with which he clipped the grass growing around the edges so that it formed a near-perfect rectangle, and then packing down any excess soil to form something like a protective mound around the whole thing before removing the desiccated flowers from the ground vase and replacing them with the fresh ones we'd picked up on our way here.

"She told me that she wanted to be buried here in the old section of the cemetery," Russell said as he examined his handiwork. "It's like I was telling you, this place, it's divided into three sections—you got this area, which mostly has people buried before 1920, then there's the area over the hill there, where folks were buried after 1920. The third section—I don't go there much—it was added about twenty-five years ago, *that's* where families with money bury their dead. This place may be depressing as hell in places, but it's got a lot of history, and people will pay through the nose to say that their loved ones are buried in the 'historic' Cedar Hill Cemetery."

After the devastating cholera plague of 1803 passed, the town began to rebuild its citizenship (many widows and widowers moving beyond the barriers of their "own clans and communities" to marry and procreate), and later, in 1905, Cedar Hill Cemetery was established as a place to permanently inter those who had died during the epidemic nearly a century before. Even though bodies of the cholera victims were scattered for nearly seventy-five miles in all directions (not counting the hundreds of bodies that had been taken out and buried on Cholera Island), groups of volunteers were assembled whose duty it was to locate and identify as many of the dead as possible, bring them back to Cedar Hill, and ensure each was given a ". . . burial befitting one of a good Christian community." Since most of the bodies were family members of original settlers, they had been buried with some sort of marker, so locating them wasn't too difficult, nor, surprisingly, was identifying them, despite the ravages of time and disease on the bodies; every ". . . Hill citizen of Anglo descent" had been buried with a small Bible, the inside cover of which bore the name of its possessor, as well as those of his or her immediate family. Once found and returned, the bodies were placed in the cemetery according to family or clan, and over the decades it remained that way, albeit by unspoken agreement; members of families directly descended from Cedar Hill's founding fathers were buried in or as near as possible to the plats where their ancestors slept. But such were the ways of over two hundred years ago that a majority of people in Cedar Hill (both the cemetery and the town) were now related by ancestral blood; some within three or less generations, others quite distantly.

Mary Alice Hubert's grave was located in front of a small abandoned church on the cemetery grounds. The long-forgotten architect who'd designed the church had evidently been an admirer of Antoni Gaudí's Sagrada Familia cathedral in Barcelona. I thought of Gaudí now because he was something of a hero to my father, a man who'd laid bricks, cut lumber, and balanced beams for a living. My adoptive parents had married on Halloween nearly forty years ago (hence that day being the Big Celebration Day in the Conover household), then honeymooned in Barcelona where Dad was awestruck by Gaudí's masterpiece. I could still recall the wonder in his face whenever he spoke of the experience, shaking his head in amazement that the plans for the cathedral's construction were so vast, complex, and precise it would take hundreds of years to complete.

As Russell gathered up the tools and supplies he'd used on Mary Alice's grave (and it looked radiant, despite its being located in the most run-down section), I stood fascinated by the church's obvious, though less extravagant, Gaudí influence, disregarding that the structure was merely the echo of another man's genius; from the blue marble inlay to the ominous gargoyles to the reproduction of the Virgin Mary over the rotting and sealed oak doors, the building seemed to apologize for what it wasn't rather than boast of its own virtues. Over the years sections of the front and side walls had collapsed, revealing parts of the interior. From where I stood I could see exposed portions of the altar area and the pulpit.

Despite the holes and gaps so big I could have stuck my head through them, the interior of the church was mostly submerged in murky shadows, some of which seemed to shift as I stood watching; animals of some kind, I gathered. The cemetery was surrounded by woods, so it only stood to reason that raccoons or groundhogs or other kinds of wildlife would make their way inside. I just hoped whatever I sensed in there weren't bats. I hate bats. It was a pity that Cedar Hill didn't do something to fix the church. Russell had told me that the city had decided that renovating the thing wasn't as important as building a new shopping mall and so dropped the project. All hail the march of progress and the history ground to dust under its heel.

Even in death, Mary Alice Hubert had to make do with second-best.

"Don't stand there looking so morbid," Russell said as he stood up. "This is what she wanted. No, it isn't the best section, but I keep her grave looking nice. I come out here every two months and fix things up, and I bring her fresh flowers every week."

"She must've meant an awful lot to you."

His voice was soft but thick with emotion. "That woman was practically the only person in town who'd have anything to do with me after the murders. Hell, even my own folks treated me like they were afraid I was gonna go off like Andy did. I started spending a lot of time with Mary Alice after all the funerals and she kind of adopted me as a grandson. I loved that dear old woman, I sure did." He looked down at her gravestone, then bent over and brushed away a few loose flower petals.

"Oh, man, you should have seen her funeral," he said, as much to himself as to me. "I swear all of Cedar Hill and half of Heath showed up for it. They had to put folding chairs up in the side aisles at St. Francis, and even then people were standing in the back. They finally had to send some folks up into the choir loft. Every cop in town was out in the street directing traffic and enforcing parking, not to mention working crowd control. A good hundred people couldn't even get inside, so they just lined the steps outside the church waiting for her coffin to be carried out. I was one of the pallbearers, and Mary Alice asked me to pick the others." He rubbed his eyes and exhaled a breath that sounded like it weighed more than I did.

"Mary Alice left me all her money, put it in a trust fund that I claimed when I was twenty-one. That's how I was able to afford to buy the janitorial company from Davies before he hightailed it to Arizona. I kept his name for the company, though."

"I noticed it on the side of the van. Hey, Russell, I have to ask, is that the same van that was—?"

"Yeah. That's the same van we used on the night of the cleanup. I've kept it in pretty good shape, I think."

"You have. How many employees?"

"Counting me? Thirty. It was a good thing I kept Davies's name. *Nobody* would've wanted to work for a company bearing *my* name, not back when I first bought it."

"Jesus! You mean that after all that time there were people who thought . . . ?"

"What do you mean 'after' and 'thought'? Shit, there are people in town who *still* believe I knew what Andy was gonna do that night. That fucking movie didn't help much, either. Don't misunderstand, I got a nice piece of change from the producers for telling them my part of the story when they were filming here in town—did you see in the closing credits that I was listed as a technical adviser? Isn't that something? It's a good movie. I'll probably even buy the DVD when it comes out, but . . . I can't help but think I come off as kind of a clueless dip-shit."

"Hey, at least you're not the hotly debated 'symbol' at the center of the story."

He looked at me and laughed. "Yeah, there is that. Must be a pain in the ass, having to go through your life now telling people you were that baby. Hey, is it just me, or did you think that the way they photographed that baby kind of made him look like the baby Jesus? All that soft-focus lighting."

I nodded. "The 'halo effect' is my favorite. No, it isn't just you. They kind of overdid it with the images of the baby. I am no saint or savior."

"And even for a baby you shit *way* too much. Should've put *that* in the movie."

"Maybe it'll be in the extended director's cut."

We stared at one another for a moment, and then burst out laughing.

"This isn't right," he said, wiping his eyes. "Us stand-ing here laughing like a couple of nutcases over her grave."

"You mean to tell me you think Mary Alice wouldn't have gotten a good laugh out of this?"

"Oh, *hell*, she'd've laughed harder than both of us com-bined. I'm glad she didn't live to see that movie—she would've hated it. That goddamn TV movie of the week back in the late seventies was enough for her." He shook his head and gave a long, low-pitched whistle. "Oh, boy, she was so *pissed* about that. It's been thirty-odd-however-many years since I saw it, but as I recall, they didn't much let the facts get in the way of the story, did they? Damn thing had more in common with *Taxi Driver* than it did with what really happened."

"It was a real puddle of suck, no arguments."

Russell checked his watch. "Suppose I should call Barb like I'm supposed to." He dug his cell phone from his pocket and flipped it open. "Barb Greer—Andy's girlfriend—she's the big lawyer in town. Has been for almost twenty years now. Lots of powerful friends—not just here, but in Columbus, Cincinnati, and even D.C. This is a woman you don't want to mess with."

"You got that right," said a voice from behind us. We both jumped a little, and then turned to see a strikingly beautiful woman in her fifties (but looking ten years younger) walking toward us, trying to maneuver the short series of uneven stone steps that led up to the area in front of the decaying church.

I looked between her and Russell. "Does *everyone* sneak up behind everyone else here?"

Russell shrugged. "Not a lot of what you'd call night-life around here, so we spend our off-hours practicing dramatic entrances. Gives life the illusion of meaning." That last comment jarred me; it didn't sound like a joke.

"A little help, please," said the woman, holding out her hand. I took a few steps forward, grabbed hold of her hand, and helped her up to even ground.

"Thanks," she said, still holding my hand. "Barbara Greer."

"Geoff Conover."

Barb examined my face for several moments, her features softening. "Oh, my God—it *is* you, isn't it? Little Joey Hamilton."

Before I could respond, she pulled me into an embrace, then cupped my face in her hands and planted a kiss on me that would have made Yvonne a little irritated.

"Sorry," she said, pulling away. "I don't usually just . . . *attack* a strange man like that but—*Little Joey Hamilton!* I can't believe it's you. Oh, I didn't mean that *you* were strange, I only meant—"

"But I *am* strange. You can ask my wife."

"Did she come with you? Oh, I'd love to take you two out for dinner."

"Sorry. I'm doing a solo this trip."

Still smiling at me, she took hold of my hand again and stood there simply *beaming*. "I used to help change your diapers."

"Seems like half the people I've met so far have said that to me. It's a wonderful thing, by the way, meeting people who look you in the face and immediately remember wiping your ass. Rumor has it that I pooped with wild abandon."

Barb laughed and playfully smacked my arm. "You were a little shit factory."

"I can't tell you what hearing that means to me."

Russell came over to us. "How the hell did you know that—?"

"The problem that you and that gang of misfits you associate with have, Russell, is that even after all these years, you still think it's possible for something significant to happen in this town that I won't find out about within an hour." She smiled at him, then reached out and touched his cheek. "How are you? I haven't seen you in weeks." There was something in her tone, her expression, and the way that her touch lingered on his cheek that told me exactly how she felt about him—and that Russell was either too obtuse or too frightened to acknowledge.

"I've been busy training a new crew to clean some banks in Heath," he said. (Even *I* knew it was bullshit.) "Aside from that, you know . . . parties at the Playboy mansion, day-trading on Wall Street, choreographing *Don Quixote* for the Bolshoi Ballet, the usual."

She gently tapped his face three times before pulling away her hand. "Uh-huh—in other words, working and hiding."

"Pretty much. Hey, listen, I was getting ready to call you. Bill Emerson—"

"—has already gotten an earful from me. I was on my way to the station and thought I'd stop by here first." She produced a small bunch of fresh flowers from the large leather shoulder bag she carried. "Looks like you beat me to it, as usual." She walked over and inspected Russell's handiwork. "You outdid yourself this time. I don't remember the last time I saw Mary Alice's grave looking this lovely."

"Thank you."

Barb crouched down and inserted her flowers in with Russell's, and Mary Alice's grave became even more stunning for it.

"How did you know I'd forget to bring yellow roses?" asked Russell.

"Because you're *you*. You always forget yellow roses."

"He didn't forget," I said. "He specifically told the florist that someone else would be bringing them."

Barb laughed. "Is that so?" She turned back to him. "Well, that's almost sweet, coming from you."

Russell looked as if he wanted to tie knots in my spine, but it quickly passed. Of course at that moment I wanted to smack both of them because I now knew that Russell felt the same way toward Barb as she did toward him. I wondered if the ghost of Andy Leonard still had that much power, that it could keep them from acting on what were obviously strong feelings for each other. I wondered how lonely they both had been all these years. And then I wondered something that I probably should have kept to myself.

"Is Andy buried here, as well?"

Listen to their silence after I asked this.

After a few awkward glances between them, Barb cleared her throat and said, "Uh, no. Andy was cremated. There was a small, private service at a chapel in Utica. It seemed the best way to ensure there wouldn't be any incidents. I have his ashes in an urn. I keep them locked in a cabinet in my office."

"I'm sorry," I said. "I shouldn't have . . . it's none of my business. I didn't mean to upset you two."

"No one's upset, Joey—I mean, *Geoff*. It's just that Andy's name will always be one of those things that we don't mention outside of our own circle—not that we mention that much *within* our circle."

"Our 'circle' being her and me," said Russell. "Barb doesn't much like the Hangman's gang."

"I like everyone there just fine—quite a lot, actually. But aside from Laura, I'm the only woman—and Grant keeps Laura so busy that I might as well *be* the only woman. It's not that I dislike your friends, Russell, it's that I get enough of a sausage fest at work. I don't need to go looking for it in my spare time."

"Well, Bill's been threatening to drag Eunice out there. If I can get him to convince her to join us, would you . . . would you want to come out there with me some night? I'm pretty sure Linus could handle the tables by himself for a couple of hours."

Barb looked astounded. "Did you just ask me out on a date?"

"Please don't be cute."

She shrugged. "I can't help it. Never could." She looked over her shoulder at me and winked. "Okay, official business now." She pulled a BlackBerry from her shoulder bag and pushed a button, bringing up a document. "I got Walter Banks—that's *Judge* Walter Banks, Geoff, a personal friend of the vice president's—to call in a favor. Until the FBI can figure out a way around it, the Cedar Hill Police Department and Office of the Sheriff have complete jurisdiction in the investigation of the kidnapping of Sharon Millhauser. Ashley's case is still hands-off, the feds want that one for themselves, arrogant bastards—but Sharon is the joint case of Bill and Ted and anyone they choose to bring in. I tell you two this because, technically, you've been guilty of Obstruction of Justice, Withholding Evidence, and Interfering with a Federal Investigation for"—she looked at her watch, solely (I suspected) for dramatic effect—"oh, about an hour and ten minutes. Don't worry, no one's going to arrest you—but goddammit, if either of you comes into possession of any further information about this, you'd bloody well better call me before you even *think* about inhaling your next breath. Seriously, guys. Ted's pretty confident that he and Bill can have the . . . *suspect* in custody before morning, and I hope he's right. The sooner they can nail this prick, the better."

"Did Sharon give them a good description?" asked Russell.

"From what Bill told me, it was an *excellent* description . . . of sorts."

"Meaning what?"

"Meaning that's all I'm going to tell you right now. Geoff, you're staying at the Marriott on the square, right?"

"Yes."

"I'll call you there if I need you, but just to be safe, give me your cell number."

I cleared my throat and looked down at my feet. "I, um . . . I don't own a cell phone."

Barb stared at me. "You're kidding? Even Mr. Anti-Social here doesn't live *that* far back in the Dark Ages."

I shrugged. "I never found a calling plan I liked. So sue me."

Barb shook her head. "*Men*, I swear. Huh—I always wanted to say that in real life, and now that I have, it's not as satisfying as I'd hoped it would be." She reached into her shoulder bag, rummaging around for only a moment or two before she produced an ultrathin silver cell phone. Flipping it open, she powered it up, pressed what looked like fifty buttons with a speed and dexterity that was—to me, at least—imposing.

I said, "What are you—?"

"*Shh*, no talking, need to concentrate." She finished punching in the numbers with almost cartoonish velocity, and then tossed it to me. Luckily, I managed not to drop it.

"*Now* you have one. I'll want that back before you leave, but while you're here, you keep it turned on. The battery is new and it's fully charged, so unless you plan on calling adult chat lines in Taiwan, it should last a few days. Yes, it works as a GPS device, so I can have your butt pinpointed in a matter of two minutes—not that I don't trust you. My number's in there, so is Russell's, Bill's, the Hangman's, Ted's, and your home number in case you want to call your wife and little girl."

"How did you know my—?"

"Because I am secretly Wonder Woman and that cell phone is my magic lasso—haven't you been paying attention? I knew who you are, who you used to be, and damn near everything else about you before I picked up the roses.

"A lot is going to be happening over the next couple of

days, and I want to make sure you two will be a phone call away, all right?"

"Aw," said Russell. "She cares."

She nailed him to the spot with a hard but not unfriendly stare. "Yes, I do. More than you think. If you had half a brain, you'd have realized that a while ago. Jerk." She looked at me. "You're not a jerk, you just hang out with one, so I'll reserve judgment." Then she winked at me again. "I'm now off to take statements and do that voodoo that I do so well. What about the two of you?"

"Thought I'd bring Geoff over to my place for dinner," said Russell.

"Is it clean?" asked Barb.

"I run a janitorial company, fer chrissakes."

"Uh-huh. *Is it clean?*"

"Clean enough."

Barb shook her head and then leaned over and kissed my cheek. "You're a better man than I am, Gunga Din. May the Good Lord protect you."

"*I said it was clean enough.*"

Russell handed me the supply carrier and moved ahead to help Barb make her way back down the steps. I stood for a moment, watching him put an arm halfway around her waist, and then Barb, with an audible sigh of frustration, grabbing his hand pulling his arm the rest of the way around. If either of them ever decided to make an actual first move, they were going to be a great couple. If the ghost of Andy Leonard would allow that to happen.

I'd just started toward the steps when the shadows within the decaying church once again shifted—only this time, instead of it being the soft thump of a raccoon or groundhog or even the moist flutter of a bat's wings, it was the heavy thud of something with a lot more weight to it. I almost called to Russell and Barb but decided to let them have a few moments alone while I moved closer to one of the wider openings in the wall of the church. I hadn't noticed before that there were still some old pieces of glass in the windows, and the afternoon sun through the trees created a mosaic of pinpoint, starlike reflections. It was actually rather pretty for a moment, and then a set of those stars turned crimson and shifted and rose and I found myself staring into a pair of searing red eyes. I tried to make out the shape of whatever animal this was—I knew that wolves were not uncommon around here—and then something else reflected in the shattered window glass and the Broken One's face, still bandaged, appeared to me. I didn't need to hear his voice this time; it was all too obvious that he was saying, "Go!"

The red-eyed thing inside the church blinked, snorted, and then shifted again, rising to a fuller height, and threw something small and shiny in my direction. Just as had happened in my classroom less than two weeks ago, my perception sputtered and things began fragmenting: there was an impression of leathery skin on skeletal arms; of long, thick, twisted fingers that looked almost like claws; of mass and deformity; clusters of ugly, seeping tumors and large scabs picked to the pink flesh beneath; of jagged, hooklike teeth; and of . . . fear. Whatever this thing was—if indeed there was anything there at all—it was as afraid of me as I was of it—and make no mistake, I was very much afraid at that moment, but I'd made an art form out of running away from or ignoring those things that frightened me, and one of the reasons I'd come here in the first place was to deal with fear, so I didn't move. The thing in the church, however, did, and when the sun flashed on the oily skin of something massive growing from a shoulder, my perception became whole once again, my left side began throbbing with low, insistent pain, and I saw the great, hunched shape drop down into the mud and ruin and begin crawling, snorting and slobbering and wheezing as it threw aside a pair of fallen, heavy ceiling beams as if they were sticks, and vanish into a maw of shadow below the altar area.

Without thinking too much about what I was doing, I bent over and picked up the shiny object the thing had thrown at me: a young girl's necklace once gold, now stained with drying blood. Hanging from the chain was a little gold heart, the type of pendant with a clasp on its side. I pressed the button and the heart snapped open to reveal two photographs inside. On the left was a photo of four-year-old Sharon Millhauser; on the right, her sister Ashley.

Ashley's face had been slashed down the center with the edge of something sharp, a knife or a jagged, long fingernail.

Though I could no longer see his reflection in the glass, I heard the Broken One's voice whisper: *Hoopsticks, bro. You just caught a glimpse of Hoopsticks. Ain't that special?*

I decided that now was a good time to put that whole dealing-with-fear thing on hold for a little while; I shoved the bloodied necklace into the pocket of my jacket and backed away, nearly falling down the steps. A raw, ugly screeching from somewhere within the maw of the altar-shadow echoed back to me, and I spun around and took the stone steps three at a time, the sound of my breathing noisy and strained, the thunder of blood pounding through my ears—but none of it quite loud enough to drown out the sound behind me of snorting, spitting, and soft, childlike wailing. I literally had Ashley Millhauser's blood on my hands, and I'd just looked into the eyes of

the maniac who'd killed her. I didn't care whether or not
Barbara Greer believed me, I was going to keep my word
and hand the necklace to her and tell her what I'd seen,
what had happened, and hope that I didn't end the day in
the psych ward at Cedar Hill Memorial Hospital or wher-
ever it was the authorities placed people who were a potential danger to everyone around them.

My left side was throbbing in pain, hammering against
my internal organs as if some invisible entity were throwing punch after punch after punch into my scar to see
how long I'd remain standing. Twice I nearly fell getting
down the steps, and the slippery grass of the small incline past the steps nearly claimed me as many times, but
I somehow managed to make it to level ground so I could
lean against the large sign welcoming visitors to Cedar
Hill Cemetery. I wanted to leave this place of the dead
and never come back, never even *think* of it again were
that possible.

It took a few moments for my blurred vision to clear
and refocus, and when it did I could see that Barb and
Russell were standing between their two vehicles—hers,
an expensive and well-cared-for Mercedes, the type of
car befitting a lawyer of her power and standing; Russell's, the classic van with the words DAVIES'S JANITORIAL
SERVICE on its side.

Russell was smiling at Barb, and she at him. It gave me
a sense of comfort, watching them, a sense of being
grounded and safe. They were holding hands.

"Kiss her, you moron," I whispered.

The Broken One's voice echoed in my head: *You got
more important things to worry about right now than playing
matchmaker, bro. Like turning over that piece of bloodied evidence that's in your pocket.*

I took several deep breaths, willing my heart rate to

slow to its normal rhythm, and reached into my pocket to retrieve the necklace. I wondered who'd given it to Ashley as a gift, if it was something she'd bought for herself after saving her allowance for X-amount of weeks; I wondered how Sharon reacted when her older sister showed her the two photos she'd chosen to put inside the heart, to protect them, to have near her the picture of the person she loved best in the world: did Sharon give her a great big hug and kiss, or did she maybe call Ashley "goofy" or something like that? I bet it was a memorable moment, whatever had happened, and wished that I'd been there to witness it.

Get a move on, pal, said the Broken One. *Fair Maid Barbara is getting ready to leave.*

I pulled myself upright and began moving toward her and Russell. I was vaguely aware of a car horn sounding once, twice, three times, and of Barb and Russell turning in the direction of the sound. My legs were filled with iron. I could barely lift my feet to walk. The thudding of my left side intensified and I cried out once, too softly for either of them to hear.

Barb laughed, then stepped forward and kissed Russell full on the lips; one of those long, lingering kisses that left no room for doubt about the intention behind it. Russell looked as if his legs were going to give out on him. I decided that there was no way I was going to make it over to them, and so opened my mouth to call out. No sound emerged. I was being held captive by my own body. This really sucked.

Another van pulled up beside Russell's and the horn sounded again. The door opened and the Reverend climbed out, smiling at the two of them.

"I don't suppose it would do any good for me to suggest getting a room, would it?"

"You are a dirty-minded man of the cloth," replied Barb, walking over to the Reverend and planting a little kiss on his cheek. "Besides, I have a house with three bedrooms."

Russell's face was turning a deeper shade of red with every word. I didn't like that shade of red. It looked too much like the eyes of the thing in the shadows of the church.

"It's not that I'm trying to rush anything between the two of you," said the Reverend. "But the gang out at the Hangman, we've got this pool going. I'm spring."

Barb took a step back. "You've actually been *betting* about when we'd—?"

"Betting is illegal in this county, Counselor. We prefer to think of it as . . . well-intended predictions with a potential profit margin."

"You are so stuffed full of wild blueberry muffins."

The Reverend laughed. "Ha! So you've seen Howard Hawks's version of *The Thing* enough times to remember that line. Russell, this is *so* the woman for you."

Russell's face grew even redder. "Could you two knock it off?"

"Fine," said Barb. "But you'd better make damned sure that Eunice Emerson comes out to the Hangman next time, or the date is off!" With that, she waved at me as she climbed into her Mercedes and drove away.

Russell—still looking like an embarrassed schoolboy—blinked his eyes a few times, turned in my direction, then at last came out of his haze and said, "What the hell took you so long?"

"I was communing with nature. Could we get out of here, please?"

"This is where I come in," said the Reverend, slapping a hand on Russell's shoulder. "I'm sorry, but I need to borrow Geoff for a little while. Something's come up that he and I need to discuss."

"Anything I can help with?" asked Russell.

"Not just yet. Details shall be forthcoming, film at eleven, and all that. Just know that part of it has to do with that little tumor discussion the bunch of you had a while ago."

Russell's face went from red to white in a blink. "How did you find out about—?"

"Ah, *come on*, Russell! The two people you guys can't keep anything from are Barb and me. One of these days, all of you will realize that, and then we shall all join forces and conquer a trembling Earth."

Russell shook his head. "We were gonna grab a pizza and go back to my place for a while."

"I'll have him back to you in a little while, I promise. Now, go. Indian Mound Mall calls you. A new wardrobe awaits your purchasing power."

"What's wrong with my wardrobe?"

The Reverend shrugged. "Nothing, if you're an extra in *Ironweed* or *The Grapes of Wrath*. You're going to be courting a very classy lady—and about time, might I add. It would be best if you dressed accordingly."

I'd managed to make it over to the vans by now, my entire body trembling as if I'd just finished running a marathon. Russell turned toward me and said, "You must feel like a hot potato, getting tossed from person to person."

"There are worse fates," I managed to say.

Russell gave me a hug, and I hugged back. This time there was nothing awkward between us. I felt as if I were embracing the older brother I'd never had.

"I'll see you in a while, right?" he asked.

"Count on it," I replied.

He pulled back, still gripping my shoulders. "Joey Hamilton."

"Who shit way too much, even for a baby."

And then he did the oddest thing—he leaned in and kissed my cheek as if I were a younger brother, or his nephew (which, in a way, I guess I was). I liked it.

"Thanks for keeping me company this afternoon," he said. "I always do this alone. I think Mary Alice would have enjoyed seeing you again."

"I hope she did," I replied.

Russell shook hands with the Reverend, took the cleaning tray from me (I was amazed to realize that I hadn't dropped it), and then climbed in his van and drove out of the cemetery, tooting his horn three times and waving at us. The Reverend returned the wave. I tried to, but the pain in my side and the iron in my limbs held me in place.

"How did you know I'd be out here with him?" I asked.

"I have what you might call mystical gifts, ethereal abilities, magic powers. I also happen to have what you might call a cell phone with the Hangman's number on speed dial. Russell comes out here on the same day every week, and he's never missed a day." He looked at me and grinned. "Not quite as dazzling as my earlier display on the square, but why try to make myself look more clever than I really am?"

"You know about anything that's happened since this morning?"

He nodded. "About Sharon Millhauser? You bet. Couldn't be happier."

"What . . . what do you need me for? And could we get the hell out of here, please? This place gives me a serious case of the willies."

He shook his head. "I'm afraid not, my friend. What needs to be done, needs to be done here, and I doubt that even this effort will bring everything to a conclusion for you, but we need to start somewhere. And for this I am truly sorry." He reached into his pocket and took out something that looked like a betting chip from a Las Vegas casino, red on one side, green on the other, and began twirling it through his fingers; an old magician's dexterity exercise. "You saw him, didn't you?"

"Who?"

Still flip/twirling the coin, he glared at me. "Don't waste time with purposefully naïve questions, Geoff. You *know* who."

I nodded. "Hoopsticks. Yes, I think I did."

"I thought my Spidey-sense was tingling. Where?"

I pointed up the hill. "In the ruins of that old church near Mary Alice's grave."

The Reverend stared in that direction. "Is he still there?"

"I don't think so. He crawled through some kind of a hole under the altar."

"*Shit!* That means we're going to have to follow him."

CHAPTER THIRTEEN

I couldn't believe what I'd just heard him say. "*Follow him?* Oh, I don't think so, thanks very much."

"It wasn't a suggestion—nor is it up for debate. You came here for answers? Some of them are in the place he's heading for right this moment."

"I don't give a good goddamn if the lost treasure of Cortez is in the place where he's heading, I am *not* following him."

Still flip/twirling the coin through his fingers— *green-red, green-red, green-red*—the Reverend gave me a look that was equal parts exasperation and pity. "You're too smart to try rationalizing all of this so it fits into tidy, comfortable compartments. You know that something is happening here that's so far outside the dictionary definition of 'normal' there's not even a term for it yet.

"Listen to me: right now, this instant, as we stand here, the hundreds of cholera victims whose bodies are buried out on that island in Buckeye Lake are beginning to stir. They're not alive again—not yet, anyway—but a form of sentience is returning to their remains, and sometime in the next forty-eight hours or so, the members of the yacht club are going to be in for one major son of a bitch of a shock when those remains begin forcing their way up through the foundation of the building and crawl out into the dining and locker rooms."

"How the fuck do you *know* all of this?"

He stared off into the distance at something only he seemed able to observe. "Because I've been a 'citizen' of Cedar Hill for over two hundred years. Because it's been part of my duties to stay here to watch and wait for *you*. Because even though you may or may not believe in God, Buddha, Krishna, or the Flying Spaghetti Monster, because you may not accept concepts like fate, predestination, synchronicity, or the billions upon billions of unseen, indefinable forces that dictate the shape and function of the multiverse, and even though you may damn well want to dismiss all of these things as delusions or flights of fancy because they don't fit into any niche that a high-school English teacher feels he has some control over, that doesn't mean your ass isn't an inextricable part of them."

The rapid, deadly cadence of his words and the intensity of his gaze were bordering on madness. I found myself stepping back before he exploded and splattered his crazy all over me. "I think I want for you to leave me alone, Reverend."

"Yeah, I get that a lot—so much so that I've come up with a standard response, and that standard response is this: that's not possible. But unlike the Broken One, I'm not fucking with you. If everything seems to be coming at you too fast, tough, deal with it. Whether you want to cop to it or not, you're strong enough to handle all of this." *Green-red, green-red, green-red*, the coin twirling with greater speed.

"You're scaring me, Reverend."

"Good, you ought to be scared. I'm damn near

terrified—and in case you hadn't noticed, *I'm* the one everybody looks to for strength and guidance. I'm sorry if I seem a bit on the . . . unhinged side. I've kind of been dreading this for a long, long time."

I looked back up the hill at the ruins of the church. "Is that why you're not exactly pushing me back up there to go after him? I mean, you said that we don't have time to waste."

"He's confused, scared, and angry, Geoff. I want to make sure there's some serious distance between us before we go after him. I know his destination, so there's no chance we'll lose him."

I pulled Ashley Millhauser's necklace from my pocket. The blood was now all but dried, turning the gold chain to a nauseating shade of brown. "He threw this at me. Look at the heart."

He took it from me and pressed the latch. "She was a lovely little girl. This shouldn't have happened."

"Why'd he kill her?"

He closed the heart and handed the necklace back to me. "Take this."

"I'd rather not."

"*Take it*. When the time comes, you'll have to be the one to turn it over. And to answer your question, I don't think he meant to kill her. I think it might have been an accident." He stared at me, still holding out the necklace.

I didn't want to touch the pitiful thing, but I took it from him, nonetheless. Yes, he scared me; yes, part of me still suspected he might be more than a little nuts; and, yes, he was right—all of this was now coming at me a little too fast . . . but despite all of that, I trusted him. I took out my handkerchief, still unused, and wrapped it around the necklace. "So what now?"

The Reverend took hold of my shoulders and turned me to face the street—specifically, he turned me to face the row of houses *across* the street, small houses close enough that I could see through the windows, houses interspersed with a couple of bars, a pizza place, and a mom-and-pop grocery store.

"How would *you* like to live across the street from this place?" he asked. "The prices are good. Which is a blessing, since it's all most of these folks can afford. And just so your education of the area doesn't go ignored, that little grocery store right there? That's where Ben Little-john's wife was killed during that robbery.

"Look at the house second from the left of the pizza place. Got it?"

A small ranch-style home (or what passed for a ranch house around here), four, maybe five rooms. The front curtains were pulled open to reveal a sparse living room and an old man, possibly in his early seventies, sitting in a well-used recliner watching a color television set at least a decade out of date.

"Okay . . . ?" I said, watching as the old man carefully peeled the foil covering off the TV dinner on the small folding tray beside him. One TV dinner in his sparse living room (I thought I saw a framed photograph of a married couple on a nearby coffee table, but couldn't be certain). A glass of milk. Eyeglasses with heavy dark frames and thick lenses. After a moment, a wobbly beagle rose up to put its front paws on one of the arms of the chair. The old man looked at the dog, smiled, scratched its head, and tore off part of the entrée—Salisbury steak—feeding it to the dog in one of those Jump-Jump! games people play with their pets who come to the table begging.

"He's all alone, isn't he?" I asked.

"Eventually, we all are, Geoff—I don't mean to sound heartless, but Chet—that's his name, Chet Beckman, a former bus driver who, yes, is a widower—isn't your concern right now. What I want you to look at is the television set. Yeah, yeah, yeah, I know, a rerun of *The Brady Bunch*, but that's not the point. The point is that every time Chet turns on that TV, an electron gun in the back of the set fires out hundreds of billions of electrons that hit that screen and give you a clear picture of Jan doing her 'Marsha-Marsha-Marsha!' bit. But the thing is, there is *nothing* programmed into any single electron which tells it that it has to hit a certain section of the screen. You following me so far?"

"I think I'm with you."

"Good. Now, since the electrons have no way of knowing what part of the picture they're supposed to reproduce on that screen, how do you suppose Chet even *gets* a picture?"

"Blind shit-house luck?"

"Close. He gets a picture because he *expects* to get one. He becomes what physicists call 'the Observer,' and by turning on the TV and *deciding* that he's going to get a picture, he collapses the wave function."

"What's that?"

"*The wave function?* Hmmmm . . ." He continued flip/twirling the coin and then, abruptly—and without interrupting the rhythm of the exercise—switched the coin to his other hand.

"What I just did? Switching the coin from one hand to the other? That's a good example of collapsing a wave function. We collapse wave functions every second of every day—do we sit, stand, cross the street, eat a peach, make that call? The wave function—despite what a lot of scientists say—does not represent *probability* but *possibil-*

ity. Here I stand; do I flip this through the fingers of my left hand or my right? Do I slip it back into my pocket or throw it into the street? An endless choice of possibilities, of roads not yet taken. So what do I do? Let's say I switch hands once more." He did so, again without interrupting the rhythm of the momentum. "And, thus, I collapse the wave function; a choice has been made, there are no other possibilities that can be chosen for this moment, for this moment has now passed, has become *that* moment, that moment *back there*, and now a fresh set of new wave functions awaits us in this latest moment. Since the quantum wave function represents the possibility of observing an event, the collapse means that the possibility has changed from less than certain to a *certainty*. Still with me?"

"Fuck, I don't know."

"Eloquence is your middle name."

I rubbed my eyes. "Would you *please* stop twirling that damn thing through your fingers? It's getting on my nerves."

Another grin. "Well, *I'll* stop with the finger exercise stuff, but . . ." The Reverend flexed his fingers and dropped both hands to his sides.

The coin, however, remained in the air next to him, twirling and tumbling in circles as if still in his hand.

I stared for a moment, then reached to snatch it from the air. It moved out of my reach. I stepped forward, made a second grab for it, and again it moved beyond the length of my arm.

"This could get seriously comical if you don't stop trying to get hold of that damn thing," said the Reverend.

"Is this some kind of magic trick?"

He seemed offended. "That's right, you nailed me, pal! Nothing up my sleeve, but watch and I'll pull a rabbit out of my ass—*hell, no*, it's not a trick! Give me some credit."

"What's going on?" My voice broke on the last word, and I had to choke back the fear and confusion.

The Reverend reached over and gave my shoulder a squeeze. "You'll understand soon enough, I promise." He held out his other hand and the coin came back to him, its flip/twirling pattern unbroken: *red-green, red-green, red-green.*

"Let me ask you something, Geoff—what do you suppose happened to all the other possibilities once I changed hands?"

". . . I don't know . . . they ceased to exist?"

He shook his head. "No. They simply no longer had a place in this universe at that moment."

"So . . . ?"

"So they were freed to be a part of other, countless possible universes, and that's where they went."

"You're talking about . . . about parallel universes?"

He almost sneered. "Oh, not you, too!" He began to pace around the small parking lot. "I'm sorry, but that term pisses me off. Too many lazy physicists with their heads up their black holes and *way* too many science fiction books and movies with writers who base their research—providing they actually *do* any—on the conclusions drawn by those black-hole dwellers. *No*, most certainly *not* parallel—that implies that they run side by side by side, that there's some sort of physical distance separating them. No, what they should actually be called are *simultaneous* universes.

"Imagine you're in a movie theater, okay, and you're sitting there with your popcorn and Coke, maybe a hot dog—I like hot dogs myself—anyway, there you are, and you're looking at the one big screen. Now imagine that the movie starts, only instead of one film being projected onto the screen, there are hundreds, thousands, *millions* of different films running at the same time . . . only you can't see them. Some apparatus in you can only see one movie at a time, even though all the others are up there, too. *That's* how the multiverse is constructed. But because you *expect* to see, I don't know, let's say *Searching For Survivors*, that's what you see, that's *all* you see. You made that choice, you collapsed that wave function."

"Okay . . . ?" I was getting really pretty seriously scared shitless by now. If it hadn't been for the Reverend's strangely reassuring presence, I might have lost it altogether.

"Look over there, on the roof of the pizza parlor."

It took a moment for my mind to register what my eyes were showing to it.

At first I thought the thing was some kind of old-fashioned box camera, the kind used back at the turn of the last century; its head was box-shaped and shone with a deep, hand-rubbed rosewood finish, and that wasn't really so odd . . . until I saw the long, sharp beak protruding from the place in front where the lens should have been. On each side of the of the box was a hand-size half sphere of brass that looked like the bulging eyes of a toad; a thin iron rod like a neck connected the box-head to a wider, longer box that looked like a small child's coffin standing on end, held upright by a pair of thick, powerful, furry legs, each ending in a wide wolf's paw, claws extended to give it purchase and balance.

So this is what going around the bend feels like, I thought. *Somehow, I'd thought there'd be more screaming and drooling involved.*

A set of membranous wings unfurled from the back of the lower box, and with another series of metallic clicks

and scrapes the creature began to move back and forth
across the roof, bending its legs at the knees and hopping
forward while its wings fluttered with a furious speed
rivaling that of a moth's.

As I let fly with one brief, barking laugh, the creature
on the roof came to an abrupt halt, its beak opening and
closing as if it were trying to either speak or snap a bug
out of the air.

"This is the fifth time today I've seen that thing," I
said.

"*What?*"

"Well, okay, technically this is the first time I've seen
it whole, but I've been catching glimpses of it all day."

"Really?" He looked at it. "That's unusual. They're
usually not so careless. How interesting. . . ."

"What's it supposed to be, anyway?"

"It's not *supposed* to be anything, other than what it is,"
replied the Reverend. "Geoff, meet one of the banes of
my existence. That creature is part of a race of beings
known as the 'Onlookers.' They don't show themselves
to mortals very often, and the only reason you're seeing
one of them now is because it's . . . well, I was going to
say it's because it was my will that you be allowed to, and
they owe me a few favors . . . but evidently it wanted to
steal my thunder. So this one in particular has been
shadowing you since you crossed the city limits? And
hasn't been going out of its way to keep that a secret?
That is surprising.

"It's the Onlookers' responsibility to watch and record
and report on reality in every branch of the multiverse.
Nothing happens in this reality or any other reality that
they do not take down for posterity, so to speak." He
glared at the thing. "Personally, I can't stand the smarmy,
self-righteous little pricks. To oversimplify their func-

tion, think of them as God's hall monitors. You know how it is that you're taught God, like Santa and the IRS, sees all?" He pointed to the thing on the roof. "*They're* how that's possible. When every millisecond a collapsed wave function in turn creates an entirely new and different universe, there's quite a bit to keep tabs on. Even the Supreme Being needs sidekicks to do grunt work. It's also part of their duties, while recording and observing all of this, to help keep all of the possible worlds—the simultaneous universes—hidden from one another, because the inhabitants of each one could not deal with that knowledge, with that . . . vision. The Onlookers chart the splits in the branches of reality; they tally up the collapsed wave functions."

As if to offer some sort of condescending gesture, the Onlooker on the roof stepped forward, bent one of its legs, and took a little bow.

"See what I mean?" said the Reverend. "It knows I can't do anything about that, but it also knows that there are things I *could* do that would make its duties a lot more difficult—*don't you, smartass? Yeah, I'm talking to you!*"

The Onlooker straightened, its brass half-sphere eyes *snick*'d as if in response, and its wings ceased fluttering; the obedient soldier awaiting its next command.

"One screen, with a million different films running simultaneously, but you can see only one." He nodded at the Onlooker. "Until now." He gripped my arm as the creature on the roof raised its camera-head higher, opening its brass half-sphere eyes.

"I need you to believe me, Geoff. With no reservations, no doubts. So stay very still and do not pull away from my grasp."

I could feel it inside my bones; something was shifting, was altering itself on a subatomic level—no, even deeper than that, beyond a subatomic level . . . yet somehow the Reverend's hand clutching my arm held me in place, protected in a frozen moment that could not be affected or altered.

Two bright pinpoints of golden light began to glow within the Onlooker's opened eyes, spreading out, widening, intensifying, and growing until they all but blinded me, and just when I thought I couldn't look any longer, the light didn't so much blink out as it did blend itself into the already-existing daylight—only now the street I was looking at was hazy, insubstantial, composed of shimmering objects obscured by the heat waves rising from a highway at the height of summer.

"Stay with me," said the Reverend. "None of that fragmenting brouhaha, not now." The pressure of his grip on my arm increased, becoming almost painful, but it kept my attention focused. The street became dozens, *hundreds* of streets, superimposed over one another. The light from the Onlooker's eyes allowed me to see different *levels* of things; sometimes, when looking at a building, I'd blink and see the ghost of a different building overlaying it in the same spot, and behind that ghost-building there would be another building, older, sometimes made of concrete, sometimes of wood, sometimes of stone—and with every ghost-building, there would be ghost-people, even ghost-creatures that came out of the stone structures—structures with writing over their doorways that resembled no language I had ever encountered. These periods of seeing ghost levels were, at first, brief but still unnerving—especially the creatures I saw scrabbling about in the miasma; they inhabited a world, a reality, a universe I did not recognize, one where history didn't exist because there was no genetic mechanism in their makeup to dictate such a necessity, a universe (or universes) of stone structures and fire and mountains made from steel and flesh and bones.

"It's beginning," whispered the Reverend. "Hold on, hold steady."

An ornate, four-wheeled circus cage sat in the middle of one of the ghost-streets. Inside the cage, lying on its side, was a huge, highly detailed stone sculpture of a woman's head. Shimmering gossamer webs blanketed the sculpture, holding it down like a weighted net; it tried rolling to one side, then the next, but the webs remained strong. Finally, defeated, the sculpture opened its eyes and pursed its lips; the air trembled with trills and arpeggios and flutings, echoes of a winter's midnight wind whispering *soon* on this spring afternoon. A flock of coelacanths and paddlefish swam around the cage as if their long-ago vanished prehistoric ocean still existed in the spot. Surrounding the cage and scattered about the area was a crowd of creatures both wondrous and frightening: a man with the head of a black hawk wearing a feathered headdress, a turtle with small antlers, a raven-headed woman in a golden flowing gown, a lion peering out from behind the visor in a suit of armor, a wolf in multicolored bandoliers, a mouse with angel's wings, a steer-skull being wearing the uniform of a Spanish conquistador, a glass owl, a crystalline buffalo, a jade spider; dressed in deerskin shirt and breechclouts and leggings, with medicine pouches and beaded necklaces, holding flutes and hornpipes and ceremonial chimes, their music and soft singing became the unbound wings of time, momentarily holding my spirit in the spell of a lullaby that offered comfort, joy, and the promise of safety. With every blink of my eyes, a new level of a different reality layered itself atop the one I'd seen only moments before, allowing me only quick glimpses of several odd-looking things that were all over the street; a lithe female figure with the head of a black horse, its ears erect, its neck arched, vapor jetting from its nostrils; another creature was tall and skeletal, with fingers so long their tips brushed against the ground; it hunkered down and snaked its fingers around the trunk of a tree, as if absorbing something within the bark. Some hopped like frogs; those without legs or feet rolled; others scuttled around on rootlike filaments covered in flowers whose centers were the faces of blind children.

Ancient, rickety, horse-drawn wooden wagons now made their way down the street, their drivers' faces hidden by thick kerchiefs covering noses and mouths. The wagons were filled with dead bodies, some of them so badly decomposed that bits and pieces of flesh fell off and were carried away by a nonexistent breeze, vanishing into dust before they reached as high as the lowest streetlight. Many of the bodies—the freshest ones—were still bloated, some slightly, some severely; all were discolored, a few were desiccated, and some were more bone than flesh. Soul-sick men and women and spirit-shattered children, dressed in clothes a hundred years or more out of date, shuffled along behind these wagons that I now realized were filled with the bodies of cholera victims; if I had any doubt about that, the next batch of bodies— these stacked seven or eight high, tied together with rope, and arranged on large tarps that were soon revealed to be the dried, sewn-together hides of animals— were being pulled along by youthful Wyandot warriors on their way to canoes.

Day became night becoming day becoming night yet again, clouds moving overhead with such speed there was barely any time to register their form or what season it was. Up in one of the night skies the moon became a shimmering silver rose, its petals formed by the wings of the hundreds—maybe thousands—of idealized angels perched around it, looking downward like excited spectators into an arena. They were watching a Quetzalcoatl twice the size of an airplane pump its mammoth wings and fly in wide, graceful circles. But the giant bird was not alone—a WWII German pursuit plane with twin machine guns mounted on its wings was engaged in an intense but playful dogfight with the flying creature; the plane turned in tight, precise maneuvers as the pterosaur tried attacking it from below. The machine guns strafed without mercy or sound, a silent-film prop spitting out bursts of sparking light, firing off round after round.

Night became day becoming night becoming day once more, and the Reverend and I were now standing on the far side of a road constructed from thousands of silently screaming faces, all of them having been cut away from the skull, stretched, and sutured to the faces above, below, and on either side. So tightly were the faces stitched together that it was impossible to tell where the flesh of one ended and that of another began. A powerful, wide stream of water surged over the faces, carrying enough force that it continued to flow even as some of it vanished down the chasms where eyes and mouths used to be. Some of the mouths stretched wide-open while others pressed their lips firmly together. Eyelids, now useless, snapped backward and were farther stretched by the churning force of the water; every so often one would be torn free and pitched about by the small but potent swells, tumbling along, mixing in with bits of fingers, chunks of tongues, bundles of broken teeth, and sections of scalp holding firm to the few clumps of hair that remained attached to them. It smelled like congealed grease, and I had to cover my nose and mouth with my hands to keep from vomiting.

Still, it didn't stop; the road of screaming faces disappeared under a rolling mist and next came a demonlike monstrosity with three bulging insane eyes and a four-fanged grin that emerged from the fog. Its body was composed of thick, bloody-looking mud, and was draped in corpse skin, riding a huge black bear. It carried an ax in one hand and a skullcap of blood in the other . . . and from every side of its form, faces peered out, faces made of black mud, dark lips working to form words, crying out in agony and terror. As it trudged past us a dozen or more police cars, visibar lights flashing, sped through it as if it were vapor and screeched to a silent halt in front of the grocery store, the officers leaping out behind their opened doors and aiming their weapons; I recognized a younger Bill Emerson as he came out of the store and fell against the hood of his car, shuddering, weeping, and then vomiting as groups of large dark dogs ran past him and the other officers, unseen by any of them, the dogs being herded along by dozens of men dressed in pin-striped suits, white shirts, and red bow ties, all of whom also wore a sharp black derby; and then a great shadow fell over all of them from the opposite direction as something so tall it blocked out the sun lumbered past on two gigantic hands, each with quadruple-jointed fingers covered in vines and dripping weeds that looked more like veins, its fingers digging into the ground as it bent low to glare down at us through empty eye sockets in a massive, skull-like head, one wreathed in worms and dead spiders, its entire mass towering nearly three feet over the top of the nearest building, water and soaked earth sloughing from its leg-stumps, its unbelievably long, lethal fingers rhythmically clawing the muddy ground that was not here in this branch of reality but rather *back there*, in the layer of time when Mr. Hands had first been given life; the thing, stinking of the rot of a thousand-thousand graves, looked down at the Reverend and me for a moment, not seeing us, not seeing the police officers behind it, the incredible creatures all around it in the ghost-buildings, the ghost-realities, the dogs running through it, the wagons of bodies passing beneath its bulk, but I could see that it, too, had dozens if not hundreds of faces staring out from within its bulk, though their expressions didn't seem terrified at all, which is more than I could say for the faces of the two little girls who were suddenly standing a few yards away, directly in front of me; Ashley and Sharon Millhauser were holding hands, Sharon clutching at Ashley's free hand with both of hers while burying her face in her older sister's side, while Ashley, trying so very much to look and *be* brave for the sake of her little sister, was looking around, eyes wide in dismal fear until Sharon tugged on her arm; then Ashley's face became that of a strong-willed, courageous heroine right out of a novel, and she knelt so that Sharon could embrace her, could kiss her cheek and tell her how much she loved her but that she was so *scared*, what were they going to do, and Ashley, smiling, brushed some of Sharon's matted hair from her face and whispered something to her, something that took away a small part of the younger girl's terror, and for a moment both of them smiled as Ashley unlocked the clasp of her necklace and they looked at the two photos hidden inside: Sharon's face became something radiant then, something filled with wonder and surprise and, most of all, the kind of awe a child's face will display when the love he or she feels toward you has just grown ten times stronger than it was a moment before, and I knew that I'd just gotten one of my wishes, that I'd been allowed to see the moment when Ashley shared her secret with her little sister, and for a moment there was no longer any fear, any doubt, there was only hope renewed, because if they shared this most intimate and wondrous of moments, then nothing, *nothing* could do them any harm—and that's when Sharon, for just a moment, turned her head away from her sister and looked directly into my eyes, I could *feel* her gaze, could sense her awareness of me, and I lifted my hand, giving her a little wave of hello as she, in turn, began to raise her arm to point at me and . . .

"Make it stop," I whispered to the Reverend, looking away from the girls, humiliated by the spinelessness in my voice. "*Please* make it stop. I believe you, I believe you, I believe you. . . ."

He moved the coin to his other hand and reversed the direction of its twirling; as soon as he'd completed this simple action, the street before me was once again as it had been, and I could clearly see through the window as Chet fed his dog another piece of his Salisbury steak.

Taking a deep breath to steady my nerves, I looked up and saw that the Onlooker was still on the roof.

"Can't you make it go away?" I asked.

He shook his head. "I've never been able to banish one of them—and believe me, I've tried. It will leave when it decides it's no longer necessary to observe and record what's going on around it." He caught me as I lost my balance and nearly dropped to my knees. "Whoa, easy there, friend. This isn't over yet."

I felt my heart trying to squirt out through my ribs. "I . . . I honestly don't know if I can take any more of this."

"Hate to tell you this, but we're going to have to find

out." Making certain that I was able to stand under my own power, the Reverend bent down and picked up something near his feet: a small brown mouse.

He looked like a man possessed as he continued. "All right, Geoff, now we get to some of the *really* weird stuff. Why this coin in one of my hands, and why this mouse in the other? Blame Einstein. He rejected the idea of 'simultaneous' universes that were created by collapsing wave functions because he didn't believe—and this is his actual example—that a mouse could bring about a radical change in the structure of reality simply by observing it. Wrong! See, old Albert made the conclusion based on his belief that—just like your sitting in a theater that's showing a million movies all at the same time but only seeing one—a mouse doesn't possess the ability to differentiate between one branch of reality and another. And since, according to Einstein, there is no wave function present in a mouse's perception, there's nothing to collapse." He held the still-twirling coin directly across from the mouse; the mouse seemed entranced.

"Say this coin in its present state represents four possible universes: Universe Heads, Universe Green, Universe Tails, Universe Red. Why doesn't Tiresias—I decided to call him Tiresias, he kind of *looks* like a Tiresias to me—anyway, why doesn't he just pick one and be off on that particular collapsed wave to whatever possible universe awaits beyond the scrim? Because our one brown mouse here knows that we *all* exist as conspiracies of simultaneous universes; all possible worlds are all around us, all the time, right here, right now, same space, same Bat-time, same Bat-channel, only we don't realize that. In his own fuzzy, innocent little way, Tiresias does. All the experiences that we say are happening in the here and now are also happening in the other universes, only with slight differences ... in one universe, Hitler got into art school, turned out to be a famous painter, and never became chancellor of Germany; in another, John Lennon was never shot; in yet another, Christ was never born, and still further out in another branch, maybe there's a universe where he wasn't even crucified, where Oppenheimer never fathered the atomic bomb, where World War I never happened—who knows? The further you journey through the various possible universes, the more radical those differences become, because endless probability waves that *never existed in this time and place* have been collapsed, giving way to new possible universes within possible universes, all of them overlapping concurrently."

He lifted the mouse closer to the coin. "Tiresias observes this coin that represents four separate universes, yet he doesn't split into four mice. Why? Because for him, the quantum conspiracy is total: he sees a *coin*, and that's it. For Tiresias, the four universes are superimposed, every movie running at the same time—the four universes are already merged into one."

I looked over at the roof of the pizza parlor, where the Onlooker still stood, watching, observing, recording. "So what you're saying is ... is ..."

"You were given a brief look through that scrim that separates all simultaneous universes. Do you have any idea why that was possible?"

"God, no."

"Because those scrims are starting to tear. There are places in this world where the corners of reality are no longer squared, and because of that, because of these tears, these gaps, these fractures ... things and places, events and times from the myriad simultaneous universes are starting to bleed through, and as they do, some of . . . let's be simplistic and say that some of the 'beams' are crossing, and when that happens, they both create and collapse probability waves that should *never have come into existence*. The structure of the multiverse is a lot more fragile than you'd think, and if this continues to go on, the base of all realities in all simultaneous universes is going to begin to crumble, and once that begins, it cannot be stopped."

I blinked but my perception did not fragment, no matter how much I wished it would right now. "So what you're telling me is that everything and every *possible* thing in all universes is on the verge of . . . what? Implosion?"

" 'Reverting to a state of nonbeing' might be technically more accurate but, yes, that's the gist of it. Cedar Hill is a border town, a crossroads, the center of a nexus where things such as those scrims are *supposed to be* kept strong and held in place. It's all starting to come apart now, and one of the reasons is because . . . is because you've come back here after all these years. I've been able to keep things more or less in balance for as long as I have because there's never been a chance that you and Hoopsticks would ever again be in the same place at the same time."

My gut turned to ice. "What do you mean 'again'? Are you telling me that . . . that that *thing* and I have . . . that we've . . . ?"

He gripped my wrist and squeezed. "There is no difference between the way Hoopsticks views the quantum conspiracy and the way Tiresias views it. It—*he*—can move in and out of any and every simultaneous universe he chooses to—but luckily, *so far*, he doesn't understand this extent of this power. He knows he can see and do things that other people and things can't, and he's been . . . experimenting. Mostly he's been moving in and out of different time streams in this reality since he was first able to understand just *how* different he is. Have you ever heard the myths and legends of, say, Abaddon the Destroyer from the Book of Job and the Psalms, or of Brenin Llwyd—the 'Grey King' in the mountains of Wales, Am Fear Liath Mòr, the Greyman of Scotland who haunts the summit and passes of Ben Macdhui? Maybe the Brocken *bow* or Brocken *spectre* from Germany? *All* of them are Hoopsticks, spotted during one of his time-slip strolls. He's not even half a century old and already he's made his mark throughout tens of thousands of years of human history because he doesn't know that he's not *supposed* to be able to move through time like that—and he doesn't know because the quantum conspiracy is total for him, so it's . . . commonplace. But because he's been doing that, because he continually goes on these little field trips, he's forsaken his duty."

"His *duty*?"

The Reverend nodded. "Hoopsticks is something of a . . . sentinel."

"Jesus H. Christ! What . . . I mean . . . how can I . . . a *sentinel*? That thing is a guard?" I took a deep breath and steadied my hands. "There's still something you're holding back, Reverend. What is it? Is it that Hoopsticks is the other 'thing' that called me here? The Broken One already told me that much."

He stared at me for a few moments, during which I swore I could feel the Earth stop spinning. "No, Geoff, Hoopsticks isn't the other thing that called you here, despite what you've been told. The thing that he stands guard over, *that* is what also called you here. Hoopsticks would never do anything to upset or harm you. Not ever."

"Why? I mean, how can you be so sure of that? I didn't exactly feel waves of respect coming from it back at the church."

"He's angry, confused, and frightened. He doesn't know how to deal with you."

"What's the big deal about me, anyway? Why should that thing give a *damn* about my presence here?"

He placed Tiresias back on the ground and slipped the coin into his pocket. "If you want to know the answer to that"—he pointed up the hill toward the decaying church—"then you and I have to go after him, and we have to go after him now. I think there's probably sufficient distance between us that he won't be looking behind him.

"Come on, Geoff. 'Miles to go,' and all that."

The Reverend started up the hill. I looked down at Tiresias. The mouse was sitting back on its haunches, staring up at me with an almost expectant look on its face.

Having no idea why, I picked up the mouse and placed it in the front pocket of my jacket. It gripped the edge of the pocket with its two front two paws and stuck out its head as far as it could, sniffing at the air, happy to be coming along.

"Why am I up here all by myself?" shouted the Reverend, already at the foot of the stone steps leading up toward the church.

"I can't do it, Reverend."

"Yes, you can."

I just shook my head.

"Look at me, Geoff."

I petted Tiresias's fuzzy little face instead.

"Dammit to hell, I said look at me!"

The volume—not to mention the anger and violence—in his voice startled me (though Tiresias didn't seem in the least bothered by it).

I glared up at him. "Don't scream at me like that."

"Then stop being such a stubborn ass. You've gotten to ask all the questions up until now—or at least, most of them—so would you agree that it's time I'm entitled to one?"

I continued staring at him.

The Reverend never once blinked. "I'll take that as a yes, then. Here is my question, Geoff Conover who was once Joseph Hamilton: why did you really come here? What's the thing you most need to find out?"

"I'm not sure."

He shook his head. "Don't. Don't you *dare* lie to me. We both know the answer to that question, so quit trying to play dumb and just answer me. *Why did you come here?*"

I took a deep breath, held it for a moment, then let it out as I said: "I came here because I want to know why Andy Leonard killed all those people."

"And . . . ?"

"And what? You asked me why I came here and I told you."

"You told me *half* of it, Geoff. You came here to get answers to *two* questions. What's the other one?"

I was shaking and my throat felt as if an invisible hand were squeezing it closed. I stood there, silent, just shaking my head.

"What's the other reason?" said the Reverend. "And bear in mind, I am not accustomed to having to ask the same question twice, let alone five times. I like you a great deal, I do, but you don't want to try my patience any further, you really don't."

Staring down into a small puddle of water near my feet, I saw the reflection of the Broken One staring back up at me. He gave his head a short, sharp, upward jerk: *Answer the man, why don't you?*

I snapped up my head and stared straight into the Reverend's eyes. "I need to know why Andy *didn't* kill me. He killed all the other children in the family, he killed children on his way to the park, and sure as hell he killed them once he got there, but he didn't kill *me*! The crazy son of a bitch grabbed a bottle of formula from my mother's baby bag so I wouldn't be *hungry* during the ride! Do you have any *idea* what it's been like to have had all of this ticking in the back of my head for most of my life? Yvonne says that I can't forgive myself for having been spared, and now I think she's right. I *can't* forgive myself for being . . . for being alive—and, yes, I know how stupid that sounds."

"Actually," said the Reverend, "I was going to say it sounds borderline self-pitying, but there's so much genuine conflict in your heart that I'm willing to overlook that whiny tone that crept into your voice toward the end."

I exhaled, nodding. "It *was* a little 'boo-hoo, poor-poor-pitiful me,' wasn't it?"

"At least you admit it." He gestured for me to join him. "I promise you this; come with me, follow me to where he is now, and both of those questions will be answered. Just remember that some answers don't necessarily bring with them resolution."

"There's a comforting thought."

"For now, will you settle for the answers, if those are all you get?"

"I guess I'll have to, yes."

"Then we'd best get to it, then. Do me a favor—get in

the van and reach under the driver's seat. There's an industrial-size flashlight. Bring it along."

I retrieved the flashlight—the thing had to have been at least sixteen inches long and weighed enough to be technically classified as a weapon. I then petted Tiresias's head once more for luck—and in the hope he might decide to let me in on the secret of the quantum conspiracy. If I'd carried a rabbit's foot, I think I would have rubbed it.

I started up toward the Reverend and the stone steps.

"Ready or not . . ." I whispered.

Chapter Fourteen

"It's a damn shame they let this church fall apart like this," said the Reverend, tossing aside a fallen ceiling beam that looked as if it would have taken three men to move. "This used to be quite a lovely little place. Sure, it could only seat maybe twenty people, but it was ideal for, you know, small services. People with no family, county-paid funerals. Of course, this was back when people still believed that no one should be buried without *some kind* of formal service, regardless of how small or humble."

He knelt down and peered at the hole behind the altar. It looked to be about four feet wide and three feet high. "Hope you don't mind getting a little dirt on your clothes."

"If that's the worst thing that happens today, I'll consider it a blessing."

"More inspiring words were never spoken. I'll go first." He held out his hand and I gave him the flashlight.

Tiresias looked around, then scrambled out of my pocket and leapt onto a lopsided section of the decaying pulpit, making himself comfortable.

The Reverend turned on the flashlight—its beam was impressively bright and wide—and began making his way into the opening. I took a deep breath, held it for a few seconds, and then exhaled as I squatted down and began crawling into the hole. After the first few yards the passageway—if you could call it that—became progressively smaller the farther along I crawled. Looking ahead, I could see the shadow of the Reverend encircled by the glow from the flashlight's beam.

"Are you on your *back*?" I called out, the sound of my voice muffled.

"Yes. I suggest you follow suit. It gets kind of tight here."

Thankfully, there was enough space for me to turn around and reposition myself so that I lay on my back, using my heels and elbows to propel my motion. I'd gotten maybe ten yards when even this became difficult, if not impossible.

"I'm still here, Geoff," said the Reverend from a few feet ahead of me. I caught a peripheral glimpse of the flashlight beam jumping around and knew he was shining it behind him as best he could to let me know everything was okay—or as okay as it could be, given the circumstances.

"I think he might have deliberately loosened some of the dirt in the walls on his way in," said the Reverend.

"So he knew we'd follow him."

"Looks like. Just . . . be careful. Try not to touch the roof or the sides. And we need to keep conversation down to a minimum. The air's going to get a bit thin for a few dozen yards, I'm afraid."

"Got it."

The passageway narrowed to a few feet in width and the roof dropped down so low I could have touched it with my fingers. When I moved—which I could do only in bursts of mere inches—my shoulders scraped the sides of the crawlway, the roof above pressing onto my forehead and chest.

As the Reverend had warned, the air grew thin. I found myself having to stop after every movement to gulp in stale, mephitic air, my lungs aching from the effort as I tried to control the quiet panic snarling to the surface. All my life I've been wary, if not outright afraid, of enclosed spaces, and now I had purposefully pushed myself into the center of one of my worst fears. I forced myself not to imagine becoming wedged in or being crushed or buried alive. Once I considered trying to go back, but the soft sounds of falling dirt behind my feet hinted that maybe that wasn't the best course of action.

So . . . forward.

The passage widened a little—not a great deal, maybe five, six inches all the way around—but it was enough that I managed to get on my side and in a burst of near panic scrabble forward, catching sight of an opening ahead and hoping it would be big enough for me to get through.

I could no longer see the Reverend, but I could see the glow of the flashlight through that opening. *Don't panic*, I told myself. *He managed to make it through, so you can, too.*

I heard more dirt falling behind me as the passageway began collapsing.

On second thought, panic.

Pushing and clawing with all I had, wriggling forward, closer to the opening, I could see the glow of the flashlight, could almost imagine the beam being a solid spear of light that I could grasp in my hands. I felt a rush of air, cool air, and smiled. If there was a breeze coming my way, that meant there had to be another opening, a fissure where air could get in. I exhaled, relieved, and crawled forward.

The roof began to crumble down around my ankles, my legs, my torso, breaking apart and disintegrating with every move I made.

"Reverend!" I shouted, never considering for a second that the volume of my voice would make matters worse, but it did because the collapsing ceiling was swallowing my chest and weighing down my arms, so I kicked forward, managing to yank free my right arm and shove it far in front of me, clawing for something—a root, a rock, anything to give me some leverage—and I felt another hand reach out and grab hold of my wrist, pulling me forward as the collapsing ceiling continued to catch up with me too fast, too fast, and as the Reverend pulled and more dirt fell around me I lunged forward, my mouth filling with dirt and mud dropping down in clumps, and just when I thought I was going to die here I was through the opening and falling down onto a ledge or platform of some kind. Shaking, coughing, hacking up dirt, I lay there shuddering for a few moments, wiping my face and clearing my eyes. At last, I was able to breathe steadily again and stand up.

"Now was that so bad?" said the Reverend, putting an arm around my shoulders to steady my balance.

"How the hell did *he* manage to get through there?" I said.

"I imagine he kicked and clawed as he went along, loosening soil all around. My guess is that tunnel was at least twice the size it was before we went in."

"Wonderful." I stood watching as the last of the collapsing dirt piled up within the passageway. "How are we supposed to get out of here?"

"Look down."

I did, and discovered that we weren't standing on a ledge, but on man-made scaffolding. The ground below—

fifteen or twenty feet below—was smooth, with what looked like a train track running along its center, disappearing into a much larger tunnel several dozen yards ahead.

That's when it occurred to me that I could *see* all of this because there was light—and not from the Reverend's flashlight; old work lights were strung along the walls on both sides and shone like decorations on a Christmas tree.

"So he knows how to string and plug in lights," I said, more to myself than to the Reverend.

"He knows how to do a lot more than just that. Listen carefully, and you might hear the hum of a generator or three somewhere out there."

"What is this area, anyway?"

"Back in the 1920s, the city made an attempt to build a subway system, but that bit the big one when there was a cave-in that killed about a dozen workers." He pointed toward the tunnel. "The tracks go for about a mile before hitting a solid wall of stones and boulders. The bodies of the workers who were killed are under and behind that wall. They couldn't be recovered. There was one boarding area completed before construction was halted. That's where we're going. Come on." He shoved the flashlight into his back pocket, swung himself over the edge of the platform, and began climbing down the steel ladder attached to the side.

"You still haven't told me how we're supposed to get out of here," I called over the side as I tentatively began my descent.

"This isn't the only tunnel that runs beneath the city," he said. "There are dozens of them—service tunnels, maintenance tunnels, ancient tunnels that archeologists haven't quite figured out yet—and at one point many of them intersect. Guess where that point is."

"The boarding platform?"

"Not too far from it, yes."

We reached the ground and began following the tracks toward the larger tunnel. The Reverend took the flashlight out of his back pocket.

"Just in case we lose the work lights," he said. There was a slight quaver of nervousness in his voice. "Believe it or not, I'm not a big fan of total darkness."

"Sleep with night-light, do you?"

"As a matter of fact, yes. Yes I do."

Without exchanging another word, we shuffled along until we entered the tunnel. The Reverend turned on his flashlight. Though there were work lights strung through the tunnel, they were much weaker than those outside, and gave too much room to too many shadows. The Reverend moved the flashlight from side to side, its wide beam giving us a more than sufficient look at what we were walking into.

"God, this place is *big*," I said.

"Yeah . . . about that . . ." The Reverend turned toward me. "There's something different. I'm not . . . not sure what it is, but this place doesn't *feel* the same way it did when I was last here. Stay close, okay?"

"If I could climb in your pocket, I would. Yes, I'll stay close."

The walls soared upward at either end like the sides of a ravine. Looking up, it seemed as if they couldn't possibly meet in the darkness overhead. The path before us, strewn with random stones and loose piles of scree around the rusted tracks, became narrow and steep; the rocks underfoot, grown fewer but larger, began stacking one on top of the other from wall to wall. Having no other choice, we climbed upward, the stack becoming higher and higher, pebbles and rocks breaking away beneath our feet, and almost before it had time to register in my brain, the hill of stones abruptly dropped and the Reverend and I were clambering down a chaotic staircase of massive, wedge-shaped boulders. The beam from the flashlight spun and jerked, zigzagging, giving me glimpses of the bones of dead things scattered at the far sides of the tunnel; animals, I assumed. Hoped. Prayed. At last, after forever, our feet touched ground in the anteroom of some vast, silent, ancient chamber.

I steadied myself. "I'm guessing that sudden uphill-downhill surprise wasn't in the original subway plans."

"That mountain of rocks is new. He's trying more and more to barricade himself down here. Look up ahead." He shone the light on an enormous slab of limestone that had fallen (or been pushed?) to block the opening at what I assumed was the opposite end of the tunnel. Beyond the topmost edge of the slab, a bluish radiance danced, haloing some kind of large rock formation, the top of which could be seen even from where the Reverend and I were standing. We managed to climb the limestone slab, scraping shins and palms every inch of the way, then pulled ourselves over the edge, scrabbling down onto an outcropping of stone that formed a sort of shelf around the chamber.

On a small plateau, under an overhang of white calcite that curved gracefully upward like a snowdrift hollowed by the wind, stood a cluster of meticulously carved stones, each roughly the size and shape of a human being, arms extended, hands outstretched as if beckoning to someone. Their bodies were complete, but all of them lacked faces. Beyond these figures the retreating blue radiance revealed the entrance to another passageway.

298   GARY A. BRAUNBECK

"What the hell is that light, anyway?" I asked.

"Damned if I know, but it's taking us in the right direction."

The odd radiance guiding us, the Reverend and I maneuvered toward the entrance. As we came closer and closer to it, I couldn't help but think that it looked like the gaping mouth of some mythic titan, frozen into a perpetual scream at the moment of its death. We moved slowly, our backs pressed against the wall, feet sliding slowly to the side, the ledge becoming tight and close, less than ten inches in depth. I slipped only once and surprisingly, it didn't frighten me. It took us several minutes, but we at last safely reached the far and much wider side of the ledge. From this vantage point, the faceless stone figures on the plateau seemed to have changed position; then I realized it was only an illusion, a parallax effect: I was simply looking at them from a different angle. But now I saw that, instead of being a random cluster, the figures formed an eerily straight line that stretched toward the center of the chamber; several dozen bluish gray faceless figures, about my height, standing silently by under their white canopy, cowled voyagers waiting with no hope on the frozen deck of an icebound ship, each holding out their hands in hope of rescue at the moment they exhaled their dying breaths. I wondered if Hoopsticks had carved these figures so that he'd have some kind of companionship.

From the depths of the passageway came a low, mournful hum, one I could feel as much as hear.

"Please tell me that sound is one of the generators you told me about," I said.

"It might be," replied the Reverend. "But if it is, *man* is it running hard." We stepped into the opening and saw the wispy tail of the blue radiance disappear around a bend. Following it, we came upon another set of man-made steps constructed from rocks and debris, and soon found ourselves stumbling downward once again. The humming grew louder, becoming a keening that filled both the air and my chest with a dull yet oppressive sense of desolation.

The ground evened out. Down here, deep in the mystery, the walls and roof, glistening with a ghostly iridescence, dripped with moisture. The keening increased its volume, growing steadily more intense, threatening to become a full-throttle roar of anguish. The radiance, churning slowly, moved forward, a worm wriggling its way into the dirt as it vanished into the mouth of yet another passageway.

I couldn't even begin to imagine how far beneath the surface of Cedar Hill we now were, and the more I thought about it, retracing our steps as best as I could remember, it seemed that the topography down here did not match that of the world above. We'd descended a great distance very quickly from the moment we'd gotten out of the collapsing tunnel. I tapped the Reverend on the shoulder and told him this.

"I was thinking the same thing," he replied. "This whole area's much more of a labyrinth than I remember. It's like it's becoming a living thing, growing and changing. I don't know about you, but I've . . . I've kind of lost my sense of direction. Don't get me wrong, I know where we are, more or less, but if I had to retrace our steps . . . I don't think I could. What about you?"

I looked around, trying to place landmarks, discern the direction from which the breeze was coming, anything that would give me a feeling of definite *placement*. There was nothing. I'd lost all sense of direction, as well.

"I think we're screwed," I said.

"Now *there's* a pep talk if ever I heard one. You inspire your students this way?"

I stepped onto a pile of small animal bones, many of which snapped under my weight and crumbled into dust. "We will be able to get out of here, won't we?"

"Yes. Even if I have to resort to . . . well, let's call them 'extreme methods' for the moment and leave it at that. But yes, Geoff, I will get us out of here. You have my word."

I looked into his eyes and knew it was true; he *would* get us out of here.

We walked forward into the darkness, carefully making our way along the rusted tracks as they curved left. The work lights strung along the walls here were bright enough that we didn't need the flashlight for now. The Reverend snapped it off but still kept a good grip on the thing. We kept moving, the blue radiance having now abandoned us, all sense of direction or place leaving with it. We were in the heart of some dark fairy tale, but hadn't thought to leave a trail of bread crumbs behind us. Time, spatial relations, reality, all of it was powerless down here. I don't know that I've ever been so scared, despite the Reverend's assurance that he'd get us out of here.

Several yards along, I stopped, putting a hand on the Reverend's shoulder and pointing. "Do you see that?"

"I certainly do."

Something was taking shape ahead of us, rimmed by faint light; the outline of a support girder along the wall. Another came into view, and then another. With each step the light grew stronger, and I could see the shine of the rails ahead. This was a tomb, this place, isolated and deep and dank, and it wouldn't matter a damn how loudly you screamed down here, there would be no one to hear you, no place for the echo of your cries to go.

Way to keep a positive attitude, I thought, then took a deep breath and continued making my way forward.

The wall curved to the left again, and we walked toward a rectangle of light suspended in the darkness. It looked unreal, like a stage devoid of props and actors. The Reverend and I pressed forward and pulled ourselves up over the edge of this stage, instantly aware of a coldness about the place that transcended temperature. So we'd found the abandoned, sealed-off subway platform. Could a person be more alone than in a place like this?

The Reverend shone his flashlight around as we took in our dim, dank, oppressive surroundings. It was a chilling sense of timelessness that touched my mind rather than my flesh. The platform was not deep, nor were there any exit stairs—so much for finding a service ladder here—only a seamless wall of cold tiles, trailing off into the distant shadows beyond the perimeters of light from a solitary bulb in the overhead fixture.

"Look," said the Reverend, shining his light onto the surface of the platform. A series of large, muddy, smeared footprints traveled away from the edge of the subway platform, disappearing into the shadows beyond.

We followed them. Even with the flashlight beam to illuminate the way before us, I could not shake the feeling of darkness, of desolation and . . . loneliness. Anger. Hopelessness. I became more acutely aware of the silence of the place. The sound of our shoes seemed so loud, so obscenely loud. I should have felt even more fear in this place, but it was replaced by a stronger emotion, one I could not articulate even to myself, a need to know this place for whatever it was.

Something was touching my face. Out of the shadows in which it languished it danced out, unseeable, and played about my cheek like fog. It became a cold, heavy mist that swirled and churned with a glowing energy of its own, and it became brighter the deeper we traveled. I could sense a barrier ahead of us, but not anything physical, nothing that could physically stop us, but rather a portal through which we must pass.

We continued to move forward and soon found ourselves standing upon a narrow, rocky ledge that wound across the sheer face of a great cavern. Above us, like the vault of a cathedral, the ceiling arched, defined by the phosphorescent glow of mineral veins. To the right a sheer cliff dropped off into utter darkness; to the left was a perfectly vertical wall. We followed the narrow winding path, each step bringing us closer to an eerie sound that was most definitely not being made by a generator; at first it was like a gently rising wind, whispering, then murmuring, finally screaming through the cavern, an uncontrollable, eternal wailing. I recognized the sound— it was the sound of utter loneliness; it was a sound made by something totally alien, and simultaneously all too human; it was a sound that, until now, I had heard only in the depths of my own mind during the worst of dreams, a primal sound from the core of the reptilian. It was difficult not to become entranced by it as we neared its source.

"What happened to the rest of the platform?" I asked.

"Like I said—the place is changing, growing, alive. It's doing what it wants, when it wants."

We stopped moving. Ahead of us, a group of shadows were assembled in a semicircle, each of them holding lighted candles.

A series of boxes and crates had been arranged to form something like a large table, and this table had been covered with several sheets of moldy tarpaulin. Atop this structure several other candles had been lighted and placed in various holders to keep the hot wax from setting the tarp aflame; discarded menorahs, broken sections of glass and plates, a piece of something porcelain that looked as if it might have been taken from a shattered statue. The candle flames snapped and burned. In other places cones of old incense burned, filling the air with heavy, spicy scents.

It was only as we grew closer to the crowd and this structure that I realized part of the sound we'd been hearing was their chanting; I also realized that the structure around which they all stood was a makeshift altar.

For a moment I stupidly feared that we'd stumbled upon some bizarre underground cult of devil worshipers or something worse, but then I saw the offerings that were scattered about the altar; old pictures of children and families, some coins probably begged from passersby, broken toys, stuffed animals that were torn open in places, their stuffing spilling out, cans of food with the labels missing, and old, stained, ripped Christmas cards.

The crowd was composed of several ragged homeless people, their faces ghostly in the flickering light of the candles.

The Reverend and I pressed ourselves against the wall and listened to the words they chanted:

"Someone come . . ." said an old man in a tattered suit who seemed to be their version of a celebrant.

"Someone come," answered the others.

"And where do I live?" asked the celebrant.

"Under the tracks of the L," replied the worshipers, "in a cardboard box that's falling apart."

All then bowed their heads.

"My quiver is once again empty," they chanted as one, "and that will not do."

"Someone please come."

The tattered celebrant then produced from one of his pockets a tin can, their version of a chalice. He also produced a pocketknife with which he cut a small section of his thumb, squeezing the blood into the tin can. Then he went around the circle and, using his knife, made a small cut in everyone's thumbs, squeezing their blood into the can to mix with his own.

When everyone had been bled, he returned to his place before the altar and held the can high.

"And where do we live?" he asked of the congregation.

"In the alleys behind the cans," they replied.

I leaned forward and saw that the altar stood a few yards away from a massive opening that resembled a drainpipe, only it was far too large; it looked almost like another section of subway tunnel. You could easily drive a semitruck into the thing and still have some room at the top.

We moved toward the crowd, peering closer at the opening.

Not a drainpipe or tunnel at all, those would have been made from concrete and brick; this tunnel—or whatever it was—was constructed of some kind of metal, now giving away to rust. As the celebrant moved around the group and my eyes adjusted to the candlelight, I saw that the tunnel extended inward for several feet, perhaps even yards, perhaps even farther.

"What the hell is that thing?" I whispered to the Reverend.

"Maybe, just maybe, it's some kind of service tunnel."

We slowly stepped from the shadows and made our way toward the congregation. "And where do we live?" intoned the celebrant.

"In songs unheard," replied the congregation.

I stopped moving.

The tattered celebrant held the tin can of blood even higher and sang: "Who will take me? Where is my Creator? When will the Second Protector show his face to us?"

The others answered: "My quiver is once again empty, and that will not do."

The celebrant set down the can of blood and nodded to the others. In silence, they dispersed. It was only as the old man I'd thought of as the celebrant moved down off the platform that I fully saw his face.

You here to fix my television?

He still carried it by its handle. As he walked away into a darkness I suspect he knew only too well, he pulled up the antenna and turned on the set. I wondered if it was time for his programs, if Katie Lynn's face would appear on the screen and smile her love and her forgiveness.

Do anything for you, she would. A sweet *girl . . .*

I grabbed the Reverend's arm. "Did you see who—?"

"Yes. I always wondered where he disappeared to. But you might want to look at that lovely old gal over there."

The light reflected off her figure, shining bronze, now fluid with life, with a form of sentience I could never have imagined, let alone accepted: Henrietta Holcomb, who liked needlepoint, Glenn Miller records, Mickey Spillane novels, and spending Sunday afternoons in spring and summer feeding birds in the park and watching children fly kites. Not only was she here, but so were all of the other bronze sculptures that were placed on their memorial benches around the square, all of them mobile, all of them alive, all of them having given their blood to fill a tin-can chalice for a reason I couldn't fathom.

I looked at the Reverend and tried to speak, but I couldn't find the words. He gripped my hand in his and squeezed.

"Don't try to make sense of this. I'm not sure I fully comprehend it myself, and I *always* know what's going on. But do you understand now why I couldn't tell you about the birdseed when we first met? If I would have told you that the statues were alive, you wouldn't have been able to run away from me fast enough."

I squeezed his hand in response.

"Okay, then," he said. "What say we go take a look in that tunnel? In case you didn't notice, the direction of the candle flames is constant. They're snapping *backward*. That means the breeze is coming from inside that tunnel. Our way out may very well be in there."

"But so might Hoopsticks."

"So?" said the Reverend as he moved toward the opening. "He's not going to hurt you, Geoff. I don't think he's ever meant to hurt anyone."

"How can you be sure? How do you *know* that he won't see us and go crazy, just tear us apart until our guts are spilling out like those stuffed toys?"

He stared at me. In the flickering candlelight, his face was ethereal, his eyes full of power and knowledge. "He won't hurt me because I've known him all of his life. I'm the one who found him when he was dumped in the woods as a baby, I'm the one who patched him up and kept him alive and kept him hidden from the world because I knew what the world would do to him. I'm the one who had to finally let him go when he grew old enough to take care of himself, living off the land, living in the shadows, in caves and cardboard boxes, feeding off the small animals he could catch, drinking water from the rivers or creeks, then later breaking into grocery and department stores through the underground service tunnels, taking simple everyday supplies so that he could at least *pretend* he was like other human beings. He won't hurt me because I am the *only* friend he's ever had, and because he knows I'll continue to protect him for as long as he lives." His voice was thick with emotion, his eyes glassy with angry tears. "There are no beatitudes for the lost or the lonely, Geoff—and believe me, of all the people I've known, of all the souls I've encountered in my time here, there has never been one more overwhelmingly lost or profoundly lonely than him. I try to ease that pain when I can, but he's been pulling away from me, as if he's *ashamed* to be seen by me. Can you imagine that? Becoming so aware of what you are, of how different you are from everyone and everything around you, that you become humiliated by your own existence? He needs to know that I still care about him, that I still *love* him, and that I'll never stop being his friend, regardless of what he might have done. *That* is why I know he won't hurt me."

I moved toward him, reaching out slowly, placing my hand on his shoulder. Though there were few tears on his face, his entire body was shuddering with anger and sadness. I don't know that I've ever felt a grief this strong, before or since.

"Are you all right?"

He wiped his eyes and took a deep breath. "No, but I'm functional." He gave me a small, cheerless smile. "I'm sorry."

"There's nothing to apologize for."

"You don't know that."

"What do you mean?"

He looked at the entrance to the rusted tunnel. "Because I've only told you why I know he won't hurt *me*." He looked back at me. "Do you want to know why he won't hurt you? Why he'd never hurt you?"

My mouth suddenly went dry and my left side began to throb. ". . . yes . . ."

"Because he's been waiting for you for a very long time. Because meeting you again has been one of the few things he's had to hope for. Because you're the only family he has left. The two of you are blood relatives, Geoff."

CHAPTER FIFTEEN

Listen to my silence after he said this.

"I probably shouldn't have told you that, but—"

". . . can't be true . . . no . . . Andy Leonard killed all of my family except me."

"He killed all of your family who were *there* on that night, yes. But he didn't kill everyone."

I shook my head and stepped back, as if physically distancing myself from him would lessen the weight of his words. "No . . . no, sorry, but I can't . . . how do you know?"

"Because he proved it to me."

"But . . . *how*?"

The Reverend looked into the tunnel, then back at me. "Why don't we go in so you can ask him yourself? We did come down here to find him, after all." He walked a few feet into the rusted tunnel, then turned and waved for me to follow. "Come on. If for no other reason, this may very well be our way out."

For the moment, that was good enough for me.

Don't think about what he said, don't think about what he said, it can't be true, something's gone wrong, just get the hell out of here and breathe in the air from the world above and then you can try sorting this out.

I followed him through the tunnel and into the grotto beyond.

I don't know what I was expecting to see—the filthy, barbaric dwelling of some subterranean madman, with bones strewn about the floor, crudely drawn pictures on the walls, and the rotting hide of a wolf being used for a blanket. I couldn't imagine in what kind of conditions something—*someone*—like Hoopsticks could survive. I just know that what I saw was arguably the last thing I might have imagined.

The area was surprisingly clean, illuminated by a series of battery-operated lanterns hung at even intervals around the walls. It was dry in here, and warm. Near one corner, tucked neatly between two large stones, a ceramic heater glowed. In another corner, set atop a metal stand, a dehumidifier chugged away. Both were plugged into separate power strips, each of which was running off a separate portable generator that could be heard but not seen. There were several tables scattered around the grotto, all of them having been made level through some often-clever means. One table held sewing materials and was piled with torn stuffed animals; another table was being used to repair broken toys; a third table—the largest of the bunch—was set up near another power strip and was evidently used for repairing household items such as blenders, radios, toasters, and the like. A large steel toolbox, opened, shelves pulled out, displayed it contents; every tool was well kept, and nothing in the box was a bit out of place.

A porcelain washbasin sat in a polished wooden stand with both side leaves locked in place; on the left was a shaving mug and brush, with a pearl-handled straight razor lying closed beside them; on the right were two stacks of folded towels and washcloths. A large mirror with only a few cracks and a couple of dingy spots sat propped at an angle between the basin stand and a large rock behind it. A few feet away, resting on top of a series of interlocked, short steel shelves, was a twin-bed mattress, with sheets and blankets. The bed had been meticulously made, and the smell coming from the sheets told you in no uncertain terms that they had been recently laundered. Two pillows lay propped against a smooth slab of stone that served as the headboard. The design on the pillowcases matched that of the bedsheets: Van Gogh's *Starry Night*—a painting that's always been one of my favorites, dear old Vincent being my favorite artist.

"*This* is the lair of a monster?" I asked.

"Terrifying, isn't it?" said the Reverend, looking around. "Trust me when I tell you—this is *much* nicer than where he was living down here last time I visited. I wonder if—ah, yes! There it is." He pointed to something several feet behind the basin stand and mirror. When I did nothing, he raised his eyebrows and pointed again.

The blue radiance that I thought had abandoned us was here, waiting, shimmering from the surface of its source. I stepped around the basin stand and mirror, taking care not to touch anything, and walked up a small incline of stones that leveled out about five feet above the floor of the grotto. (I almost looked into the mirror's reflection as I moved past it, but the thought of seeing the Broken One down here with us would not have helped anything—at least, not that I could think of at the moment.)

I reached the top and the blue radiance shifted, churning in on itself, until it faded away like the iris in an old silent film, revealing what it had brought us—brought *me*—here to see.

For a moment I forgot to breathe, I was so stunned.

A massive curtain of bluish gray flowstone, its surface shimmering and shifting like sand beneath incoming waves at high tide—there was no other choice but to think of it in terms of liquid, for everything about the image embedded in the curtain seemed to ripple.

The image was of myself, lying on my back, naked from the chest upward, arms crossed over my center, the right somewhat higher than the left, fingers slightly bent as if about to clutch at something unseen, unknown. The rest of my body was hidden underneath a wide sheet composed of smaller stones and slates and uncountable fossils: toads, lizards, prehistoric arachnid crustaceans the likes of which I'd never seen, praying mantises, eels, and serpents slithering over faded, ancient symbols and primeval drawings.

Even my skin was not as I first perceived it to be: thin and transparent, misted with a fine scintillance like lavender spiderwebs, it allowed me to see through my own surface to the millions of swarming, teeming, multiplying cells and legions of bacteria-like clumps within. There was an odd, damaged beauty to the sight, a vague impression of transcendence, of the human becoming the elemental, then the infinitesimal, and I was drawn toward it but, at the moment of communion, something in the image pulled back and became cold, alien, unreachable, hiding as if ashamed to be seen, leaving me to stare into my own exhausted eyes, balanced atop dark crescents. They were near-lifeless eyes, unfocused, with no inner light remaining, eyes beyond caring. The mouth was curved downward, trapped somewhere between a grimace and a groan, but as I moved a little to the side a parallax effect took place again; viewed from the right, this image of myself was a sad, dark, twisted thing, but viewed from the left, it appeared that the image was about to smile, as if it had just awakened from a dream to see the face of the one it most wanted to see.

"It took him *years* to finally get that right," said the Reverend. "I don't know how many slabs he ruined or chisels he broke over that time."

I could only shake my head. "How did he know what I looked like?"

"He didn't. Why do you think that damned mirror is so big? It's a self-portrait."

I turned away from the carving—something that was much more difficult to do than I'd expected—and began to make my way back down when I noticed another steel shelving unit, this one at least five feet tall, a few feet farther back, almost hidden by the shadow cast by the slab of flowstone. The unit's legs had been pounded into the ground, while small spikes and chicken wire were used to secure it to the stone wall. It wasn't the shelving unit itself that caught my attention so much as its contents: two items, each covered by a section of heavy cloth, and roughly the size of a good chunk of sculpting material. He was keeping his latest pieces from view.

I called for the Reverend to join me but didn't wait for him before pulling the covers off the two pieces.

Large medical specimen jars. The one on the left was the older of the two, its lid having been sealed with paraffin many years ago, judging from the discoloration of the seal. Inside it were the remains of a malformed baby, nestled on a bed of cotton, soaking in what I assumed was formaldehyde or alcohol; whatever it was, years of being saturated in the chemical had turned the baby's skin a ghostly white.

The child had been born . . . incomplete. It had a head and torso, part of a groin, a right shoulder, arm, and hand . . . and no more. Extra cotton had been packed behind its neck, around its shoulder, and underneath the stump of its torso to prevent it from lolling forward or around; only close scrutiny revealed the clear, thin wire that ran down from the lid of the case, snaking through the dense layers of cotton to attach itself—via a small silver hook—to a catch protruding from the base of its skull. Something about the sight of this pitiful thing struck me—I'm ashamed to say—as almost absurd. Which doesn't excuse what I did next, but at the time it was all the more reason I needed.

Feeling myself beginning to fragment again, I reached out and began turning the jar around so I could see the baby from the side—parallax viewings had been nothing if not enlightening so far. As the jar turned, a series of small ripples spread through the liquid, jostling the body.

A pain more intense than any I'd ever experienced before ripped into my left side and dropped me to my knees, clutching at my stomach and trying desperately not to vomit. The pain came in waves, lessening with each attack, and by the time it was over I was in near-total darkness, feeling myself lifted up and carried away. . . .

. . . I opened my eyes to find that I was lying on the bed on the main floor of the chamber. The Reverend was kneeling beside me, pressing a warm washcloth against my forehead.

"You shouldn't have done that," he said. He looked as if he might also have gotten ill; his face was pale, his eyes glassy.

"Did you see it?"

"Yes, I saw it, and I saw the contents of the other jar, as well. Just in case you get curious again and want to try and sneak a peek—don't."

"What's in the other jar?"

He swallowed. Once. Loudly. "Ashley Millhauser's head."

"Oh, *God*. . . ."

From somewhere far beneath us, a heavy vibration of something massive shifting sent a short but serious tremor through the earth. Everything in the chamber shook, but nothing fell.

"Was that an earthquake?" I asked, realizing how stupid the question was before I'd even finished asking it.

"You could call it that, I suppose. Are you feeling all right? I mean, do you think you can stand?"

I pulled in a deep breath. The pain in my side was still there, still throbbing, but it was nothing compared to before. I nodded, and the Reverend helped me to my feet.

"Thanks for carrying me down here," I said.

He shook his head. "I didn't carry you—*he* did." He put his hands on my shoulders and turned me toward the entryway.

Hoopsticks stood there, towering over us. It–he–*they* had to have been at least seven feet tall.

As in my fever-vision of him during class, he was a large, hunched creature of grayish white mottled flesh and impossibly long, muscular arms ending in skeletal hands. Hs legs were equally well muscled, his feet so large they couldn't be fully contained by the army boots he wore; the front had been cut away from both boots so that his toes weren't crushed together. His pants were held tight around his waist by a section of heavy rope, but so thick were his calves that the pant legs reached only halfway down his legs. His massive chest was covered in cuts, scabs, and other wounds, as well as small clusters of tumors. His hair was long and thick, tied back

in ponytail so that his face—*this* face of his, anyway—
was easily seen.

And it was so very much like my own; the bone structure, the eyes, cheeks, the dimple in the middle of the
chin, all of it. There were several minor differences—his
nose had been broken at least once and had not been
properly set, and so healed at an ugly, crooked angle that
made it difficult for him to breathe through, judging
from his wet, thick wheezing; there were several large
scars on his forehead, and one that ran from his left
temple down the side of his face and neck, disappearing
into the numerous wounds on his chest.

He breathed through his mouth, occasionally drooling a mixture of saliva and blood because at some point
during his life his tongue had been torn out.

"There are no beatitudes for the lost or the lonely,"
whispered the Reverend.

". . . there should be . . ." was all I could manage to say.
Here before me was the terrible monster of local legend,
the nightmare dread of every child, the horror beyond
all horrors . . . and I felt not even a twinge of fear, even
after looking at the thing growing from his back.

It was another body, only it was fused to Hoopsticks's
body at the base of its torso. He'd fashioned a complex,
heavy leather harness to hold his brother upright, the
straps crisscrossing his chest. His brother was an abomination of a human being; compacted nostrils leaking
black oil; puckered, scarlike knots where eyes should
have been; mouth drawn downward, stretched wide to
create a triangular maw of teeth, flesh, and black-red
gums; two long and seemingly useless arms that hung
down, flapping from side to side every time Hoopsticks
readjusted his stance . . . and its flesh was spotted with
clumps of tumorlike growths. No wonder Hoopsticks

walked hunched so far to the left; there was no other way for him to maintain his balance, not with that diseased thing attached to him.

"Now do you understand why I had to hide him from the world?" asked the Reverend.

". . . yes . . ."

"See his face? Do you believe me now?"

". . . yes . . ." I didn't know how it was possible that I could be related to him, but looking at his face—his scarred, ruined, *smiling* face—there was no doubt whatsoever.

His smile widening, spattering blood and saliva down his chin, Hoopsticks lumbered forward, his arms outstretched, his mouth working to form words he was incapable of speaking.

The abomination growing from his back jerked from side to side with every step, its head lolling around like a baby's, its arms smacking into Hoopsticks's sides with a moist, dead sound.

Hoopsticks gripped my shoulders—it hurt only a little—and bent lower to get a better look at my face. I stared at his mouth as he again tried to form words, and somehow was able to discern what he was attempting to say.

Thank you. Thank you.

The force of his loneliness, the weight of its compiling over the decades, hit me in the center of my chest. Never in my life had anyone been so overjoyed to see me. He shook his head as if he couldn't quite believe I was real, and then, with great tenderness, touched my face with one of his hands.

Thank you. Thank you.

My chest hitched and I stepped closer to him. "I'm sorry," I said. "I didn't know. I didn't know. I didn't know."

Still touching my cheek, he bent down and kissed the top of my head, then pulled away, pointing at me to stay where I was. He scuttled over to the table filled with broken toys and tugged a small box from under a pile of stuffed animals. Reaching into the box, he removed four rubber balls, each a different color, and began to juggle them, his smile growing even wider.

Not knowing what else to do, I found myself laughing and applauding. Hoopsticks stopped juggling, took a bow, and then stood up, removed a fifth ball from the box, and began again—only this time, the thing fused to his back came alive and joined in, its right arm shooting out to catch and release the fifth ball so that all of them were in continuous motion. As the two of them continued to juggle, Hoopsticks's brother *smiled*, his head bobbing back and forth, a sound not unlike laughter emerging from its horror of a mouth. It was feeling joy, and I immediately felt ashamed for having thought of it—of *him*—as an abomination.

"I was right," said the Reverend, standing by my side. "He didn't mean to kill her. Ashley and Sharon were down here with him. He'd juggled for them just like this, and they loved it. So he decided to show them his self-portrait. They were up there when a tremor occurred. Ashley lost her balance and started to fall and he panicked. He tried to get hold of the back of her dress but grabbed a handful of her hair and her necklace instead.

"He's incredibly strong, and didn't realize what would happen when he yanked his hand back." He watched Hoopsticks and his brother juggle for a few more seconds, and then said: "Sharon went into shock. He was scared, so he ran away with Ashley's body and dumped it in the same place he'd been abandoned as a baby. He came back here and found Sharon almost comatose. He cared for her until she started to come out of it, then took her out of here to a place he knew she'd be found. It was an accident. I *knew* it had to have been an accident."

Hoopsticks and his brother finished their routine with a flourish, and bowed. Both the Reverend and I applauded, which seemed to please the performers to no end. It almost appeared both of them were blushing.

"What now, Reverend?"

"What you came here for. Don't be pissed, but I could have answered your two questions hours ago. You might even be almost back home by now, as a matter of fact."

I glared at him. "Then why *didn't* you?"

"Because you needed to see this. You needed to meet him again. You needed to believe everything that I had told and shown to you was the truth."

I blinked at him, exhaling. "Fair enough."

Hoopsticks came over and gave me one of the rubber balls, then put his arm around my shoulder and stood there, smiling, just like his brother, both of them wheezing from their efforts.

"You know how much violence there's been throughout Cedar Hill's history, I assume," said the Reverend.

"Yes . . . ?"

He nodded. "There's been a pattern to it. Not an obvious one, far from it—I think it would probably give most mathematicians strokes if they tried to figure it out. But it's there. You'd have to possess intimate knowledge of every act of violence that's been committed since this town was settled, but if you had that kind of knowledge, you'd see there is a definite pattern to the outbursts."

"So says the man who's been here for over two hundred years."

"Indeed." He looked at me. "Don't ever let anyone try to tell you that all wisdom is good wisdom, Geoff. I read that in a fortune cookie once, paraphrased it here for my own purposes.

"Every act of violence that has ever been committed here is because of the creature that Hoopsticks stands guard over. The tremors are because it's beginning to awaken from a slumber that has lasted tens of thousands of years. It's been drawing its strength from the violence and death that's occurred here. I don't know when it first became aware of its imprisonment, or when it first experienced a moment of near wakefulness, but what I *do* know is that since that moment, it has *willed* these acts of violence. In awakens for only a moment, demands bloodshed, and then sleeps again as it absorbs all of the life forces it has taken. This has been happening for centuries, but I'm not going to waste time trying to explain the pattern to you. What you need to know is this: Andy Leonard was just one of the tools it's used over the centuries to carry out its demands for bloodshed. Once he had been touched by this thing's will, it was all over. He killed everyone that night because he was compelled to.

"I have struggled a very long time to ensure that the balance of suffering in this branch of the multiverse remains constant. This fucker that's trying to wake up, it wants to tip the scales. Forever. I can't allow that to happen. And so I trained Hoopsticks to be my sentinel. By the way, his name isn't 'Hoopsticks,' that's something that was dreamed up by some overzealous, superstitious Bible-thumper looking for a way to burn the fear of God into children's minds. No, his real name is Kerubim, a name taken from the names of the Angelic Hierarchy. It means 'Strong One,' an angel of the foundation of the universe. Yes, I gave him that name. It suits him."

Hoopsticks—*Kerubim*—smiled at the Reverend and proudly nodded his head.

"As to your second question. Andy Leonard didn't kill you because Kerubim protected you. You were to be Andy's last offering before taking his own life, but Kerubim slipped back into the time stream and took the bullet intended for you. There was no one else alive in the park to see him. Look at his left shoulder."

I did, and saw the puckered scar.

"He waited until Andy shot himself before returning to this time. Don't look at me like that, I *told* you—hell, I *showed* you a glimpse of the multiverse. There is a branch that now exists where you aren't alive. It was supposed to be *this* branch, but Kerubim kind of took care of that. And like it or not, that's where and when one of the ruptures in the multiverse was created."

I felt my knees go weak and would have fallen had not Kerubim held me. "You're . . . you're telling me that I'm not supposed to be alive?"

"Nice to know that the Hangman's gang aren't the only ones with a firm grasp of the obvious. Yes, that's what I'm telling you. But you are alive, and barring any stupidity on your part, you're going to stay that way until you're a very old man, so deal with it. You might want to thank him, as well. Just a suggestion. No pressure."

I reached up and squeezed Kerubim's hand. I couldn't find the strength to speak, nor the words to say. I was so dizzy with everything I'm amazed I was able to remain conscious.

"So, you have your answers, Geoff Conover, formerly Joey Hamilton. You have finished what you came here to do. So it's my turn to ask you—what now?"

I shook my head. "I don't know."

"You can leave if you want. Regardless of the empty threats that the Broken One might have made, no one will try to stop you."

Kerubim was shaking his head, his eyes wide with fear. *No, no, no, no. . . .*

"What good will my staying here do?"

"If you stay—*if*—you can help us. I'm going to need all the help I can get to fight what this thing is trying to do. It has a name. The *Popul Vuh* calls it 'The Sorcerer of Night, Unkempt.' It used to be one of the Good Guys, a long, long time ago, but there have been a few too many ruptures within the multiverse and now the thing is simply . . . insane. And I have to figure out a way to stop it from fully awakening, even if it means killing it. I could use your help, because if it *does* come fully awake, it's all over—literally.

"I could also use your help because the series of tremors that have occurred here over the past few weeks means that sometime in the next five days, someone is going to go on a killing spree. Night, Unkempt has made its will known. If we can stop this spree from happening, we'll have the upper hand for a little while. Please stay."

Kerubim nodded his head, squeezing my arm. I knew then that I would stay, but I had one more question.

"Why here? Why someplace like Cedar Hill?"

"Because every place in Heaven has a counterpart on Earth. Hell is located on the north side of the Third Heaven. Care to guess the location of *its* earthly counterpart?"

Everything inside of me went cold.

"That's right," said the Reverend. "And allow me to be the first to officially welcome you. I'd appreciate it if you'd keep it between us, though. Somehow I don't think the folks around here would embrace the idea of their literally living in Hell on Earth. Will you stay and help me? Help us?"

"Yes."

"Even though you have what you came for?"

"Yes."

Kerubim embraced me.

The Reverend rubbed the back of his neck. "Okay, then. So now it gets weird. Are you sure you're up for this?"

"I think so, yes." I almost sounded as if I believed myself.

"Then let's go." He nodded to Kerubim, who took hold of my hand and began guiding us deeper into the grotto, into areas where we'd have no choice but use the flashlight.

"So," said the Reverend as we entered into darkness, "all in all, how would you rate your first day here?"

Beneath our feet, the ground trembled. I held fast to Kerubim's hand and waited for my eyes to adjust to the shadows. I had a feeling I was going to be spending a lot of time in them over the next several days, if not forever.

W. D. Gagliani

"GAGLIANI REDEFINES THE WEREWOLF MYTHOS FOR A JADED TWENTY-FIRST CENTURY AUDIENCE."
—SCI-FI HORIZONS

Some people are afraid there's a wild animal on the loose, savagely tearing its victims apart. Others, like Nick Lupo, know better. Lupo knows a werewolf attack when he sees one. He *should*, since he's a werewolf himself, though he's been able to control his urges and maintain his secret. He's also a homicide cop, so it may be up to him to hunt down one of his own kind. It looks like there's a new werewolf in town, a rogue out only for blood. But looks can be deceiving.

Wolf's Gambit

ISBN 13: 978-0-8439-6249-9

☐ YES!

Sign me up for the Leisure Horror Book Club and send my FREE BOOKS! If I choose to stay in the club, I will pay only $8.50* each month, a savings of $7.48!

NAME: _____

ADDRESS: _____

TELEPHONE: _____

EMAIL: _____

☐ I want to pay by credit card.

☐ VISA   ☐ MasterCard   ☐ DISCOVER

ACCOUNT #: _____

EXPIRATION DATE: _____

SIGNATURE: _____

Mail this page along with $2.00 shipping and handling to:
Leisure Horror Book Club
PO Box 6640
Wayne, PA 19087
Or fax (must include credit card information) to:
610-995-9274
You can also sign up online at **www.dorchesterpub.com**.

*Plus $2.00 for shipping. Offer open to residents of the U.S. and Canada only. Canadian residents please call 1-800-481-9191 for pricing information.
If under 18, a parent or guardian must sign. Terms, prices and conditions subject to change. Subscription subject to acceptance. Dorchester Publishing reserves the right to reject any order or cancel any subscription.